ONE OF THE WICKED

A MICK CALLAHAN NOVEL

ONE OF THE WICKED

HARRY SHANNON

FIVE STAR
A part of Gale, Cengage Learning

Detroit • New York • San Francisco • New Haven, Conn • Waterville, Maine • London

GALE
CENGAGE Learning

Set in 11 pt. Plantin.
Printed on permanent paper.

LIBRARY OF CONGRESS CATALOGING-IN-PUBLICATION DATA

Shannon, Harry.
   One of the wicked : a Mick Callahan novel / Harry Shannon.
  — 1st ed.
    p. cm.
   ISBN-13: 978-1-59414-703-6 (hardcover : alk. paper)
   ISBN-10: 1-59414-703-5 (hardcover : alk. paper)
   1. Radio broadcasters—Fiction. 2. Mafia—Fiction. 3. Drug
dealers—Fiction. 4. Las Vegas (Nev.)—Fiction. I. Title.
PS3619.H355064 2008
813'.6—dc22
                                          2008032114

First Edition. First Printing: November 2008.
Published in 2008 in conjunction with Tekno Books and Ed Gorman.

Printed in the United States of America
1 2 3 4 5 6 7 12 11 10 09 08

For my best friend and AA sponsor Hal Cornelius,
who died 28 years clean and sober back in 1991.

ACKNOWLEDGMENTS

I have to thank Leya Booth, Ed Gorman, Joe Donnelly, Marty Greenberg, John Helfers, Pat Wallace, the staff at Five Star Publishing and of course my wife Wendy and my beloved daughter Paige.

I greatly appreciate the many folks who have taken the time to stop by my Web site at harryshannon.com to say hello. Likewise all the booksellers, authors, fans and libraries that have helped spread the word about Mick Callahan and his exploits. As usual, nearly everything on these pages was either made up or deliberately distorted, all for my nefarious purposes. Rest assured that any errors are my own.

"Now am I, if a man should speak truly, little better than one of the wicked."

—Shakespeare,
Henry IV, 1, ii, 105

PROLOGUE

Midnight. The young man in the torn Armani suit ran through the desert sobbing like a schoolgirl. His name was Calvin, and he was barely twenty-four years old. He tripped and fell, rose again. The shadowy earth was an uneven mix of rocks and earth, dried sage and cactus. His Gucci shoes were tattered and full of sand.

Calvin risked a look back over his shoulder. He saw a small group of people watching from a flat rock, next to the giant red Hummer. The presence of one man in particular made his stomach roll. Calvin paused for a moment, bent forward sharply at the waist and spewed what was left of three shots of Skyy Vodka and a few cocktail sausages. Bright headlights pinned him there, alone on the pocked surface of a moon.

By the Hummer, someone said, "That is how a man drowns."

The voice was low and raspy, with only the faintest of accents, and it carried. The speaker was a huge man, nearly seven feet tall and very fit. His grey eyes were as clear and cold as those of a sled dog. He wore his hair in a buzz cut.

"What you mean, Nicky?" The blonde took a pull on her tepid bottle of Crystal. "I not understand."

Nikolaou Argetoianu spat at her feet. "Slut, you are in America. Learn to speak English."

The girl flinched. "I am sorry."

Nicky ignored her, cupped his hands and shouted, "Wait, Calvin, perhaps I have another deal for you. And then you do

11

not have to die tonight. You are interested in this new deal?"

The terrified young man in the distance was still vomiting. Finally, he stood up a bit and waved one hand. He was interested all right.

"A man drowns because he panics," Nicky said to the girl, who hugged herself as if against a nonexistent cold. "He forgets the water will hold him up, and that most things work out when one stays calm. You see? Now, watch."

Nicky yanked the hunting rifle to his shoulder, aimed and fired. The silenced weapon emitted a muffled *chuffing* sound, and a spray of earth appeared inches from the terrified runner's feet. The boy called Calvin jumped up, pinwheeled his arms, falling backwards into the sand like a snow angel.

"Listen to me," Nicky called. "I'll say this one last time. Are you listening, Calvin?"

Calvin sat alone in the sand, crying and praying. Finally he sat up, took a deep breath and forced himself to respond. "Please. Anything." Calvin hated the weakness in his voice almost as much as the urine staining the crotch of his expensive trousers.

"Oh, but of course you are frightened. This is because I killed your friend, yes? You must understand our position, Calvin. You two were scamming us. Mr. Big Paul Pesci cannot allow such a thing. He must remain a man of respect. So my superiors decided that something had to be done."

"Please don't kill me."

"Do not beg. Now stand up."

Calvin stood up.

"Walk this way." Nicky's voice became both gentle and firm. "And I promise we will not kill you."

The blonde took another step backwards, closer to the Hummer. "Nicky, I don't feel too good. Can I go lay down in the car, please?" She knew what that very sudden tone of kindness meant, and she suddenly wanted to be somewhere, anywhere else.

Nicky frowned, as if pondering something. He scratched his fashionable stubble. "I can never get this one thing straight, is it 'lie' or 'lay'?"

"Excuse me?"

"No. Stay here, little bitch. And keep your mouth and legs shut until I ask you to open them again."

Nicky tossed the rifle to the third figure. "You, keep him covered." The muscular man named Lucky complied mutely. He glared down the scope and tracked Calvin. The rifle made a small red dot flicker on the kid's sweaty forehead.

"Calvin, I said come closer. Quickly."

The kid in the desert shivered like a man with the flu. His last shred of courage deserted him. He stumbled back toward the red Hummer. *Why did I let you talk me into this, Rudy? Why? We had enough money to go home; we didn't need more. Why did I let you get us caught?*

Calvin kept his eyes on the ground but tripped anyway. He stared down at the shadowy dirt, forced himself back to his feet and kept walking.

Nicky cleared his throat. "As I was saying, your partner had to be executed. His disappearance will serve as a message to other grifters that it is most unwise to fuck with Big Paul Pesci. I take no pleasure in such things. Violence is one of the more unpleasant parts of my job, Calvin. It is an ugly necessity of life, nothing more."

Calvin was weaving like an extra in a zombie movie, but he was making progress. Nicky checked his watch. "Come on, hurry up."

The kid paused, perhaps twenty feet away. "What is it? What's the deal?"

"Wait there."

Nicky sighed dramatically. He moved to the left a bit, so Lucky would have a clean shot, and stomped out into the dried sage. As Calvin watched the tall man approach, a stress flashback loosened his bowels. He saw his lover and partner screaming in terror.

"Where is it?"

"What? What?"

"Where is the item that was with the cash?"

"What item? Please!"

"The disc."

"Disc? I don't know what you mean!"

"I think you do."

This seemingly amiable giant had clutched a screaming Rudy's hair in one hand, yanked that handsome face back, and used a saw-toothed hunting blade on the exposed throat. One clean swipe had nearly severed Rudy's shrieking head. A second cut had done so.

And then the man called Nicky had left Rudy to rot in the bloody sand and drove further out into the desert. He'd been toying with Calvin for at least thirty minutes now, ordering him to run around in circles, sniping at his feet with the hunting rifle, laughing good-naturedly.

Nicky closed the distance rapidly, boots snapping twigs and silencing insects. The night took on an even bigger chill.

Calvin raised a flat, thoroughly useless palm. "Stop right there."

The giant called Nicky grinned. He had long, white front teeth. *The better to eat you with, my dear.* "Relax, Calvin. As I said, I am here to offer you a deal."

Calvin pictured Rudy again. The pain, the blood. "I'll take it."

"No, no," the huge man said and chuckled. "You must hear me out first, and then decide."

Calvin cringed. "One option is you shoot me down?"

"Oh, no. Much worse."

"That's just great," Calvin sobbed. "Okay, then what's my other choice?"

Nicky reached into his pocket. He produced a small pair of garden clippers with wicked, shiny blades. Smiled. "You carry a message for us."

"A message?"

"We do not like wasting our time on something as mundane as locating stolen property. We have better things to do, you see. But we will not rest until this item has been returned to us, yes?"

"We didn't know. We thought it was just money. Just money."

"Oh, it was much more than just money, my friend."

"This fucking disc you keep asking about? I never saw it. We don't know anything about that . . ."

"Okay, here is the deal. I want a message to reach whoever holds our property. The disc. Perhaps then he will send it back and save us all a great deal of pain, time, and trouble."

The boy wailed in terror and misery. "What do you want from me?"

"Nothing much, my little thief." Nicky clicked the garden clippers. He showed large, white teeth. "Just hold out your fingers."

ONE

"I know who I am," the new client said. His voice cracked. He lowered his head and rubbed the left knee of his new slacks like a fortune teller struggling to get an image from a crystal ball. "This can't be happening."

Clearly it was happening, so I couldn't offer much in the way of reassurance. He was battling himself, close to tears, so I just sat back in my chair and opted to wait him out. Sometimes silence works better than words. In fact, it can be a counselor's best friend. Ticking seconds rapidly gain weight and a minute creates a black hole in the universe.

It takes a lot of effort to repress and divert those pesky emotions we'd all rather not have to examine. They want to express themselves. Don't believe me? Just turn off that television and take away alcohol and drugs and sex and spending and gambling and eating and exercising and all those expensive hobbies and fetishes and obsessions and your deeper feelings have a way of rising to the top. Handle them. Piece of cake, right?

Quentin was a slight man with short grey hair. He'd turned fifty years old and lost both of his parents in an automobile accident within the same year. Quentin had been married twenty-four years. He and his wife Suzanne had three children; a daughter in middle school; a boy who played high school football; and the oldest son, who was now in college studying law. Quentin had followed a beloved uncle into the film business, and was currently producing and distributing documentary films and DVDs. He was miserable, despite being rich, active in his church, and dedicated to his family, or at least he claimed to be. He was also three weeks into a hot and heavy extramarital affair.

Despite my second career hosting talk shows, I still get most of my clients through personal referrals. It's not difficult to keep the two occupations separate. To me, they are two very different worlds. Show business is a job, counseling my vocation. Doing radio and television just lets me make enough money to offer a sliding scale that goes from a hundred and fifty dollars an hour down to free. I do the pro bono stuff, mostly chemical dependency, on my own time.

My poor client Quentin was tied up in emotional knots and grappling with the decision of a lifetime. Finally, I gave him a nudge.

"This must be a very painful choice."

Quentin's tired eyes overflowed. He touched the tear on his right cheek with two fingers and sobbed. I weighed the possibility of leaning forward to touch his hand, but it didn't seem necessary. He was probably integrating the situation and beginning to accept responsibility. That would be step one in the long process of properly dealing with a rather large mistake.

Let it be.

I glanced out the window, where a light breeze moved a row of patterned green leaves across a pavement damp from sprinklers. Spring was inching into a long, hot summer. I'd been in Los Angeles for almost a year. I was back on the radio, although my job wasn't secure. This was what I'd fought hard to achieve, but now that I had something of an entertainment career and a practice again I found myself longing to be back in Nevada. Doing what? I had no idea. I've always been restless and maybe more than a little crazy.

As if reading my mind, Quentin raised his head. His mouth

turned down at the corners like in a clown painting. "Do we ever really know ourselves?"

I weighed my response. "I can offer you a personal, highly subjective opinion. Like most great truths, the answer is probably yes and no. We don't really know ourselves but can figure a lot out by cool and steady observation."

"Mr. Callahan, I never thought this could happen to me."

"Mick. A friend of mine says your conscious mind may be on a diet, but your unconscious will keep stopping for a cheeseburger and fries."

A thin smile. "You're saying Patty is junk food?"

"She is a human being." I shrugged and smiled back. "Still, maybe that's an apt metaphor. She has admitted she tends to pursue married men. And junk food can taste damned good sometimes."

"What should I do, Mick?"

"I can't answer that for you. It's your life. However, I can tell you some things that might help you decide on a course of action."

"Please do."

I had his full attention and the advantage of the moment. "Someone once wrote that integrity is 'obedience to the unenforceable.' That's a solid definition. It means that we all need a code to live by, something we can turn to when things go dark. Without integrity life can turn you inside out."

"I'm a Christian." A bit defensive. "I have my beliefs."

I opted not to go there. "I'm not here to debate theology with you, Quentin. However, it seems to be that there is a qualitative difference between dogma and integrity. One comes from the outside, and is hammered down our throats from an early age. We believe because we've been brainwashed to believe, or to be kinder maybe because it comes naturally. We get upset when someone makes us question dogma because our world is rooted in it, kind of like a foundation. Are you with me?"

"Yes."

"Okay. In my opinion, integrity is something that comes by trial and error, it's open to new information on a daily basis, and is chosen from the inside. As my sponsor always says, 'there is no outside answer to an inside problem.' The spot you're in now demands real integrity that can translate into decision making and action. Mere faith won't cut it."

Quentin struggled with that for a long moment. Had I insulted him, or perhaps his belief system? Well, yes and no. His features gradually darkened. I could tell that he wanted to be angry with me, maybe find an excuse to reject that statement and storm out of my office for good. I held back, for fear of setting him off, and let him digest things.

"So I have to give her up."

I almost didn't hear him, his voice was so low. I pretended not to. "Excuse me?"

"I have to give her up." It wasn't a question. He was trying a difficult sentence on for size. I didn't respond. Quentin said it again. "Give her up." He screwed his face up like a little boy and wiped his nose. "But I can't do that."

"You can do whatever you decide to do."

He didn't seem convinced. I allowed some more space. Way down the block a squeal of tires followed by silence announced that someone had narrowly avoided a fender bender. The clock ticked forward. I wanted a drink of water but sensed it was important to remain still.

"Oh, God," Quentin whispered. "Oh, God."

Time was running out. If I didn't strike now, I sensed he might not be back. I went for the throat. "I'm going to offer some final thoughts, Quentin. Just listen and consider what I'm saying. This won't fly. What you're feeling is similar to a physical addiction. It will pass."

"You promise that?" A trembling lower lip.

"Objectively, you have been seeing this woman for a matter of weeks. Weigh that against all those years with your wife. You tell me."

"I see."

"You've been honest in business, a good dad, and a man who believes in life having a purpose greater than the satisfying of appetites. The right stuff is in there, just look for it. If you dig deeply enough, your integrity will tell you what to do."

"Okay, okay."

"We'll have to stop here."

"Okay." Quentin took out his pen and began to write me a check. I got up and went over to my laptop to check for E-mail. I found one cancellation for the following Monday, and a note that I saved for later. Came back, sat down.

"It may be old-fashioned, but when I'm looking at marital issues, I always start with what is best for the children. They didn't ask for this mess, and have no vote. You've been married for a long time, Quentin. Your wife deserves a chance to keep it all together."

"I know that . . ."

I pressed on. "Your sons will look to you as an example of manhood, for better or worse. Your youngest, Mandy, is female. If you are found to have been unfaithful to her mother, you have cheated on her as well. She may never forget, much less forgive."

He looked stricken. I ignored that. I was hurting him for surgical reasons. "Now let me give you some painful statistics. Around eighty-five percent of new relationships that begin with an affair will not succeed. The essential trust necessary has already been damaged. Your girlfriend will watch you lying to your wife, and never believe you when you say you're working late. You'll go through every day knowing she cheerfully jumped into affairs with married men."

He was absorbing the trust issue, I could feel it. He was probably already jealous of her, and vice versa.

"So, if you do leave your family and want this new relationship to work, you'll need immediate and serious therapy to pull it off. I will give you the number of someone new who can be neutral and might be able to coach you through. But believe me, the odds are not good."

I had his full attention. I bored in further. "Also, she is too young, Quentin. I tell men that if a woman is under thirty she's too small, throw her back. Let's do the math. When you are sixty, she will be thirty-four, so when you're seventy, only forty-four. I've seen people beat this one, but it is rough. And the most likely outcome is that she'll eventually leave you for someone younger, and you'll have a heavy burden to carry."

"You're probably right." I wasn't telling Quentin anything he didn't already know. It just helped to have it coming from the outside. That made it a bit easier for him to focus on the truth.

"When we drift into an affair, it is usually because we've ignored the signs that our marriage has gone off the tracks. We feel so disconnected from our spouse that we withdraw that mysterious spark of attachment and allow it to begin to flicker elsewhere."

"Yes." He closed his eyes as if to soak in that idea.

"You probably started with harmless flirtation, right? Then some private time and sharing personal information you would otherwise have held back. And being in the same church group created a kind of false intimacy. You stopped talking to your wife about the things that matter. A crush became an emotional affair and then finally sex. But what if the proper connections had been nurtured months or years ago? What then? You've had crushes before, but never allowed an affair to start, right?"

"There was a woman in the choir maybe ten years ago,"

Quentin said. "She was married, too. We talked about it, but never did anything. She and her husband went into therapy."

"I rest my case. She did the right thing. And it would have been smart for you to have followed in her footsteps back then, for your own sake. Once the communication clears up, we often rediscover why we're together and save things."

"I don't like hearing this, but I get your drift."

"What I'm saying is that it's generally more about the problems in the existing relationship than the appropriateness or desirability of the third party in a triangle. There's still a chance you can fix this thing."

"You've seen it work out?"

"Lots of times." And that was the truth. People constantly amaze me with their resiliency and capacity for change. In fact, that's what keeps the work so interesting and rewarding.

"Can we still be friends, Mick?"

"After this?" I shook my head. "No. My advice is to lose her phone number. Send no E-mails, arrange no more meetings."

"That seems cold."

"Every young woman has read a dozen articles warning her not to get involved with a married man because he usually stays with his wife. Her friends will spank her and remind her that what she did was foolish and wrong."

"I can never speak to her again?"

"If you want to call her once to tell her you're going into therapy to try and save your marriage, keep it brief and not romantic in any way. Believe me, if she really cares about you, she'll get it. She may even be relieved."

Quentin cocked his head. "I don't understand that remark."

"People have affairs for lots of reasons. One reason younger women pursue older men who are married is a buried wish to take Daddy away from Mommy."

"Ouch."

I stared at him. Quentin's face was pink with shame. He'd deserved it. "Our time is up, Quentin. You have the card I gave you? Joan is a good marital therapist. Call her, set something up and take your wife in for a few appointments." I also told him about a book by John Gottman, PhD that I often recommended. Quentin found some tissues and wiped the tears from his face. His jaw settled. He looked like a man on a mission.

"Do I ever tell my wife about the girl?"

Now just "the girl," no first name. We'd won some ground. "That's another one I can't answer for certain, but my gut feeling is no. I'd just keep your mouth shut. It doesn't seem fair to unburden your conscience at her expense, especially if you decide it's completely over."

"I should go, it's late." Quentin looked me up and down as he decided on his next move. I'd stung him, but helped him at the same time. Finally, he said, "Can I come back?"

"Of course you can." I opened my appointment book. "How about next Saturday? We could keep this as a regular time."

TWO

Later that night I drove to the Kitty Kat Club, a dump located in a grey strip mall out by the Burbank Airport, just north of Vanowen. It's pretty much the same as any other bar of its kind; a darkened, neon-addled pit reeking of urine, smoke, and alcohol. The female dancers are a cut above average, mostly because a drunken businessman on the road with an expense account is generally the best tipper. I know, because I've had a few of those working girls as clients. Well, and I used to be a regular customer, but that was a long time ago.

When I pulled in, the parking lot was nearly empty, except for a Jeep Cherokee with rental plates, a panel truck, a BMW, and a geriatric station wagon that looked like it had been tenderized with a ball-peen hammer.

I drove to the back of the lot and parked sideways, so I could see the entrance and the alley at the same time. I turned the radio down and watched the door for a while. Eventually I heard my own voice. I should be used to that by now, but I'm not. I winced as I listened to myself pitch a brand name comfort mattress for the station. That reminded me that my job status was shaky again. Did I even care? I shut the car off and sat listening to some crickets and the ticking of the engine.

The Bone was back. *Unbelievable. . . .*

There are moments in life that have an odd, almost leaden resonance to them. They give you the distinct feeling that a decision you're about to make could have magnificent or

25

devastating consequences. This was one of those moments. I
had no reason to feel so scared, no logical reason at any rate,
but my gut was a plastic sack full of ice cubes. I hadn't seen
Bud Stone in nearly nine years. I'd loved him like a brother
through boot camp, leaned on him when we suffered through
Hell Week in the SEALs, hated him for hitting on an officer's
wife I was seeing at the time, even knocked him flat one Tequila-
fueled night in San Diego. I washed out of the Navy because of
that affair, and we'd eventually lost touch, but Bone proudly
wore the trident until grievously wounded in Iraq. Then he'd
returned to civilian life. Other than an occasional E-mail or
phone message, I'd not heard a word from him in years.

Until now.

As if on cue, a man in a business suit opened the door with
the ponderous gravitas of the dedicated inebriate. When he
stepped outside, under the lights, his bald pate gleamed like a
polished diamond. He struggled to light a cigarette, but couldn't
hold the match steady. Finally he walked over to the rented
Jeep, stood weaving like a cobra and searched his pockets for
the keys. The door opened again and I instinctively slid down in
the seat, out of sight. The drunk looked vaguely like Bud Stone,
but I couldn't be sure. And Bone wasn't the type to wear a suit.

Two other customers emerged; both broad shouldered, with
buzz cut hair and tight, stylish jeans. One wore a cowboy hat
and a wife-beater tee with Old Glory on it, the other a faded
green windbreaker. The two looked reasonably sober, though
pretty worked up. They stood near a black Nissan, talking in
low tones. Meanwhile, the drunken businessman leaned on the
hood of his own vehicle and projectile vomited into some night
blooming jasmine. I got a good look at his face, and it wasn't
Bud Stone.

The guy in the windbreaker stayed blocking the door. The
cowboy strolled after their mark, cracking his knuckles.

Two thugs mugging a drunk. Great.

This was clearly none of my damned business. I was here to see an old friend, not to get my nose broken again. *Ah, shit.* I made a show of getting out of the car like a man who'd had a few, whistling and mumbling to myself, figuring maybe a witness would be enough to throw a monkey wrench into their plans.

It didn't work. The guy on the door just leaned back, folded his arms.

"Closed, pal. Take off."

I looked at my watch, started walking. "Don't let them bluff you, bro. Last call is one-thirty."

"You don't hear so well? It's my bar, and I said take off."

I kept moving, hands loose at my belt loops to show I was harmless. Out of the corner of my eye, I saw the cowboy closing in on the drunk. "One beer, a look at Tina's tits, and I'm out of here."

I was on him now, maybe two yards away. A brief, confused look crossed his face. "They ain't got any Tina."

Cowboy popped the businessman who looked like Bud; hit him once on the jaw. The drunk went down in a heap. Cowboy was lifting his wallet before he hit the ground, maybe looking for credit cards. My guy went for something in the pocket of his windbreaker, probably a small gun. I feinted giving a kick to the nuts. When he raised his thigh and got off balance, I ran him into the door, slammed my elbow into his temple a couple of times. He dropped hard, but still breathing. I spun and sprinted for the cowboy. He was already up, crouched with his hands loose like a man who'd gone a few rounds.

"This ain't smart," he said, not unkindly.

I sighed. "I know."

"Then don't throw down."

I pointed to the drunk, who was struggling to sit up. "Give

the man his stuff back, and then maybe we can talk."

Cowboy studied me for a long moment. I saw him replaying how quickly I'd dropped his partner. He opened the wallet, took a twenty and held it up. "Figure I should get a few beers out of this. I walk away now, we straight?"

I shrugged. "He'd just blow it anyway."

Cowboy nodded. He went back towards the club, eyes on my face. He took the long way around, to avoid getting close. Picked up his friend from behind, under the arm pits, and half dragged him over to one of the trucks. They got in and drove away.

The businessman that looked like Bud was back on his feet, leaning against the rental car. His suit was speckled with vomit and some blood from a cut just over his right eye. He glared at me.

"Buzz off, man. I didn't ask for your help."

"True enough." I raised my arm, pointed. "There's a Motel Six just down the road. Check in and sleep this off. Otherwise, a squad car is going to nab you, and you'll spend the night in a cell and lose your license."

He wiped his nose and spat, turned to open the car, and then I heard him mumble something obscene.

"What?"

"I said . . . thanks."

I nodded. "Try AA. It works."

"Not for me."

"Give it ninety meetings in ninety days. Keep at it. This is no way to live."

"That so?" He got in, slammed the door and started the engine. Now he felt safe. "Yeah, well fuck you too, Mother Teresa."

I watched as he backed out, clipped a metal trash can, and finally managed a U. He drove out of the lot onto Vanowen, then floored it to well over the speed limit. It was no surprise that he went the wrong way, down toward the next line of strip clubs. I crossed the lot.

Some Rick James tune was thumping, scratching, and growling at the other side of the entrance. That tired old one about a girl being super freaky. I opened the dented metal door and went inside.

Bud Stone was parked alone at the end of the bar, before a half-empty pitcher of warm beer, watching two bored girls pretend to have lesbian sex. He wasn't wearing a suit. The years hadn't been kind. Like the drunk, his hairline was trekking steadily towards Bolivia, and his massive chest drooped a bit. He still had huge guns straining his tee shirt; arms festooned with tattoos and clumps of thick, reddish hair. Bud Stone worked out harder than any man I'd ever known. And he was one of the good guys, even after two combat tours. I owed him. A lot.

Bone saw me coming, and his face split into that familiar, toothy grin. "Well, if it ain't Mick Callahan his own self!"

"Was last time I looked."

We shook hands, palms slapping together, grips hard and short. "You're in good shape," Bone said. "You've been hitting the iron?"

"I go over to Golden Gym, on Laurel Canyon, but only three or four times a week these days. Know the place?"

"Yeah, I know it. I know right where that is."

"You could meet me there some time."

"Sure, let's do that. Well, then." An awkward silence ensued. Finally, he motioned for me to sit down. "Want a Coke or something?"

"Not at five bucks a glass. How are you doing, Bud?"

"I'm a happy camper." Bud didn't lie well.

I slid around him, so my back was to the wall. The two dancers saw they'd lost our attention and slithered off to bother the only other patrons, three drunken Hispanics in work clothes.

"Same old Mick."

"What?"

He grinned. "What did you call it, Hitchcock fixation?"

"Close." My face felt hot. "But it's the cowboy, not the director. Wild Bill got shot in the back playing cards. I just hate to turn my back to a room. Like to see what's going on."

"Okay, bro, I got a riddle for you. Picture this, okay? You are on a horse, galloping at a constant rate. On your right side is a sharp drop, and on your left side is an elephant traveling at the same speed as you. Directly in front of you is a galloping kangaroo and your horse is unable to overtake it. Behind you is a lion running at the same speed as you and the kangaroo. What must you do to safely escape this highly dangerous situation?"

I grinned. "Okay, I'll give."

"Well, son, the very first thing you better do is get your drunk ass off that merry-go-round!"

We laughed loud and warm. The homely waitress sauntered over wriggling her fake breasts. I gave her cash for the cover charge without being asked. "Just bring me some ice water with a slice of lime in it." She started to remind me that I'd be paying for booze. My eyes told her I already knew. Bone watched her haunches as she walked away.

"Killer body, with a face designed to protect it."

I grabbed a swizzle stick from one of his dead soldiers. "Been a long time, Bone."

"A few years. You may not recall, you seemed pretty blitzed, but we said howdy at Burbank Airport one night. I was on my way to Vegas. You were going to tape that show in Denver, that one where you punched some guy on live TV."

I winced. "That was my downfall."

"Every time I saw that clip replayed on the news shows, it cracked me up all over again. The guy was an asshole, Mick.

Had it coming to him."

"Let's talk about something else. I'm reformed."

Bone wasn't going to let me off easy. "Then I heard about that stuff up in Nevada, where you busted up some kind of drug ring. I was hoping the good publicity would kick start your career. Damned glad to see you land on your feet here in LA."

"You ever listen to my show?"

Bone grinned hugely. "Not often. You know me. I've tuned in now and again, but I'm way past saving."

The girl brought my ice water and slipped away. Bone and I clicked glasses. "To old times, bro."

"Mostly good times."

We caught up a bit more. Showed off a few scars like boys who'd played high school football together. The Navy had done a hell of a good job fixing his bum leg. Finally, Bone looked around for a moment, as if embarrassed to finally have to come to the point. "Mick, you said one time that if I ever needed help, you'd have my back. Did you mean that?"

"I'm here, Bone, just like you asked." He was calling in the favor of a lifetime, and we both knew it. "Even though it's way past my bedtime."

"I need you to do me a solid."

"What is it you want?"

"For you to watch out for somebody who means a lot to me."

"How serious is the situation?"

"Hey, it's probably nothing, man. I just want you to look in on her the next few weeks, maybe make sure she's okay."

"Most things aren't that simple."

"Well, it's that and if necessary maybe scare some bad guys away. It's become sort of a mess."

"Rats. We were fine until that last part. Who is it?"

"My girlfriend." He reached into his shirt, produced a photo of an attractive young woman. I leaned closer. She had bottle-blonde hair, bright blue eyes, and a nice figure. In the picture she wore glasses, but I was willing to bet she had contacts in the bathroom cabinet. One of those ubiquitous LA actress/model/dancers.

"I thought you were married."

"I am."

I stared at him for a stiff minute, trying to decide what, if anything, to say. I deal with this sort of soap opera all day long, but Bone wasn't a client. I decided to skip the lecture unless he asked for my thoughts. "What's your wife's name again, Wendy? What the hell happened?"

"What happened? Well, I guess real life doesn't measure up to combat. It gets dull. I made a mistake, bro. I became a statistic. I started to take Wendy for granted. My son is all grown up, moved away to New Orleans to get in on reconstruction stuff after that second hurricane. I started fooling around now and again, nothing serious."

"And your wife found out."

"Not about the light stuff. It was a lot worse than that. I got serious about one of them, and my wife saw a couple of hot E-mails. It got pretty ugly. She left me last year, man, and went to stay with her mom. Maybe I didn't mention that in the card I sent at Christmas, I don't know."

"No, you didn't."

"It took me months to convince Wendy to come back, but she finally did. We're doing okay again, at least lately."

I looked around the bar. "You sure about that?"

He ignored the barb. "That girlfriend I mentioned? She ain't there to tempt me anymore." Bone shrugged, but his eyes glinted. "Got involved with some yoga teacher, even said she wants to have kids with the prick. I was going to lose out to a granola eater. Can you believe that? Cheated on while I was cheating on my wife. Anyway, it finished us, but that's who this is about. The girlfriend."

"I'm listening."

He handed me the picture. "You keep it, okay? Just so you'll know her when you meet her. Her name is Brandi, last name DeLillo, originally from Omaha. You can probably tell she was in the life a ways back, but she got herself into a program, and now she's in school at UCLA. It's over, but I still give a shit."

"Bone, the obvious question is why me? Why not watch out for her yourself?"

"Figure you owe me?"

Back in the day, Bone stood by me in numerous barroom brawls, even took the rap for a DUI hoping to protect my ultimately failed status with the SEALs. There were other incidents, including a couple of things I should have gone to jail over. Still could. Those days had to stay buried. "Yeah," I said, without resentment. "I owe you."

He looked down. "I got myself in a little trouble is why. Nothing I can't straighten out. I'll watch out for Wendy, but I can't be two places at once. So I'm only asking you just in case, if you know what I mean."

"Like as in case you do time? Get blown the fuck up? What?"

"That doesn't really matter, does it? You don't need to know."

I shook my head. "We're old friends, Bone. I keep my promises and pay my debts. But if you want me to get involved in something where there's real risk, I have to know the whole story. It's better that way."

"Can I count on you to keep your mouth shut? Even to the law?"

"Give me some money."

"What?"

I held my hand out. "Give me some money."

Bone shrugged, dug around in his pockets and produced a

ten-dollar bill. I tucked it into my jeans. "Okay. Tomorrow, when I go to the office, I'm putting you down as a cash client."

"Huh?"

"Then anything you tell me will be kept confidential, unless you're planning a murder or molesting kids. Sound okay?"

"Okay." He looked down at the bar, moved some moisture around with his fingertips. "I was a cop for a while. I should know better than to be in this fix. I did something really stupid, Mick."

"What, and why?"

"Why? Money, what else? The what of it is that I wanted to help Brandi with her school. I wanted her to think I was cool, look up to me and be grateful. Okay, and maybe give me another chance. Anyway, I gave myself all the same lame excuses we all use when we're young, dumb, and full of come."

"You're not that young anymore, Bone."

"Yeah, but I'm still dumb and horny."

I checked my watch. "Just tell me what happened. I wasn't kidding about this being past my bedtime."

"I was shooting pool with a guy I know, and he said he was sure he could make a big score through a pal of his, some guy named Toole. He just needed some cash to make the first buy. Said it was an easy double-your-money type thing, okay? Piece of cake." The waitress wandered our way again, and Bone fell silent. He resumed when she vanished into the ladies' room. "And you know something funny? I can't believe I went for it, because I hate those fucking drug dealers, I really do."

"Go on."

"I sold a couple of my old cars, borrowed from a few people, and gave him my stake. He went to make the move. I was supposed to get paid the next weekend."

"Let me guess. He disappeared."

Bone picked at his fingernails. "Dumb, huh? Faber never

showed up for work after that. Neither did this Toole guy. They just left my sorry ass twisting in the wind. Mick, I got cocky. I figured they'd never risk pulling a fast one on someone like me. Looks like I was wrong."

"How much money are we talking about, Bone?" I was running numbers through my mind, wondering if I could float him a loan instead.

He mumbled something. I stared at him until he managed to say it louder. "It's maybe a hundred and change."

My shoulders slumped. "Oh, man."

"I know, I know. Like I said, dumb."

I slapped his leg. "So face up to it, work hard, pay everybody back."

"I'm trying to do that, but it gets worse."

"Doesn't it always?"

Someone came in the front door. The hair on my neck fluttered. It was the cowboy from the parking lot. He saw us and waved at me. No sign of his friend, who was probably waiting outside to rearrange my facial features. This night had started bad and was going downhill fast.

"Some of the money I borrowed, like maybe fifty grand, it was from the Pesci crew." He expected me to recognize the name. "As in Big Paul Pesci, who I hear is one bent-nose, spaghetti-chomping motherfucker. And he doesn't go to a shrink like that guy used to on TV, okay? I figured the vig was low enough that if I doubled the fifty in a week and paid everybody back I'd still come out thirty large ahead of the game, enough to cover all of Brandi's tuition. I meant well, man. I really did."

Cowboy sat at the other end of the bar. He flashed a shark grin and wriggled his fingers. I waved back this time, with a growing sense of anxiety. All I needed now was my name in the newspapers because of a fight outside some strip bar. My ratings had slipped, my radio job was getting iffy, and that could really flush it all down the toilet.

Bone didn't notice. He finished his beer. "Anyway, I missed the due date, so Pesci sent a couple of folks by my place of employment to adjust my attitude."

"Did they?"

"They tried, but I adjusted back some. I'm sure they're a bit pissed. Anyway, here is the rest. Fucking drug dealers, I hate those pricks. Some clown name of Rico Diaz from Guatemala? It seems he sold a bunch of primo smoke to this Toole fellow, who took down his man and skipped town with the whole shipment of weed I was supposed to be helping to buy."

"He sure about that, that he's gone?"

"At least it looks that way, which is just as bad. So this Diaz, now he also likes me for repaying his money, too. Mostly because I'm the only asshole anyone can find."

"How much do you owe there?"

"Another fifty."

I rubbed my temples. "Jesus, Bone. So you have yourself on the hook for a hundred and fifty thousand dollars, and it's to the mob and a drug ring?"

He forced a shark smile. "Genius, isn't it? Like I always said, you're going to fuck something up, do it big-time."

"Why not go to the police? Wear a wire on both crews."

"Not a chance. These folks play too rough, even for witness protection, and I like having my balls attached to my crotch. I'll find a way to get the money together. In the meantime, Mick, you can help put my mind at ease by promising me you'll look after the girl. Just in case anything bad happens. If they can't get to me and my wife, they may go after her. Okay?"

"Wow."

"Like I said, I'll find a way to make this right. Do this thing, Callahan. Please. I don't want to have to worry about Brandi, too."

36

"She already got sober, right?"

"More than a year ago."

"I know a lot of women in the program."

"She doesn't really go to those meetings much anymore."

"Just a backup plan. I'll ask a friend to keep an eye out, maybe." I patted the photograph in my pocket. "Okay, Bud. If anything happens, I'll help her out. You have my word."

He sighed with relief. "Thanks, Mick. You have no idea how much better I feel."

"Bone, what are you going to do?"

"I'll figure something out."

"Like what?"

He stared at me. Something in his eyes said he was enjoying himself more than he was letting on. Warriors always have a hard time packing it in. They want to recapture living on the edge. Hell, I was more that way myself than I wanted to admit.

"Never mind," I said. "Way better I don't know."

"True."

I looked around the room, thought for a moment, leaned closer to Bone and whispered in his ear. He nodded, slammed his fist on the bar. "Well, I got to piss like a racehorse. I'll call you next week, tell you what's up."

"You do that. Take care of yourself, Bone." We slapped palms.

Bone wandered off, in search of the toilet. I slid off the bar stool and considered my options. Cowboy was waiting for me, grinning like a possum licking peaches off a wire brush. His friend was probably right outside, maybe in the bushes by the trash cans. I checked my watch, thought about things, and decided to just get it over with.

I walked straight past Cowboy without looking back, paused briefly in the doorway, and then went outside. The night air was crisp and welcome after the stench of the bar. I listened carefully, heard the guy in the windbreaker quietly change positions in the brush.

After a long moment, I moved further out into the parking lot. Heard the door open and close again behind me.

"I thought we were straight," I said, still facing the other way.

Cowboy belched and chuckled. "Guess I lied."

He rushed me from behind, boots in deep gravel, while Windbreaker clanged past the metal trash cans to jump me from the right. Things slow down a bit when you can see the fight coming. I tend to feel pretty calm.

I dropped low, spun around, and my shoulder hit Cowboy in the lower belly. He gave up a whinny and a burst of foul breath. Tried to grab at my face, gouge my eyes. I straightened up, got my knees into it, and brought him high into the night before slamming him down on the pavement. When he hit, I heard the air whoosh out and something go *CRACK*, maybe the plastic handle of a hidden gun. I kicked his head, made sure he was down and out for a while.

I turned slowly, looked. Windbreaker lay facedown in a pile of trash, writhing in pain. Bone had slipped out the front of the bar, jogged down the alley, and ambushed him for me. My friend removed a pair of brass knuckles, shook his fingers. We stood, chests heaving, staring at each other under the stars. Bone grinned.

Kind of like old times.

THREE

One hour later, I was in my small house in the San Fernando Valley, talking to my sponsor, Hal Solomon, via Tag World. The connection was especially good.

"What I want to know," Hal said from the computer screen, "is how you manage to create so much drama without even breaking a sweat."

My best friend, virtually always in a suit and tie, currently wore a thick pair of red pajamas that somewhat robbed him of intrinsic dignity. His silver hair was freshly washed, almost sparkling. The camera showed me a large bed and part of a rustic executive suite in the background. If memory served, Hal was at a lodge somewhere in Canada, ostensibly to learn how to fly fish. Or maybe it was upstate New York.

Personally, I figured he was there because of the cuisine. Hal was comfortably rich and semi-retired. He could do any damned thing he wanted on a daily basis, and generally did.

"Without even breaking a sweat? Hal, you almost sounded like a country boy."

"I've been hanging around you long enough."

"I'm not at all sure the world can handle two opinionated, sober, educated rednecks."

"Promise me you won't get dragged into anything messy. I realize this fellow is an old friend, but things have been somewhat peaceful of late. This is indeed a welcome change."

"I know that."

"Was that the sound of you giving me your word?"

"Hal, I have no intention of getting into trouble."

Hal sighed. "Semantic judo. You should have become a lawyer instead of a therapist."

"I should have become a lot of things."

"So, young stallion, the television show is on hold and you're still on a contractual probation at the radio station. Yes?"

"True, and so I should stay out of this."

"Unless you're tired of paying a mortgage and having a pot to urinate in, I would think that a reasonable proposition. Look, I'm still not sure I understand what exactly has gone wrong at work. Can you fill me in? Is it your ratings?"

"My ratings are decent, Hal. They've slipped a bit, that's all. The manager doesn't like my act all that much. He's got a thing for this so-called conservative commentator, a bozo named Zachary Marks. He's been pushing the guy to take over my time slot, one of the best for late-night talk."

"So he has no legitimate reason?"

"Okay, one. Maybe his numbers are sort of closing in on mine, but the guy's a first-class prick, and ignorant as a bullfrog."

"One of many, although their numbers seem to be shrinking. Only a few brave souls still admit to having voted such incompetent thieves into office."

"A bit late. If this country had turned any further to the right it would have met its own ass coming the other way."

"Your manager, this Bill person, is it a matter of politics with him, or just advertising dollars?"

"He'd never admit it, but it's just about the money."

"Then it would behoove you to shake things up a bit, get your ratings back up where they belong."

I leaned back in my desk chair, rolled from side to side. "I know, I know. The truth is I'm a little bored with the show. Maybe I need to take on a partner or something. Two hours can be one hell of a long time all by your lonesome."

"I noticed that the last time I was in the ER."

"Don't remind me. I thought we'd lost you. Still feeling okay?"

"Fit as the proverbial fiddle." Hal glanced at his watch. "I'm going to have to jump off soon and get my beauty sleep. Have you managed to patch things up with Ms. Hernandez?"

"She won't call me back."

"You're still fighting."

"She is."

Hal stared at me. He required a better explanation than I was prepared to offer. I drummed my fingers on the rim of the computer keyboard. Sergeant Darlene Hernandez and I had been an item for several months. At first things had gone wonderfully, but as soon as some of the initial chemistry wore off, as is so often the case, we started to bicker; senseless, low-key arguments that left us exhausted and hurt and confused. I call them "evil twin" fights, because afterwards you can't even remember what started it. Your evil twin just takes over, sticks a hand up your behind and starts running your mouth. To Darlene, it had something to do with our relationship being only about sex. To me, it had something to do with her trying to encroach on my precious freedom to be driven and self-absorbed.

"Callahan?" Hal was still waiting.

"Sorry. I was just thinking 'physician, heal thyself.' It's amazing I can know so much about psychology and counseling and so little about keeping a woman happy."

Hal chuckled. "Not that I'm a black belt in these matters, but I'd say you've made a critical error right there, stallion. It is not possible to keep a woman happy. In the final analysis, they've got to make themselves happy, just like the rest of us. All we can do is be there for one another in a pinch, and perhaps be friends."

"I'm going to think of a good argument the second we sign off."

"I doubt it, Mick. And one other thing, at the risk of sounding like a broken record . . ."

"Hal, they don't play records anymore."

"Don't nitpick." He leaned forward, closer to the camera. "You have a fierce anger that is rooted in your childhood, needless to say. I'm no therapist, but it seems to me that if my stepfather beat the feces out of me on a regular basis and forced me to fight other children for money, I might have a tendency to confuse love and hostility."

I grimaced. "Hal, I'm not the one starting the fights here."

"But you'll damn well finish them?"

"What's that supposed to mean?"

"It means that when Darlene lashes out at life, maybe you instinctively think about winning the battle instead of loving her through an emotional experience."

He stared, I stared. "Old man, sometimes I just want to strangle you."

"Take your best shot," Hal said, then laughed and touched the computer screen with his fingertips. "Just do it now, not the next time we're in the same room."

I grinned. "This fellow is selectively courageous."

Hal leaned back in his chair. "How are those nightmares?"

A shrug. "Some okay, some terrible. I don't dream about him very often anymore, if that's what you mean." The man in question being Donny Boy, a violent psychopath who had nearly killed me on two occasions, and was now fortuitously six feet under the Nevada desert. One of my finer achievements. "Most of the time they're fighting dreams. No surprise there."

"I wish I could help you get a good night's sleep," Hal said sadly. "What do you think these bouts with the demons are really about, counselor?"

"A man named Robert Simon wrote a book on forensic psychiatry called *Bad Men Do What Good Men Dream*. He views human behavior as nothing more than a continuum from the rare instances of extreme good, all the way in an arc to the thankfully rare instances of extreme evil. He says we're all capable of just about anything under the right circumstances. I happen to agree."

Hal sighed. "I learned that when I examined my own drinking and drugging history, and finally did a fourth step."

"As did we all. Anyway, Simon makes the simple observation, similar to Freud's, that our dreams solve problems, work out violent and inappropriate impulses, and therefore protect us against our antisocial tendencies. Any good therapist learns rapidly that some part of him completely understands his most disturbed clients in a very visceral, sometimes upsetting way. Like bad dreams." Of my violent past; getting tossed from the Navy SEALs for drinking, brawling, and that affair with an officer's wife; the humiliating crash of my television career. *Booze, drugs, and rage. Sex. Booze, drugs, and rage. On and on.*

"What about understanding Darlene, then?"

I hate it when Hal uses logic on me. I sighed. "I hear you. Her anger may have nothing to do with me. I'm being too self-centered when I react that badly."

"You said it, not I."

"You manipulated me into saying it."

He cocked his head. "Promise me you'll try again. She's the finest young lady I've ever seen in your company."

"Well, that's certainly true enough. That's a promise I don't mind making. I haven't given up on her. Not yet, anyway."

"Glad to hear that."

"Hey, did Jerry e-mail you those pictures of his little palace at the beach? He's surrounded by sand, surf, healthy young ladies in tiny string bikinis, and enough sunshine to give a rattlesnake a bad case of sunstroke."

He laughed. "The lad is probably in heaven."

"Jerry likes California a lot more than Nevada, that's for sure, and the security job lets him consult and telecommute more often than not. I think he is one happy camper."

"Are they going to do that work on his face?"

My hacker friend was badly disfigured. His foster mother had gone psychotic and burned his face with a hot iron. The new job in aerospace security had a nice package of benefits, and Jerry had recently consulted a plastic surgeon about having the scars removed.

"I don't think he's made a decision yet."

"Odd. That would seem to be an obvious call."

"Actually, I can understand what gave him pause, Hal. We are what we are."

"True enough." Hal checked his watch. "I have to run, Cowboy. We have an early day tomorrow, and I've been promised some great scenery. You getting to meetings lately?"

"Not really, hope to fix that this weekend."

"A likely story. Stay sober, and watch that temper."

"Over and out."

I checked my E-mail and then walked out of the room. The house was so silent I could hear a low, moaning wind whistle through the yard. Leaves scraped the windows. Up until recently, I'd had company—one scarred up, geriatric tomcat I'd called Murphy, short for Murphy's Law. The old dude had passed away in his sleep, and I hadn't had the heart to adopt another pet.

I made a club soda and lime in the kitchen, took it into the living room and channel surfed. After a time, I turned both the television and the lights off and sat alone in the dark, sipping and thinking. I missed Darlene and the gentle vibe of a female in my home. My thoughts briefly caressed her skin. I made them change direction.

Damn, Bud Stone was in a hell of a mess. My old friend had clearly been finessed, but by whom? The easy answer was his so-called partners, Faber and Toole. It seemed likely they still had either his money or the drugs, or both, and thus offered a way to take Bone off the hook. I didn't want to get very deep into this. My situation at work was already precarious enough. Why get arrested due to some misunderstanding? Or killed, for that matter. Hey, you can't work if you stop breathing.

I went back into the office, sat down at the computer. I sent a quick note to my agent, Judd Kramer, asking about the status of my contract with the station. Then I e-mailed Jerry to locate two ex-cons named Joey Faber and Frank Toole as quickly and quietly as possible. I didn't say why. I checked and found Larry Donato online. Darlene's cousin had once helped out with a messy situation, got mistaken for me and shot. He'd ended up in a wheelchair for his trouble. Hal had set him up to run his own company supplying off-duty cops for private investigations and security. We connected and his face filled the screen.

"Larry, how goes it?"

"It goes," Donato said. "Have you heard from Peanut?"

My old sober pal Suzanne Walton, whom I had once dubbed Peanut, had dated Larry for a time. Peanut was currently living in Dallas in order to care for her mom. "Nothing lately, not since her birthday. You?"

He shrugged. "I think she bit off more than she can chew. Her mom is a piece of work, and still boozes it up."

"Well, we are what we are."

Donato yawned. "What can I do for you, Mick?"

"I may need someone to keep an eye on a girl, Larry. She's an ex-stripper, used to see a friend of mine. I'll let her know what's happening."

"Any rough stuff?"

"Maybe, but I doubt it."

"Let me think on who. Can I call you guys tomorrow?"

"Tomorrow is fine. You can just let Jerry know."

"How are you and Darlene getting along, Mick?"

"Touch and go."

"Ouch. Okay, talk to you soon."

" 'Night, Larry." I stretched, meditated, and crawled into bed with my mind still buzzing. We'd get Faber and Toole. Hell, Jerry could find anyone, any time. He'd tracked me down for a gig in my hometown of Dry Wells when I was struggling to make a comeback, after years of alcohol and drug abuse. That short job had taken us from acquaintances to friends when a young girl was murdered. Jerry had persuaded me to investigate. We were lucky to escape with our lives. Hal had found consulting work for Jerry, who had opted to follow me to California and live at the beach.

I reflexively reached over to the other pillow, petted thin air, and then remembered Murphy was dead and gone. The towel I'd kept there for him to sleep on was now packed away in a box in the garage. I missed that mangy old coot.

Well, and Darlene.

Women. I'd spent years working my way up to being a talk-show host and media therapist, crashed and burned and come back again, written hundreds of thousands of words in term papers, and past a certain point, still didn't understand anything about them. So fascinating, so emotionally fluid, so mysterious.

I rolled over and tried to go to sleep. My mind replayed horrific images, pictures of several violent incidents from my return to Dry Wells, the Burning Man Festival in the high desert. I remembered fear, blistering heat, the salty taste of fresh blood, the wicked crunch of bone, and the flat splat of a bullet striking meat. *Think about a Bach cello solo, then some flowers in the breeze. Let everything else fade.* My pulse sprinted anyway. *Easy, let it go, get some sleep.*

Another tough choice. Except I didn't feel I really had much of a choice. Bud Stone was an old friend. I owed him. Yet somehow my sobriety had become almost as violent as my drinking career.

It made no sense for me to risk getting seriously involved with Bone's messy situation. It would be far smarter to just hang back and hire someone to look after his stripper girlfriend.

Come on, Callahan, do the smart thing for once in your life. Just back off. Let this one go. Stay out of it.

Yeah, right.

FOUR

"Okay, let's talk about impulses."

I was pacing the studio, wearing a headset to keep my hands free, trying to keep my energy level up. Sixteen minutes to go, and the show felt flatter than the ass-end of an anorexic stripper. *Lift some, damn it. Lift.*

"It's a natural impulse to hop out of the car and punch the crap out of the guy who cut you off in traffic, right? But we learn, or hopefully we learn, to restrain that natural impulse. Therapists call this 'impulse control,' and if you didn't have it, you'd pee in your pants. Well, impulse control has a lot of functions. It can keep you from sleeping with your neighbor's wife, punching the hell out of your kids, stealing from the company you work for, right? So, it has a lot of uses."

The caller was a young man from Encino named Don. "How is that different from having a functioning conscience?"

"Good question. I'd say because it gives us choices, not motivation. Look at it this way, Don, a sociopath can have some impulse control, albeit pretty poor in most cases. He could refrain from killing someone in the heat of the moment, and wait for a better time. A conscience would keep most of us from committing murder in either case."

"Got it."

"Thanks for calling."

I checked the clock, reached for the console and brought up some background music. "Go grab a snack, guys. I'm Mick

Callahan, and we'll be right back after this brief message."

I popped a commercial into the deck and stretched. I looked out through the glass partition, and saw Zachary Marks coming in to tape an interview with the Mayor. The station manager, a rotund bald spot named Jim O'Brien, was sucking up like the oldest whore at the Chicken Ranch. As I'd told Hal, O'Brien wanted the station to go right-wing talk, despite the current political climate, a posture which struck me as a little like betting heavily on tech stocks back in 2002. Still, Marks had a loyal following and ARB numbers that now rivaled mine, though God knows where they came from in a city as liberal as Los Angeles.

O'Brien saw me, gave a halfhearted wave. Zachary Marks acted like I wasn't there. The Mayor nodded the way people do when they know they've seen you somewhere before and figure they'd best be polite. I went back on the air and brought my theme music up as I spoke.

"I've got time for one or two more callers, and that's about it." I glanced down at the phone. Three lights were blinking. I chose the middle.

"Hi, you're on the air with Mick Callahan. Make sure your radio is turned down. What's on your mind?"

A female, low-voiced with a slight drawl, kind of scratchy and sexy. "You were raised in Nevada, right?"

"Yes, up near a small town called Dry Wells."

"Were you born there?"

Something about her voice was familiar, but I couldn't pin it down. "I'm not sure," I said. "I think so." That was an honest answer. "My stepfather wasn't exactly forthcoming about such things."

"I'm curious; do you have any family still there, or anywhere else?"

"Not that I know about, ma'am. Did you have a comment or

a question on tonight's topic, by any chance?"

"No, thank you."

Dial tone. "Okay, then I will consider myself dismissed." I found another blinking light. "Hello, you're on the air."

"I love your show," an older woman said. "And tonight's topic." She sounded sincere. "I just want to toss out a question, and see how you respond. What are we?"

"What are we, in *your* opinion?"

"Violent, selfish, down and dirty, kind of evil."

"So you're saying Freud was right, and we're all just a raging ball of destructive id in a thinly wrapped package, ready to explode?"

"That's it exactly. Sometimes I think we're all kidding ourselves, you know? If I'm good, I'm just wasting my time trying to pretend to be a bad girl. If I'm evil, there's nothing society can do to reform me. I'm one of the bad guys, and that's it."

"I see where you're going, and I'm enough of an existentialist to agree with that to an extent, but even if it's wishful thinking I'd like to believe we can grow out of things and change. For example, I think I have."

"Think, or know?"

I laughed. "Touché, what do any of us really know about ourselves? Have a good night and thanks for calling."

I checked the time. "This is Mick Callahan, and tonight's discussion was about who and what we are. Now it's time to wrap things up. Stay tuned for news on the hour, and then some cool nighttime jazz to help you sleep. Thanks to that last caller, I'm going to offer a new twist on Callahan's thought for the day. It comes from Walt Whitman. 'This is what you shall do: Love the earth and sun and the animals, despise riches, give alms to everyone that asks, stand up for the stupid and crazy, devote your income and labor to others, hate tyrants, argue not concerning God, have patience and indulgence toward the people . . . and your very flesh shall be a great poem.' Good night."

I dialed down the music, started the pre-recorded news disc, and removed the plastic headset. The door to the recording studio was already closed, and as I watched, the red light came on. I knew I was being neurotic, but I had a sinking feeling in my stomach. Maybe I'd be out of a job again soon. My agent was scheduled to have lunch with the brass to raise the issue of a new contract. I didn't want to think about how I'd cover my mortgage if they failed to renew. Hal would certainly help out, but accepting money from him would be yet another exercise in humiliation.

Those thoughts made me queasy. I packed up my stuff, grabbed my briefcase, and left the soundproofed room. The hallway was empty and, as usual, the receptionist was long gone. I went out into the parking lot, and the motion detectors kicked on. Shadow to bright light. I briefly flashed on the night I'd been jumped by a masked assailant. My skin rippled.

I crossed the lot without incident, tossed my briefcase in the trunk, and stood there for a long moment. Opened my cell phone, started to dial Darlene Hernandez but closed it again. *What do I say? I'm sorry, but I'm so screwed up I can't handle how screwed up you can get?*

I heard tires crunching gravel and looked up. A white Toyota with rental plates cruised slowly down the alley. A pretty woman sat behind the wheel and stared back at me. She had long, dark hair and large eyes and wore a jeans shirt and jacket with what looked like a cowboy string tie. I smiled and waved, just in case I knew her. Although she clearly recognized me, the girl did not react. The car went behind a concrete wall and I turned back to my own vehicle. *That's probably what's left of your fan club, Callahan.*

I got in, slammed the door, and drove home. Along the way, I turned on the radio. I'd left it set on a Classic Rock station, and noticed it was playing an ancient hit called "Dust in the Wind." That got my Buddha going. In the scheme of things, what the hell were Darlene and I fighting about, and why did it even matter? All we are is dust, blowing in the wind. *Carpe Diem,* seize the day. Besides, what kind of man would I be if I simply backed down from a woman's emotions?

Be a man, Callahan. Enough is enough.

At least I now had something to talk about. As I took my exit from the freeway, I dialed her cell number.

Darlene, in her lightly accented English. "Hello?"

I hung up the phone. *Okay, so what if I'm a coward. No one has to know.* My cell phone rang. *Oh, shit. Caller ID.*

"Callahan? Did you just call me?"

"I'm sorry, Darlene. I hit the memory button by mistake."

She sighed, a feathery breath that sparked a memory and lit my candle. "Jesus, you're a terrible liar."

"I am, aren't I? See, that and my lack of big boobs is probably why I never get out of traffic tickets."

"I was just thinking about you." She was in a bar or something, probably with a few colleagues. I could hear male voices, arguing in the background—something about a perp who was a real scum bag. Some of Darlene's fellow officers spoke like extras on a bad cop show.

"Missing me?"

"No, not exactly, just thinking about you."

I pulled into my driveway, went into the house. I closed and locked the front door. "You there?"

"Yes, I'm still here. Are you home for the night?"

"Just walked in."

Too much time passed. We both coughed nervously, and that made us laugh. "I don't understand what's happening between us. You're the shrink, Callahan, can you explain it?"

"Maybe." I stuck my neck out. "Can I try that in person?"

"Sure, in a public place and during daylight hours." She covered the phone and sent someone away.

I took a shot. "I was hoping for some oils and a fireplace and candlelight."

"Keep dreaming, Cowboy."

"Noon tomorrow for chili burgers?" I was reminding her of how we'd first met for lunch, hoping to strike gold.

"Not tomorrow and most assuredly not there." She remembered, too. "In fact, I'm having a pretty crazy week. I'll have to call you."

"Darlene, you're making me work too hard at this." *Do you have some balls, Callahan, or what?*

"Like you're some kind of cake walk?"

"I didn't say that. Don't twist my words."

"Don't tell me what to do."

"Time out."

"Look, Mick," she said quietly. "I will call you sometime tomorrow. I promise. Let's not fight about making up. Deal?"

"Deal. Don't let them grind you down." But she had already broken the connection.

Well, that went well. Now, with a little luck, I'd have to do some difficult couples counseling that week, just so I could feel like a complete hypocrite.

I put the phone down and found a vegetable drink in the fridge. I walked out into the backyard. The motion detector kicked the lights on. It was cool, and a light breeze rippled through the palm trees at the end of my small property. I sat in a lawn chair and looked up at the stars. They just don't look the same in the city. Hell, everything in the sky seems smudged and greasy when you're staring up from a yard in LA.

Careful what you pray for, you just might get it. After years of busting my hump, I was feeling homesick. I'd grown up in the northeast part of Nevada, just outside of a nothing little town called Dry Wells. My mother died when I was just a boy, and I couldn't really remember her. Despite the ugly part of those memories, and ugly was pretty much the largest part, visiting there again had reawakened the country boy. Now I missed the smell of sage, the silence, and the flat and open heat of the desert.

So what if you lost this gig? Maybe that's not so bad. Sell the house—hell, it's already worth twenty percent more than you paid for it—pack yourself up and go home for a while. Think things over.

I sipped the drink, felt sleepy. Damn, I missed old Murphy, too. At least the cat was a living presence. I'd thought having my own house would bring comfort, but some nights it only seemed to accentuate my loneliness.

My stepfather Danny Bell emerged from the shadows in my mind and whispered: *Callahan, you're just like me. Your problem is you don't fit anywhere, with anybody.*

I tried to think of a comeback . . . and failed.

FIVE

"Okay, who do you want first, bro?"

"Are you done already? Damn, you're the best, Jerry."

"Flattery will get you everywhere. Are you going to get us back in trouble sometime soon? I'm starting to find the good life a little boring."

"You're a sick guy."

"There's only so much money, pussy, and sunshine a country boy can stand, you know what I mean? I like the superhero-sidekick thing we got going. Let's kick us some ass. Let me hear you say 'well, that should stir things up' one more time."

"Relax. Unfortunately, I may be about to step on my dick again."

"I was hoping you'd say that. Is your camera on?"

"Oh. Sorry." I flipped the equipment around, yawned, and sat back with my cup of double espresso. "Do you have pictures for me?"

"Does a bear shit in the woods? Have a look."

I squinted. The mug shot that appeared on the monitor was of a dark-eyed man in his late twenties, with a buzz cut designed to hide a badly receding hairline. Poor bastard. He had pig eyes, a pug nose, simian brows, and a large jaw that looked like it had taken a pounding in a boxing ring.

Jerry said, "Meet Mr. Joey Faber. Joe was born and raised in a dinky town up near Sacramento. His mother drank like a fish, married three times, and beat the shit out of him. According to state records, Child Welfare Services came to their trailer so often they should have been charged admission."

"Never took him away from her?"

"Twice, but always gave him back to his loving mommy. Couldn't make it stick for some reason. Social Workers are always overworked, underpaid, and poorly supervised. The State records are a mess."

"State records?" The kid seemed to be able to hack anyone, any time. Legal or illegal. Which often made me wonder if someone else just as good could follow the trail back to Jerry's computer and get his sorry ass arrested.

"Don't ask."

"Ask what? Okay, go on."

"Faber lifted cars as a teenager, broke into a couple of homes, just small-time shit. Got caught a few times, prosecuted once. When he was sixteen did half a year, unfortunately in the kind of place that cranks out seasoned cons with very sore assholes."

I was still studying the face. I knew Jerry would send me a file with all the facts and numbers anyway, so I just let the information wash over me while I tried to get a sense of the man we were discussing.

"You listening?"

"Yeah. So what happened when he turned eighteen?"

"Faber decided to be all he could be."

"The Army took him?"

"You know how it was, Mick. We'd just gone into Iraq. They would have taken Paris Hilton if she'd buffed up and sworn off pink."

"He got sent over there?"

"Quicker than a politician can lie."

"Combat?"

"He saw some action backing up the locals in and around Basra. Faber got one purple heart."

"IED?"

"Strangely enough, the kind where you actually get shot. Incident report says insurgents ambushed a truck he was driving. The unit got into a firefight."

"How did Faber do?"

"No John Wayne–heroics or anything, but they wrote him up okay. He returned fire, may have hit one of the insurgents, that sort of thing. His commanding officer skimped on praise all the way around. Maybe the boys half-assed it."

"Can you find out more?"

"Not without risking prison."

"Screw it, then."

"Here's something interesting, though. Just a few weeks later they changed his papers and sent him home."

"Any reason given?"

"None."

"So you figure . . . ?"

"That he got in hot water, of course, kind of like you and the SEALs."

"As in fighting?"

"Bet on it, because there are write-ups after he came home, both for fighting and boozing. Army records show him reprimanded three separate times, and he finally got a Dishonorable Discharge after doing less than two years."

I drummed my fingers on the desk. "Wonderful. A violent drunk with military experience."

"Alert the media. And hey, you turned out okay."

"Funny. What happened to him after the service?"

"I lose him for a year or so, but then he turns up in Nevada."

"Go on."

"I tracked him through the next period off credit card receipts, parking tickets, the post office and stuff like that. Faber started in that little dump near the California border, the one by the lake, and then bounced around working at a few different casinos. You know, Jackpot, Elko, Sparks, Lake Tahoe, and finally Vegas."

"He lives in Vegas?"

Jerry chuckled. "You were expecting maybe Little Rock? The guy is mobbed up, Mick. Are you going to tell me what's going on soon, or what?"

"Or what."

"Prick."

"Look, I just expected him to be located here in LA for some reason. Who does he work for in Vegas?"

"The last couple of years he's been working for an outfit called The Valley of Fire Corporation. According to their payroll records, Faber works in security. I guess they own some new casino and resort that's going up in a toilet called Loose Change, out by the Paiute Reservation near Moapa."

"Did you run down who owns this Valley of Fire Corporation?"

"Does a bear shit in the Vatican? Is the Pope living in the woods? If you dig through a mountain of legal bullshit, Valley of Fire turns out to be run by a very bad individual. The guy is one of the last of the outlaw Italian boys, from what I can tell. The rest have gone legit or caved in to the mobs from Russia and Eastern Europe."

I leaned back in the chair and examined patterns in the ceiling. "Okay, so we're looking at Big Paul Pesci."

"So you already knew that. Now you're beginning to piss me off."

I took a few moments and filled him in on Bone's story, though I knew Jerry should stay out of it. He'd already had my back a number of times; maybe too many. And this situation felt like it could go south in a hurry.

"How do you figure on handling this one, chief?"

I shrugged. "I called Larry Donato to put someone on the girl. Beyond that, who knows? I just want to gather information and see where it takes me. The only thing I see for certain is that I can't let my friend go down hard, not without trying to lend a hand."

"Donato already has that biz up and running? Cool of you to toss him some work. All his guys are qualified cops and ex-cops."

"That's what I was thinking." I rubbed my temples slowly, and my weariness probably showed.

Jerry cocked his head. "You have a lot on your own plate these days, Mick. How's it going at work?"

"It doth proceed. Excrement inevitably rolls downhill, yes?"

"Now you sound like Hal."

"I learned pedantry from a master."

"You wouldn't be looking for something to distract you from the mess at the station, by any chance?"

"There's that. But Bone is an old buddy, Jerry. You know how it is."

"I know. And if you need me, I'm in. I just don't want you trying to handle too many problems at the same time, especially if it gets hairy."

"Tell me about the other guy, Frank Toole."

Jerry shuffled papers. "He's a 'Southie,' born in the slums around Boston. No juvenile record I could find. Did one bit in the Marine Corps, got an Honorable Discharge. Two arrests, one for assault and battery, charges dismissed when the victim refused to press charges. The second beef went to trial. Toole was nailed for contracting to do a hit, but a high-powered Vegas lawyer named DeMartini got his ass out of that one by claiming it was entrapment. Oh, and that Toole was actually looking to get evidence on the guy who wanted to whack his wife and planned to turn him in and write a book about the experience.

The jury bought it. The scum bag walked."

"Easy on the tough-guy talk, Jerry."

"Why? Can you tell I've been practicing?"

"Toole was already connected by that point, is that what you're telling me?"

"No way Toole could have afforded DeMartini on his own, Mick."

"And this attorney does a lot of work for Pesci."

"Give the cowboy a prize."

"You have addresses and other information on these clowns if we need it, right?"

"My man, I could steal their identities and fuck up their credit in a heartbeat, just say the word."

"Who knows, maybe we will." I got up, paced and stretched. "Okay, likewise the stripper?"

The picture arrived a second later. She was a real looker.

Jerry said, "Brandi DeLillo was born Barbara Ann DeLillo, in Newark, New Jersey. She's twenty-eight years old. Brandi dropped out of high school, moved to Atlantic City, then Nashville, and finally Vegas. She did a six-month stint in drug rehab, under court order. Prior to that, our girl had a couple of busts for prostitution and some speeding tickets, but other than that she's clean."

"Credit history?"

"Brandi tends to live large, but you'd expect that from a working girl. In the past few months she has paid off and closed down some credit card accounts, downscaled to a less expensive apartment. She's drawing pay as a waitress, so maybe she dumped her sugar daddy and plans on going back to college to become a surgeon."

"What?"

"Hey, she's probably got great hands, right?"

"Very funny."

"Thanks. Oh, and Larry Donato just e-mailed me. He's going to give us Dave Lopez to watch out for the girl. Lopez has a lot of free time the next couple of weeks and needs the extra money."

"Sounds good." I sat down again. The computer announced that I had mail, too. "Thanks, Jerry. Great job, as usual. I'll look this stuff over and let you know when I decide my next move."

"*Our* next move?"

"Jerry, I have a bad feeling about this one," I said. "Other than hiring Lopez, I'm thinking maybe I'd better keep this one simple and take care of it on my own."

Jerry shook his head. "What was that? You're cutting in and out. Can't hear you. I'll call back when I'm packed and ready to drive up."

"Hold on a second . . ."

The screen went dark. Jerry was gone.

SIX

"You must understand one thing," Nicky said. "An organization such as ours survives by demanding absolute loyalty." He held up his glass of red wine, swirled the glass and sniffed the bouquet before continuing. "And absolute honesty as well."

"Honor among thieves?"

"Quite."

The young attorney nodded vigorously. His collar was over-starched so the action made his neck itch. The two muscle men on either side of him did not respond. They were too busy searching the restaurant with lidded, suspicious eyes. They reminded the attorney of giant lizards. Maybe aliens from a dinosaur planet.

"Very nice," Nicky said. He put the glass down without finishing it and tapped a brief note on his BlackBerry. "I shall have to order a case for my collection. Are you sure you don't want to try it? This is a fine California Cabernet. It would be superb with any red meat."

Jacob Mandel shrugged. "I've never cared much for alcohol."

"But a man must have a vice. Yours?"

Mandel weighed the question, visions of a fat retainer dancing in his head. "I've been known to smoke a bit."

"Marijuana?"

"Never," Mandel lied. "Only tobacco. I have a weakness for Cubans."

"Wonderful. I have a few aged Cohiba in my cellar. As you

know, they are exceptional, and no longer manufactured."

"I'm impressed. They're impossible to find these days."

"I'll send some over before the ink is dry on our agreement."

The taller of the two bodyguards sat up in his chair. At six foot two, Lucky was still several inches shorter than Nicky. He stretched, popped his neck, and spoke through clenched teeth. "Three o'clock."

Nicky sighed. "Lucky, what is it now?"

The second man got up, as if to head for the bathroom. His name was apparently Andy. He answered the question. "That couple over there, pretending to be cuddling? They're cops, Nicky. The broad works vice."

"I shall refrain from asking how you know that, Andy. Sit down and relax, please. I was almost finished anyway." Nicky snapped his fingers, and a waiter appeared from nowhere. "Check."

Mandel squirmed in his chair. He hadn't expected the police to be on to their arrangement, at least not so quickly.

"Relax, counselor," Nicky said. "It's not you. We're often followed and photographed. In our organization, we consider this a badge of honor."

Mandel focused on the fat, six-figure retainer again. *What the hell.* He leaned back in his chair.

"Do you know Shakespeare?" Nicky asked.

Mandel shrugged. "Not much call for him in law school."

"A man in our line of work should be well rounded, Mr. Mandel. He should know his classical music, Shakespeare, some poetry. This is in order not to become an absolute barbarian." Nicky fixed his gaze on Andy, then Lucky, as if to say, *You see what I have to put up with?*

"Makes sense, Nicky. Where would you suggest I begin?"

"I enjoy the tragedies myself," Nicky said. "*Macbeth, Othello,* and *Hamlet* in particular. They are studies in human weakness."

"Mel Gibson did a Hamlet movie once, right?"

Nicky looked pained. "Please. Watch Sir Laurence Olivier's *Hamlet,* even the old BBC version with Christopher Plummer if you must, but not Mr. Gibson. That one was edited to shreds, just butchered."

Andy decided to chime in. "I saw some of that on cable," he said. "It's about a crazy guy wants to fuck his mommy."

Nicky lowered his gaze, studied the wine again. Some time passed. The three men with him began to perspire. When he raised his head his eyes were flat, his mood obfuscated. "It is about quite a bit more than that, actually. I should not expect you to understand, Andy. Shall we go?"

Mandel blinked. "Go where?"

"I thought you might want to take a run out past Moapa to see our new hotel and casino, Mr. Mandel. We're calling it Valley of Fire. After all, it will soon be your primary client."

A quick glance at the undercover cops. "But they'll follow us."

"Relax. They'll be taken care of." Nicky snapped his fingers. The sound made all three men jump. "Andy, go over nicely and have a chat with them. Lucky, you go outside and cut their tires."

The goons rose and left without looking back. Nicky smiled, shrugged. "Such morons must be good for something, yes? Violence is unpleasant, but one never knows when it may become necessary." His piercing eyes pinned Mandel to the chair, then a half smile caressed him with cool fingers. "To be candid, sometimes I feel like I am living in a Godfather film."

Mandel swallowed. "Can't imagine why." He started to get up, but Nicky waved a finger. Mandel sat.

"We still have a few moments," Nicky said. "Tell me about yourself, Mr. Mandel. What made you decide to practice the law?"

"My parents," Mandel said. He flushed, embarrassed by the involuntary honesty. "I got okay grades, but I was drifting. My dad was a police officer, and my uncle went through Special Forces and worked for the government."

"Special Forces? Impressive."

"I thought so. Those guys are tough."

"Go on."

"Well, in families like mine, you get pressure to be a cop, a soldier, a doctor, or at least a lawyer, and since I can't stand the sight of blood, I passed on the first three."

"Is that so? The sight of blood makes you queasy?"

"My own, anyway," Mandel said. He tried to grin. The big man did not smile back. The look in Nicky's eyes made Mandel shiver.

"Ha!" Nicky suddenly got it, laughed and looked around the room as if inviting everyone else in on a great joke. "My own! Ha! Go on, go on. About the law."

"I did really well on the LSAT, and got into UCLA. From there I went to Ross, Goldfarb and Kramer in Century City. I left there to work for Mr. DeMartini, which is how I met Mr. Pesci, and now I've been on my own for about a year."

Nicky nodded. "It is good to be king, no? I mean, to employ one's self."

"Yes," Mandel said cautiously. "Although I still take orders from my clients, naturally."

"Ah, this is the way of the world. No one is ever completely free, yes?"

"Indeed."

Nicky slapped the contract on the table with an open palm. Mandel jumped an inch up and two more back. "This agreement says you work for us, for Mr. Pesci to be exact. Most of the time you will be left alone to do your job, because we respect a man who has the eggs to start his own company. However, if we ask for a specific thing at any time, you will do it without question. This is understood?"

"I understand."

"And we do not need to be concerned that members of your family have worked in law enforcement?"

"No, not at all."

"Mr. Mandel, your face asks a question."

Mandel swallowed. "Well, as for that last thing, please understand, I will keep your business confidential at all times, but I don't know that I can personally do anything illegal, Nicky. I don't mind bending rules, of course, not so long as I still have plausible deniability, but I cannot promise to flat out commit a crime. You'd have way too much on me, then. Besides, I could lose my license. I'm sure you can appreciate that."

Nicky cocked his head. His lips pursed. "How sad."

"Excuse me?"

"Your hearing problem. So sad in a man of such tender years."

Mandel summoned courage, started to rise. "I don't wish to disappoint you, Nicky. So perhaps we'd best shake hands and call off the transaction while we can still be friends."

"Sit."

Again, Mandel sat.

"We shall put our differences to one side for a few moments. Why, you ask? This is because I have something to show you before we consummate the deal, something that should clarify the circumstances and requirements better than anything I could personally do or say. Let us go."

"Just to the casino, right?"

Nicky did not answer. The bodyguard named Andy quietly seized Mandel's Armani-smothered sleeve. They all rose as one, shoved aside tourists, crossed the nerve-jangling, blindingly pat-terned carpet and rode down in an elevator that seemed silent as a tomb after the clang and clatter of the slots. Time seemed to speed up.

As he got into the long, shiny limo with Nicky and the two stereotypical goons, Mandel couldn't help but recall that in every mob movie he'd ever seen the victim was hustled into the backseat of a car and driven somewhere.

Don't think like that. . . .

They left the strip and went north and east on the 15, to the edge of the Wildlife Range, past very long stretches of shadowed sand and dots of dried sage that clawed at the sky like fingers. The night was bleak, black, and speckled with stars that seemed like pinpricks of clear ice. Time slowed down again.

Nicky cleaned his fingernails and listened to some music via satellite that sounded both faint and classical. Mandel studied the night sky. Lucky drove the limo while Andy worked feverishly on what appeared to be a zit at the back of his neck. A few words would have been nice; something to break the strained silence, but no one said a word. Perhaps no one dared.

Now it seemed like a very, very long drive. Mandel wondered how the hell they expected to entice tourists to wander such a distance from the strip. Then it hit him that they must be figuring on the unique angle: high-stakes gaming, luxury suites, glamorous shows, but also legal female and male prostitution, all located in one, convenient resort. Hell, it would be one-stop shopping for everybody with the money and the hormones.

Mandel did not know whether to be excited or frightened when several tall, dinosaur-like shapes appeared on the horizon. He knew they were the metal girders of a complex still under construction. Although its casino and hotel were both soon to open, the full Valley of Fire resort would not be officially completed for another six months. The metal skeletons would soon become the rest of the huge resort.

As they parked, Mandel squinted and made out that the place had been carefully sculpted into a reasonable facsimile of a mountain. This establishment would have outdoor swimming pools placed on several plush levels, with flowing waterfalls lushly connected to one another. The area below the hotel, soon to be a bright red and orange casino lit by flames, would then become the proverbial Valley of Fire.

The site seemed deserted. Lucky drove the limo off the highway and onto a bumpy dirt road. Only every other streetlamp was operational. The visual effect was disconcerting—pools of yellowing light followed by ribbons of darkness. They bounced along through potholes. The rocking motion somehow allowed Andy to finish popping zits. He emitted a simian grunt of satisfaction.

Nicky turned the radio off and pointed to a huge square marked off by tape and sticks. Fresh cement. Some of it had been poured into what was rapidly becoming a giant parking lot.

Lucky slowed down as they approached the unfinished section, where three trucks sat quietly. As they moved closer, Mandel studied them and noted that the huge rotating concrete drums were still moving.

That's funny, he thought. *What union crew works this late?*

And then it hit hard. The world snapped sharply into focus, the night turned lush with shadow, the stars became bright, crisp and clear. Mandel's stomach inflated with gas before twisting into a knot. Three connected guys had just driven him out into the boonies, to a deserted lot. Oh, shit.

I'm a dead man. . . .

Mandel swallowed bile. They'd caught him padding his hours. That had to be it. But it hadn't been by all that much, just enough to cover the down payment on the Beemer. The other guys did it far worse, and more often. And how had Nicky found out about it? The fucking bookkeeper? That piece of dog shit! Or maybe it was for dealing grass. *Oh, man. God, get me out of this, please get me out of this, if you do I'll believe in you and hit the high holidays every year, I swear it. . . .*

"Park here, Andy." Nicky's voice, cold as steel leaving a scabbard. The big man pulled the car over, turned off the engine. Nicky undid his seatbelt. "Everyone out."

Mandel felt his knees shaking. His mouth went dry. "Nicky . . ."

"I said out."

Within seconds, the four men were standing by the edge of the unfinished parking lot. Lucky stuffed his ham-sized fists into his pockets and stared out into the night. Andy eyed Mandel with a vague smirk, like a man delighted by another's misfortune. Nicky stepped over the string outlining the empty patch of dirt.

"This way, Mandel. I'm going to show you something important."

It's true, Mandel thought. *Your life does flash before your eyes.*

He stepped over the string. By now, he realized there was nothing he could say that was going to make a difference. Mandel decided to be as strong as possible, perhaps that would earn him some respect, and an easier death, if not save his life. He'd give Nicky nothing to mock. Well, try hard not to cry.

"Andy?"

"Yeah, boss?"

Nicky's brow furrowed. He pointed to the cement truck. "Go check that out."

Andy looked down at his fancy shoes, shot Mandel a dirty look. He stepped into the dirt, hopped a couple of rows. Behind him, Lucky drew a 9mm Glock from a shoulder holster and held it pointed down at the ground. Nicky eyed Mandel with amusement, as if aware of what was going through his mind.

"Mr. Mandel, I told you there is honor among thieves, yes? That there is a covenant one should never break?"

Mandel couldn't talk, so he nodded once. And again. Unfortunately, his head kept moving of its own volition, like a broken puppet. He knew he looked ridiculous but couldn't make it stop.

Nicky nodded to Lucky, who raised the huge handgun. Mandel moaned. Lucky aimed, fired. Mandel shuddered as his bladder let go.

Out in the dirt, Andy grunted and fell to his knees.

Mandel looked down, stunned to discover that he hadn't been shot after all. He discreetly covered the small damp spot on his crotch with both hands.

"Shit, they got me!" Andy cried. He clutched at his back, tried to draw his own weapon at the same time. Lucky fired again, and Andy's hand vanished, along with his gun, in a spray of blood and bone. Andy shrieked; fell to his knees, then over on one side.

The cement truck revved its engine, backed closer.

"I believe you have been stealing from us, Andy," Nicky called. "I am so disappointed in you."

The thug whined and crawled in circles, clutching his ruined wrist. "No, Nicky, I didn't do nothing!"

"Maybe not," Lucky said under his breath, "but I never liked you anyway." He started to fire again. Nicky shook his head, waved for the truck to back closer.

"Observe, Mr. Mandel. An objective lesson, yes?"

The truck began to spill cement. Andy realized what was about to happen. He screamed and struggled, but he was too wounded to get away. The huge, grey wave rolled closer. Andy babbled, thrashed, but finally got partially covered, which slowed him down just enough to go under except for his face, bloody arm, and one leg. The truck left and another took over. Andy kept screaming until the cement filled his mouth and he vanished from sight.

Mandel threw up.

The second truck left and was replaced by another.

"Mr. Mandel, do as you are told, and you will prosper." Nicky slapped Mandel lightly on the cheek. "And you do not speak of these matters to anyone, not your policeman father or your hot-shot fucking uncle who worked for the government. Yes?"

"Yes," Mandel said, shivering. "Yes, I promise."

Time crawled. Eventually, they filled in the whole area of the parking lot and raked it flat. When the job was done, the trucks drove away into the night. Nicky took the shattered attorney back to his hotel.

No one said another word.

Seven

"I've never gotten over it."

"Maybe you don't want to get over it."

"What's that supposed to mean?"

I shrugged. "A brilliant existential therapist once composed a Mobius strip sentence. It goes like this, 'Mom and Dad, I refuse to grow up until you love me the way I needed to be loved when I am seven.' "

JD was a cop, and a good one, but the concept of holding on to one's childhood in a vain effort to change it seemed to elude him. "Don't you think finding out you're adopted after your parents died would upset you, too?"

"It doesn't matter what would upset *me*. The point is you're going around in circles, JD. Booze won't cure hurt feelings, and in fact it exacerbates them. Believe me, I know all about that. Don't wimp out."

His eyes narrowed with anger, but he released it seconds later. JD was powerfully built but on the short side for LAPD. He still looked like he bench pressed three hundred, easy. He leaned forward and hunched those broad shoulders. "I read your bio at the station Web site," he said. "You didn't have it so easy."

Not much point in avoiding disclosure when the information is out there on the Internet. "Okay, I never knew my parents. I was raised by an abusive stepfather. To be candid, I still struggle to come to terms with some of the things that happened."

"Sounds like *you're* not over it." He thought he was being smart.

"Not completely, JD, but I understand better now that I'm an adult. I have forgiven as best I can, because that's the only sane alternative. Holding on to that stuff eats you alive, rots you from the inside out."

His face turned to granite. "I'm not joining AA."

"I don't expect you to, JD. The program's not for everyone. But we both know you're going to have to take a hard look at the drinking."

His eyes went out of focus. He looked out my office window to study a squirrel that was busy tap dancing along the wooden fence. "What's wrong with me?" Just the hint of a little boy.

"Low frustration tolerance, poor impulse control, signs of PTSD. Post Traumatic Stress Disorder. You have one hell of a difficult job, and losing your partner didn't help."

I reached over the coffee table to get my note pad. JD shrank back, a suspicious look on his face. We still had a ways to go.

"I'm going to write down a couple of books. You can pick them up just about anywhere. I want you to have the information you need to make some good decisions for a change. Then we'll talk again. Sound fair?"

When the session was over, I took a quick bathroom break and splashed water on my face. I looked puffy. I was still weight training, but had slacked off on the running. My job stress demands a pretty consistent exercise regimen. I used my cell to check for messages, and picked one up from Jerry.

Later: "Are you going to return her call?"

Andre sat quietly, head in hands. A balding man in his forties, he wore slacks and an expensive silk shirt, gold chains and watch. His right hand trembled. Andre hadn't spoken to his aged mother in months, ever since he'd come out to her that he was in a gay relationship.

"It's your decision, Andre, but the only thing we know for sure is that not speaking to her is making you miserable."

"What if she attacks me?" he asked softly. "I hate when she does that."

"She probably will."

"Then why bother?"

"It's for your own sake, not hers. Want my suggestion?"

He looked up with wet eyes and nodded.

"If she starts to lecture you on the Bible, or criticize your decision, say 'I love you, Mom. Let's talk again later.' And then just quietly hang up the phone."

"I see, just don't get drawn into a fight." He nodded. "I can do that."

I leaned forward. "Send me an E-mail. Let me know if it works. If not, we'll come up with something else."

He left happier. Andre was my last client; it was a short day. I gathered up my notes, reviewed them, and then ran them through the shredder. No written notes means less risk of having to respond in detail to a subpoena. I locked up my office and went out into the early-afternoon sunshine.

It was time to switch gears and see what I could do for Bud Stone.

Jerry's message encapsulated the credit card trail for Mr. J. Faber, who had rented a vehicle from an Enterprise outlet on Oxnard Street in Van Nuys on the very same day he'd disappeared. I jumped on it; called the business directly and drove over straight from work. When I got to the address, the girl behind the counter had an enormous grin, red gums, and a name plate that said TINA. It seemed safe to assume that she was the same Tina I'd just spoken to on the phone.

"I'm such a fan. Mick Callahan, I can't believe it." Tina rested her ample bosom on the counter, like someone putting ripe melons on display. "What can we do for you?"

I showed her a photograph of Joey Faber, and one of Frank Toole. "Like I said on the phone, this is kind of off the record. It's for a TV pilot I'm working on. I think you may have rented a car to these men a couple of weeks ago, on the fifteenth. Mr. Faber signed for it. Do you happen to remember them, Tina?"

She blushed as if I'd said something forward. "Let me look Mr. Callahan, maybe I can help you out here. Give me a few minutes."

I went outside to wait. A large family returned a van. I watched some jittery squirrels square dance atop a cement wall festooned with graffiti, walked a few feet away and called Jerry on my cell. "How's it going?"

Jerry's voice was brittle, cutting in and out. "We're leaving Laurel Canyon, heading down the hill. The lady seems to be on a shopping binge."

Probably with the Bone's money, I thought. "Okay, just keep an eye out without scaring her. Stay on her tail."

"Hey, no sweat. It's a very nice tail. You coming over?"

"Soon."

"How soon? I'm hungry."

"Don't wait to eat. When I'm done here, I'll try and catch up with you. First, I'll call her and try to meet face to face. Right now, just see if anyone else is following and stay out of trouble. Jerry? Thanks for the help."

"No sweat, I kind of like doing this stuff."

I closed the phone and paced the parking lot. The sun burned my neck. Two young guys in shorts started washing the van that had been returned. A plane came in low, heading northeast to land at the Burbank airport. The squirrels scattered.

"Mr. Callahan? Mick?"

It was Tina with the expansive gums. I went back over to the counter, and she stepped away from her station. A small man in a dark suit gave me a foul look. Tina whispered in my ear, "By the way, Mr. Callahan, how did you know to ask for me?"

I wasn't about to tell her that Jerry was the smartest hacker on the planet. "I can't tell you that," I whispered back. "Part of the TV pilot."

She nodded vigorously. "Oh, I see, sure. Well, anyway, you were right. Mr. Joseph Faber rented a black Range Rover. Here is the license number. I didn't remember at first, but I do know that car because it was in an accident just after."

"Just after?"

"After they turned it in. Well, maybe before, we're not sure."

"Can you clarify that for me, Tina?"

"Mr. Faber rented the car and drove it to Las Vegas. He turned it in there, later on the fifteenth, but it sat in the lot for another day. The report shows some minor damage to the driver side and the front fender, but we don't know when that happened exactly."

"Because it sat in the lot?"

"Yeah. Anyway, he came back and rented it again."

"The same car?"

"Apparently he asked for the same car. And they hadn't had a chance to fix anything. He said he was bringing it back to this outlet, but he never showed up."

"So the car is still missing?"

"Yes, it is overdue and missing, but people are a day or two late all the time. I'm sure he'll turn it in soon."

"Oh, I'm sure, too."

"Anyway, I ran you a copy of the rental form, but don't tell anyone or I'll get fired." She slid it across the counter and winked.

I already had the form, thanks to Jerry. I shook my head. "That won't be necessary, Tina, thanks anyway. If we get this off the ground, I'll have my people be sure and get you tickets to the first taping."

"That would be cool! And can I have your autograph?"

Some days things are just *too* easy.

The day was turning hot. I drove over Coldwater, then turned on Sunset and doubled back. As I drove down the strip I had a bit of a scare. I thought I saw the same white Toyota I'd seen by the radio station, with the identical dark-haired young woman driving. I flashed on a girl named Frisco, who'd once followed me in disguise and led me into a trap. The sun blinded me for a second. I blinked and looked again, but the car, if it had ever actually been there, was gone. *Sure. Someone following you following Jerry following Brandi to see if she's being followed?*

During my conversation with Tina, Jerry had tailed Brandi DeLillo to the posh Beverly Center, where he planned to turn the function over to an off-duty detective named Dave Lopez. Lopez was moonlighting for Larry Donato, the ex-cop cousin of Darlene Hernandez.

I parked in the loud garage, blended into the crowd and rode up the escalator behind two young women in black Goth clothing. One was Hispanic and skinny, the other white and heavily muscled. They were engaged in a fierce argument about the quality of some rapper's new CD.

I flipped my cell open, hit auto. "Where are you now?"

"She just went into the Pizza Kitchen. Dave Lopez is here, and he's going to pick her up when she leaves. Like I said, I'm kind of liking this cloak and dagger stuff . . . except for the feeling like a pervert part."

"Why start regretting that now?"

"Funny."

"Okay, you can take off. Give Lopez my cell. I'll call you later."

I paused at the top of the escalator, stepped to one side, and dialed Brandi DeLillo's cell phone number. I pictured her groping through a large purse, looking for the instrument. She answered after four rings. There was a brief silence, perhaps as she checked for a Caller ID.

"Hello?"

"Brandi, my name is Mick Callahan. Bud Stone may have mentioned me somewhere along the way."

She didn't answer. I heard her take a deep breath. I turned away from the mall and towards the busy street. "Hello?"

"I'm here. Did he give you this number?"

"Yes."

"Because he really shouldn't even have it."

I looked back at her. From a distance, she seemed genuinely angry. "To be honest, I'm a little confused. Bud asked me to call you, Brandi. He wanted me to see if there was anything I could do."

"About what?"

"I guess there's been some trouble."

"Is he okay?"

"As far as I know."

"Then I don't know what Bud led you to believe about me, but it's over. Bud and me, we're finished."

"I understand that part. Look, can you spare me just a few minutes?"

"I don't even know you."

"I'm harmless, I promise. I often walk old ladies across the street. Dogs never bark. Cats love me and generally purr."

I looked up, watched her sit back, saw her smile. "Why should I meet you?"

"You can help me understand. Maybe I got fed a line of crap. I'd like to sit down with you, and tell you what Bud said. About the trouble."

"Well . . ."

I took a risk. "I'm in Beverly Hills right now, about to go

down Santa Monica. Can I ask where you are?"

She pondered. "Oh, I'm down around the Beverly Center. Why?"

"I can be there in no time. Just let me meet you, somewhere very public is fine. I'll buy you a coffee since I'm sober. I'll fill you in, and then you can tell me your side of the story."

"I'm sober, too." Brandi turned in circles for a minute. She told me where she was and that she could only spare a few minutes. "Okay, how will I know you?"

"Like I said, my name is Mick Callahan. I'm the radio guy. Or maybe you caught my television show?" *Oh, for Christ's sake, Callahan, that sounded pretty arrogant.*

"Actually, no. Never heard of you."

That'll teach ya. I described myself and told Brandi that Bud had shown me a photograph. Then I killed a few minutes looking at puppies in a pet store. Maybe fifteen minutes later, I walked right by Lopez, who was waiting outside, but didn't acknowledge him. I opened the door and strolled into the restaurant. Brandi was worrying the hell out of a paper napkin. My size threw her for a second, and she edged back. I sat down across from her, leaned my elbows on the round glass table and shook her hand. Her palm felt damp.

"Hi, I'm Mick."

"Brandi. Can we make this fast?"

"What's the story with Bud? You sounded pretty upset that he had your number. I got the impression you were on good terms. Was I wrong?"

She sighed. "It's not that I hate him or anything, okay? Bud keeps trying to get back with me, and I'm not into the married man thing anymore. Never again. I'm not sure what that was about, except maybe I was looking for a dad or something."

Since Bud Stone was only a couple of years older than me, maybe forty, I winced. *Better start getting used to it.* "He told me you guys were an item but called it off. I'm not here to bother you."

She leaned closer. "You said he was in trouble. What kind of trouble?"

I told her some of it, but watered things down a lot. Bone owed people money, and was worried they might hassle her to get back at him.

"What are you, some kind of bodyguard?"

"Not at all. When I'm not on the radio, I'm a shrink."

"Bullshit." She laughed. "You look like a boxer. How many times have you broken that nose?"

Charmed another one. "I lost count." I tend to lose control of the conversation when it comes to pretty women. Well, when I'm not working. I covered by sipping some water. Meanwhile, Brandi looked at me like someone studying a math problem.

"I guess it was nice of him to think about me."

She didn't blink. I didn't, either. "I thought so."

Brandi came to a decision. She got up so abruptly a glass of water started to tip. I grabbed and straightened it. "Nice reflexes, Mr. Boxer."

"Gee, thanks. And it's Callahan."

Brandi leaned over the table. I enjoyed her perfume. "Callahan. Okay, I'll just try to keep an open mind. Any woman who says she doesn't like handsome men worrying about her safety is a liar. But I can take care of myself."

"Somehow I believe you."

"Leave me your number if you want. I'll call if I need something, but you're in for a long wait."

I gave her a business card. "Mind if I have someone check in on you from time to time? You'll go right past him when you go outside. He is an off-duty cop."

"Whoa. This is kind of creepy, dude."

"Just a precaution."

"All right, as long as he stays out of my way."

"He will, I promise." I looked up, waved to Lopez and motioned with my hands that I'd filled her in. "Hopefully this will all blow over in a day or two, Brandi. Thanks for indulging us."

"It's a free country."

Brandi got up like I'd never existed; walked away briskly, swinging her purse. She walked right by Lopez, who was reading a newspaper, and gave him a quick smile. He wriggled his eyebrows at me, gave her maybe ten yards and picked up the tail.

Jerry was right. Young Brandi DeLillo had a very *nice* tail.

EIGHT

"I've got good news and bad news," Judd Kramer said.

My dour agent wasn't generally much for joking around. I felt my stomach tighten. "As long as we're spouting clichés, how about you just cut to the chase." I was pacing outside, sloppily watering my backyard. To the west, the sun was sinking into a bright pool of watercolor smog.

"Hang on a second."

He put me on hold. I watered the roses, wrapped up the hose, and plopped down on a lawn chair. Shadows lengthened and a light, welcome breeze whispered through the tall, purple magnolia. My jeans were wet at the shins. Judd had been trying to renegotiate my contract with the station. He'd had lunch with O'Brien, the station manager, and an attorney for the mother ship.

The music in my ear was an old Beatle's tune that had been cruelly hacked to pieces by some bored arranger and now consisted of insipid electronic strings and bland choral voices. I let the phone rest on my shoulder and struggled to pick a theme for my next show. It crossed my mind to do politics. Maybe offer an examination of the general personality differences between liberals and conservatives. Someone once wrote that conservatives were ruled by fear, liberals by guilt. That the root of liberal was "generosity" and the root of conserve meant "to hoard." It didn't take long to discard the idea; my bias would be far too obvious, but the thought of doing that show with Zack

Marks listening made me grin.

Judd was taking a while. I thought about my options. Did I really want another one-year contract, assuming they offered one? I'd been feeling interfered with lately, pressured by management to shift from what I was comfortable doing to a more traditional talk-show format. That heat was likely to continue. On the other hand, I really needed the money for the mortgage. I wondered how Jerry and Lopez were doing with Brandi, and what was going on with Bud Stone.

I checked my watch. Five minutes. I don't enjoy playing diva, but the long delay was starting to feel rude.

If you sit alone and still for a long time, without meditating, you'll start to feel empty. Me, if I don't give my mind something else to eat, it eats itself. I wondered, did I really even want to be a homeowner? Didn't the idea of hopping in my car and driving back to the desert sound good sometimes? Being free enough to do that on a whim? But then I also wanted a family some day. Women don't take too kindly to a vagabond husband, so I wanted to prove I could put down some roots. *Is that what this is about, then? Proving something to Darlene, or a woman you haven't even met yet? Pretty weak, Callahan.*

What would you tell a client?

Judd finally came back on the line. "Sorry about that, Mick. Had to take that call. How did your show go last night?"

"Pretty well." We made small talk; his kid got in to UCLA and the wife was still mean as a badger with hemorrhoids. I noticed that Judd's speech seemed pressured and tight and that he was much cooler than usual. We circled the issue without tackling it. I got tired of stalling.

"The lunch, Judd?"

He sighed. "Which do you want first?"

"I don't mean to be rude, but let's quit screwing around. Just tell me what's going on, okay?"

"You're fired, and it's as of last night."

I sat up. *"What?"*

"O'Brien wants to go with Zachary Marks and his new talk show. To keep things simple, he'll pay off the last month of your contract and use re-runs until Marks is up and running."

"Conservative radio has been dropping like whale poop, Judd. What's he thinking?"

"His numbers aren't far behind yours, man." I winced. Judd mumbled to someone else in the room, probably his secretary. "Anyway, he figures he can corner the market in LA, and since they skew older he can sew it up for years. He'll settle for a smaller piece of the pie, because the ARB numbers stick."

"I can't believe he's backing that idiot."

"Easy there, Mick. I may not always agree with him, but Zack is actually a pretty smart guy."

The air grew even colder. Short hairs fluttered. "Wait a second. Hold on. Since when are you on a first-name basis with Marks, Judd?"

A long pause. "Since a couple of hours ago."

"You took a meeting with my competition?"

"Business is business."

"I don't believe this, you took him on as a client?"

Kramer sputtered. "You know I like you personally, but a man in my position can't afford to turn down work. It's nothing personal. O'Brien assured me there was nothing I could say or do on your behalf that would have changed his mind. He just feels it's time for a change."

"You know something? So do I."

"Excuse me?"

"Nothing personal, Judd, but you're fired, too."

I closed the phone. Just like that, back to square one, with just enough savings to last me a few months. I could always sell the house, but I sure didn't want it to come to that. I pondered my suddenly bleak future. Yet in a weird way it was also exhilarating to be free again.

It got very dark outside. A chorus of dogs screamed along with distant sirens. I thought about drinking the way you think about an old girlfriend who lied and broke your heart. You wonder what she's doing, but it's not like you're in the mood to get raked over the coals again, not any time soon. When I got tired of feeling sorry for myself I went back inside.

I did the dishes, dumped the trash, and listened to Emmy Lou Harris. The woman is magical and can make sadness a blissful thing. I played "Too Far Gone" twice. Then I went to the computer.

Hal looked rested and a little pink from the sun. His lips moved silently for a couple of seconds before I remembered to turn up the sound.

". . . I got your E-mail about the job," he said. "That is somewhat depressing."

"Yeah, but to be honest, I'm ready for a change anyway. As you know, I've been feeling pretty restless."

"As you generally do, stallion. Why be upset? Consider it a month-long vacation with pay and rather fortunate karma."

"I've made Kramer a lot of money and yet he just stabbed me in the back, Hal. That hurts."

Hal's eyes popped open with feigned astonishment. "An agent lacking in scruples? Heavens to Betsy! I shall alert the *Los Angeles Times*."

I laughed. "Touché."

"Have you considered your next move?"

I sipped diet soda. "I'd still like to go back to television at some point, but that's not in the cards for now."

"You could sell the house, take a year away from things, and perhaps write a book. Then come back and I'll get my people to set up a tour."

"You know me better than that, Hal. I love to read but hate to write."

"One does what one must."

I crumpled the soda can and sailed it toward the metal trash can. NBA caliber, nothing but net. "I'll think of something."

"Don't wait too long. Any news with respect to those missing miscreants Faber and Toole?"

"I have a sense of where they may have gone. Haven't decided what I'm going to do about that yet, if anything."

"Have you heard from your friend Bud?"

"No." I filled Hal in on the meeting with Brandi and the rest of what we had on the two missing thieves, which wasn't much. "I asked Jerry to help out, so he and an ex-cop will keep an eye on the girl."

"How close?"

"I don't want him hurt. They'll just trade her off, light and easy, mostly just keep an eye out to see if anyone else is following her."

"Nothing too serious."

"No."

"For once this looks like a boring story."

"Let's just hope it stays that way."

Hal rubbed his eyes. "Getting to any AA meetings, Callahan?"

I was in no mood to be scolded. I grimaced. "I'm just kind of off the program for now, Hal. I'll go back."

"Do I need to remind you of what can happen if you stray too far from the well-worn path to happy destiny?"

"Just looking at your face reminds me."

"Ouch," Hal said. "He's grumpy. Still, I must ask. Any random urges?"

I shook my head. "The only urge I'm aware of is that it's been too long since I've had someone in my bed."

"And how is the lovely Sergeant Hernandez these days?"

"Don't ask."

Hal cocked his head. His eyes oozed concern, and for some reason that annoyed me, too. "Mick, this isn't the wisest time to call her."

"I know, but I may do that anyway. The breast nurtures, you know?"

"Ponder carefully," Hal said. "And perhaps wait until the morning to decide."

I looked around the room to avoid meeting his gaze. Finally, I nodded. "You take care of yourself, old man. I'll keep you posted."

"You are valued."

"And you."

I surfed for a while and then shut down the computer. The black screen became oddly fascinating. After a long moment I opened my cell, looked at Darlene's phone number as if expecting it to morph into her face. Closed the phone and leaned back in the office chair. It squealed loudly, as if in sympathy.

It's a bitch being a loner who gets lonely.

I wandered through the house looking for something to do. Examined my large stack of unread books, but they all seemed uninteresting. Went outside into the front yard and sat on my porch steps. Another one of those perpetually low-flying planes crossed west to east, lights twinkling, rumbling toward Burbank. I could hear Mariachi music playing several blocks over, across one of the invisible jigsaw lines that separate middle-class San Fernando Valley from the barrio. Los Angeles is strange that way, six-hundred-thousand-dollar homes surrounded by apartments full of people on welfare.

The street began to settle in for the night. Yellow and white porch lights went on and off. Two feral cats got into a loud duel down the block. Homes, side by side, unique yet all the same.

Places where it seemed like mostly contented people sat in mostly comfortable rooms; sharing dinner, watching television, getting their kids bathed and into bed. Making love.

Don't go there.

I opened the cell phone again. Closed it with a metallic snap. Wondered what the hell had gone wrong. Darlene was a cop, given to the mistrust of outsiders that damned near went along with the job description. She'd been molested as a girl. We'd fit so comfortably at first, maybe because we had both been abused as children. Then something subtle had begun to go wrong. The lulls in conversation, calls that weren't returned. Odd questions that seemed to have suspicion layered thickly between the words spoken aloud. Finally, that dreaded request for "time off" and "some space."

Come to think of it, a cold beer sounded pretty good.

I looked at my watch. There was an eight-thirty meeting at Beverly Glen and Dickens. I considered taking a quick shower and running over there. I'd probably arrive just in time to catch the main speaker. My legs didn't move. As I'd told Hal, I'd just felt out of place at the meetings lately, bored with the rhetoric, weary of the routine and the structure. *Physician, heal thyself.* I was getting pretty burned out on sad stories. Shrinks call that state "compassion fatigue." Too much work, not enough of a personal life. And that led me back to the cell phone and Darlene's number. I strolled out onto the sidewalk and paced in a circle.

Okay, say you call, what the hell will you say to her, "Hi, can I come over?"

The hulking shape of a dark van came down the street, rocking from side to side as it passed over the new speed bumps. The driver had not bothered to flick on the lights. I turned away, feeling embarrassed for some reason, as if a host of adolescent feelings were stapled to my shirt.

I opened the phone. The screen lit up. My finger was actually trembling. Screw Hal, what did he know about women? He'd been single since the Jurassic Period. I dialed Darlene. Maybe I'd do this the simplest way possible. Admit I was an asshole and I missed her and just needed a hug.

The van parked almost in front of my house. Someone inside was smoking a cigarette. I walked closer to the porch, into the light, and hunched over with the phone to my ear. Darlene answered on the third ring. She sounded sleepy. I remembered her next to me on the pillow and the scent of her perfume. A need burned in my chest.

"It's me."

A sharp intake of breath, as if Darlene knew what was coming and couldn't decide how to answer. That happens sometimes, when people are on the same emotional page about a relationship, half in and half out. . . .

Feet trotted up the slanted grass behind me. My adrenaline kicked in, and I ducked low and spun around. A baseball bat glanced off my left hand and sent the phone flying. My fingers went numb. I feinted to the right as my eyes darted around in search of a weapon. My vision narrowed to take in the bat. It came at me from above, so I closed with the assailant and drove him back into some potted plants. He lost his balance and grunted harshly. He smelled like cigarettes. I clubbed him twice with the side of my clenched fist, mindful of suddenly sore and possibly broken fingers. Our eyes locked.

It was the man from the strip club. He wore a different shirt but still that same faded windbreaker. I threw myself off him and rolled through the plants and out onto the cement. The second man was closing fast. It was the one I'd called Cowboy. I backed toward the house, palm up and circling. Cowboy went left, Windbreaker—looking a bit dazed—broke to the right. I didn't bother trying to talk them out of it. They both looked pretty determined. Cowboy spoke.

"You could come quiet."

Not likely. Windbreaker tried to rush me. I backed into the wall, and felt the handle of a rake. I brought it up and blocked the bat as it came down. Cowboy was faster this time. He grabbed at me. I used the end of the handle to whack him, got lucky and caught him in the abdomen. His own momentum cost him a lot of wind. He staggered backwards into the bushes. Windbreaker tried for my testicles but I turned in time to catch most of it on my thigh. The bat grazed my skull. I got woozy and my knees weakened.

"Don't. Kill. Him."

Cowboy, trying to yell but sounding like a feeble old woman. Windbreaker tapped my temple with the bat. The world went white, spun in a circle, and I went down. I snapped out of it for a second and tried to stab upwards with the prongs, but he kicked me in the throat. I thrashed around like a trout, clutching at my neck. Another blow to my head and the lights went out.

NINE

Bud Stone was the neighbor you loved to hate if you lived in LA. He had a lot of used cars and at least two would be up on blocks in his parched brown yard on any given day. Late that same afternoon he had gotten an old red Mustang running for the first time in years. Once it cranked up, belched and farted fire, the Bone looked in all directions, left it running, and went back through the metal wrecks and into the cluttered garage. He got up on a small folding ladder and took down a tackle box, put it on his wooden workbench, opened it up and removed the top row of wrenches.

The sack layer held a saw-toothed hunting knife in a sheath, some old field glasses, two handguns, and worn holsters for a 9mm Glock and a .38 Smith and Wesson. Bone had cleaned and oiled the weapons the night before. He loaded them, tucked the Glock onto his right hip and put the smaller gun at his ankle, cop style.

My friend put an extra clip and a speed loader full of hollow-points into the pockets of his bulky, grey sweatshirt. The wicked knife sat in the back of his belt. He stretched and did some breathing exercises to calm himself. He heard a floorboard squeak.

Bud looked up, saw his wife Wendy standing in the kitchen, peeking out through the doorway. She wore a pale blue dress and a stained white apron that read BOSS. Wendy was a plump redhead, almost blind without her glasses, and she worried too much and too often. Bud loved her dearly. Since it was hard to know how much she'd seen, he assumed the worst and forced himself to produce a broad smile. "Now, don't get all worked up. It's no big thing."

Wendy's eyes filled with tears. "Guns again, Bud?"

Bone shrugged. "They're mostly for show, okay? I have to bluff. I've got to meet some guys. It's a business sit down, but these clowns fancy themselves badasses, you know? I might have to show them I'm not scared. Believe me, I know better than to sign on for the real deal. Relax. Just finish packing. Did you call your sister?"

Wendy nodded. "She said to come on ahead."

"You're overdue anyway, Wen. She can use your help on the farm, with her husband laid up and all. You've been homesick. Consider this a vacation."

"Bud, I'm scared. We're both too old for this."

Steel entered his voice. "Just go inside."

Wendy shook her head and backed up two steps into the kitchen. Her hands busied themselves with a worn dish towel. Bone could hear water boiling. She was making pasta for dinner before she left for the airport. Wendy always had to freeze a week's worth of meals.

"Sometimes it's like I don't even know you anymore," she said.

The look on her face stung him. *Sometimes I don't know myself. Guess I'm just one of the wicked.* Bone turned back to the tackle box, closed it up and put it back on the shelf just to buy time. He composed a reasonable reply, but by then she was gone.

My friend went back into the yard and turned on the hose. The car was still running because Bone didn't dare shut it off. He soaked the ground a bit, got down near the front of the old Mustang and muddied up the license numbers and then did the same at the back. They were junkyard plates anyway, but Bud wanted to be extra careful. He cleaned himself up.

After a time, Wendy opened the front door and handed him a cold beer and a huge plate of rigatoni with tomato sauce, steamed vegetables, and a big hunk of homemade garlic bread. He thanked her, took it and sat down in the front yard to eat. Wendy went back inside to finish packing her suitcase. Soon Bud could hear the game show she liked, canned laughter and a pretty woman spinning a wheel. He finished the food, washed the plate with the garden hose and left it on the steps.

The TV went silent. The front door opened and Wendy came out rolling her luggage. Bud helped her take it to their best vehicle, put things in the trunk, slam it shut. They looked at each other for a long moment. Then he kissed her on the cheek and they hugged. Bud Stone watched his wife drive away. After a while he went to the running car, got in and closed the door. He rolled the window down and stared at the empty home he was leaving behind.

My friend sat there nursing the beer, car running, until the sun was almost down. Then he drove down the driveway and headed north and west, toward Pacoima.

Bone used to tell stories about how bad some of the gangs were in the San Fernando Valley. He said the leaders rotated in and out of jail, and some ran small empires based on drugs and a new kind of sex trade. They bring girls in from all over the world, tell them they'll be working off their passage to America in some sweat shop but then hold them in Mexico, where they addict them to drugs and break them in to be hookers. Some have set up safe houses in parts of LA where underage girls can be arranged for a cash price. They bring them over the border in dresses and curls, rent them to perverts, pay them with heroin or Oxycontin and return them to Mexico when they're all worn out.

There were stories about what happened after that, about

home movies of cold-blooded murder that could be purchased on DVD or over the Internet. Some folks think snuff films are an urban legend. Other people know better.

Bone had one particular gang in mind that night. The one that sold what appeared to be some of those genuine snuff films. A group of sociopaths flush with cash and far, far beyond redemption. Bud probably figured their reputation would assuage his guilt, make him feel better if he had to shoot. He was willing to play for keeps tonight.

He went into Panorama City and stared through the open window at neon signs and broken windows and gang markings. Gang bangers glared at him, shaved heads shiny with sweat, beige pants hanging loose below torn and stained white wife-beater tees. Some grabbed the crotch of their trousers and shouted epithets. The streets were filled with trash . . . of all kinds.

Young hookers were everywhere, skinny girls with needle tracks teetering on high heels flashing as much skin as possible, goose bumps like Braille dots on their shivering, pale skin. Bud drove on.

The night was like a pulsing, purplish vein when he pulled into the parking lot behind the empty chain market. This area was so rough the place closed down right after dark. No one would take a night shift. Rap music assaulted the ears. There were cars everywhere, kids blowing weed and drinking wine and beer. Bud drove into the lot. His old car blended in with the others. He didn't plan on getting close enough to stick out as a gringo. He sank low in the seat, drove along the fence and parked the Mustang in the side alley by the store.

Nothing to do now but wait.

Across the lot, two girls necked and fondled one another while a group of drunken boys cheered them on. For the first time, Bone allowed himself to feel afraid. A little fear could sharpen the senses. If these kids discovered an armed white guy among them, he'd be dead meat.

The man he was expecting was nicknamed Gordo; just huge, a fridge with a head on it, a wild mane of red hair and tats. Gordo was rumored to be half Mexican and half Irish, some such shit, but born and raised in East LA. Bone had sat in more than a few cop bars, listening to stories about the prick. He had the dope and hookers and snuff porn cornered, so much money behind him that the law couldn't get around his high-powered attorney long enough to nail him on anything serious.

If anything went wrong, Bone knew that the rest of the gang might come after him, but other than that, hell, the kid's own mother probably wouldn't give a shit. He opened the glove compartment, got some chaw and let the bitter taste fill his mouth. He didn't use it often, but it was an effective stimulant. The blast of nicotine added to his nervousness, gave him more fire. He gagged and patted his guns like a man trying to calm down nervous pets.

About a half hour later, a loud horn blared out a tune that Bone thought might have been *La Cucaracha.* Some of the boys hopped into their cars and backed out of the way to create an opening. A caravan of three shiny black BMWs drove slowly into the middle of the wild, noisy circle. The kids partied on and sprayed beer everywhere, but no one went near those three new cars. Bone sat up in the front seat, heart thumping.

Trouble.

Into a pool of light came a skinny kid with terminal acne. The boy was stumbling his way, maybe looking for a place to hurl without being teased by the others. Bone swore and slipped further down in the seat. The kid paused, leaned on the wall and pissed. Steam rose up and faded. *Stay there, damn it.*

The kid zipped up, and started walking again, but the wrong way. He was too drunk. For a long moment it looked like he'd crash into a soft drink machine by the market, maybe knock his sorry ass out, but he bumped into a metal cart instead, stumbled and fell to his knees.

Back in the circle, the crowd was starting to go quiet, perhaps with anticipation. The kids were all staring at the middle BMW like they knew who was in it. Bone figured Gordo would be in that one, with protection front and back. *That's what I'd do.*

The drunken boy started his way again, completely lost, just wandering around. He seemed to be singing to himself. Since the rest of the gang had fallen silent, Bone could hear his voice, all hoarse and boozed up. *Time to make a decision.*

Bone divided his attention as best he could, half on the approaching boy and half on that middle car. The front doors opened, and tall bodyguards got out on either side; black steroid junkies in those ubiquitous blue jogging suits with all the requisite gold chains. The crowd murmured.

The boy was closer now and had seen his car. Bone swore, and moved to the passenger side. He slipped out onto the cold cement and duck-walked backwards to vanish into the overflowing trash bins. Let the kid look, find the vehicle empty, move on. The garbage reeked. Bone peeked over the top of the trash can.

Back in the circle of headlights, a wide man with red hair got out of the Beemer at his own leisurely pace. The crowd erupted into cheers.

Gordo.

The boy was at the red Mustang, peering in the open driver's window. He slipped a bit, leaned on the car. Stuck his head inside. *You barf in there and I'll break your fucking neck,* Bone thought. *Damn it kid, your karma sucks.*

The kid opened the door and got in. He studied the dash for a while and then vanished from view. Bone shook his head, stunned. He edged closer and could just make out what was happening.

The boy was trying to hot wire the Mustang.

Back in the center of the crowd, Gordo was turning in a wide circle, arms raised. The gang cheered him on. Bone took advantage of the noise, opened the passenger side, reached in and grabbed the kid military style, one hand over his mouth. The boy whimpered and struggled. Bone dragged him back out onto the pavement in a choke hold and rendered him unconscious. He dragged the kid further into the alley. He pulled his knife, held it to the kid's throat for a long moment.

Bone sighed. He tied and gagged the boy and left him by the loading dock. The staff would find him the next day.

My friend got back into the waiting car. *You should have wasted him, just collateral damage.* The kid was a gang member. His hands weren't likely to be clean. *Getting soft in your old age.*

The party went on a while; Gordo and his bodyguards doing coke lines off the bare tits of a tall hooker in a black thong. Somebody put out a kit and a few of the gang members shot up, but most stuck to booze and hits of grass.

At one point the cops showed. One lone squad car started up the driveway, but when the first two lines of gang bangers turned and glared, the cop, probably some rookie getting initiated by an amused partner, discovered that discretion was the better part of valor. He drove off quietly.

Bone waited and watched. No one else came his way. Finally Gordo got back in the Beemer and the other cars parted again. Bone sat up, prayed silently and started the Mustang. It ground around some but wouldn't start. He tried again. Finally realized the kid must have done some damage. Frustrated, Bone slid down and checked the ignition, found the problem, started the car. It roared to life.

Bud Stone got behind the wheel and began to coast down

the alley toward the front of the parking lot.

The BMWs were maybe forty yards away, going back out onto the main drag, when Bone hit the side street and turned. A few heads turned out of curiosity, but the car was old and the plates were a mess. Nothing out of the ordinary. No one followed. He stayed half a block behind the procession, low in the front seat like one of the locals. Bone opened the door a crack and spat. He got a fresh pinch of chewing tobacco. He kept his tired eyes glued to the back of the car bringing up the rear. If it braked, he braked. If he felt made, he planned to drive on by and try again some other night.

Gordo stopped at a battered, boarded up liquor store near the freeway. Bone pulled to the curb and waited. Gordo stayed in the car while one of his bodyguards went inside to buy a fifth of Tequila and a couple of six packs of bottled beer. The Beemers kept driving. Bone discreetly followed.

The neighborhood turned into large chunks of undeveloped land or decaying wooden crack houses with dying grass around them. Tall succulent plants grew everywhere; the world was darkness, shadows, splintered boards and phallic, spiked undergrowth.

The cars finally slowed. They ended up driving onto a large piece of what looked like horse property. There were two houses. The one out front had men camped at the windows, but they seemed drunk and careless. The cars headed for the back house. At first glance, it was another dump.

Bone left his Mustang and slipped into the bushes. He used his field glasses. The windows were clear and clean. Inside, he could see decent furniture, paintings, and a large-screen, high-def TV.

The black guys collected some cash and left together in one of the BMWs. Maybe their shift was over, or they were hired for show. Either way, the odds had just improved. Bone eyeballed the property. No signs of an alarm, and the only guards seemed to be in the front house. He had to get closer. A long, wooden rail fence wove in and out of thick ivy that offered the only decent cover. Bone went flat and started crawling at a steady, patient pace.

It took an hour, but by the time Gordo closed the thick curtains Bud Stone was squatting right outside the side door, picking the lock. He eased inside and sat there on the kitchen floor, alone in the dark, scared and excited at the same time. Listened. Someone said something and a woman giggled. *Wait.* Another. There were *two* women. But was that it? Would Gordo allow himself to be so careless?

Bone forced himself to wait, and a few minutes later heard coughing. There was at least one other man, on watch in the living room, probably smoking a cigarette. Bone crawled into the hall. The living room was two doorways away and the lights were on; the big TV fired colored shapes at the wall. He crawled closer to one of the doors, heard nothing. Peered inside and looked up. Someone fast asleep in a bed, one foot half on the floor. The guy was out cold and snoring.

Bone choked him out, tied and gagged him.

My friend moved on and soon heard what sounded like a bad horror film coming from the next doorway. He crawled again, froze when a floorboard squeaked. After a time, he continued forward and peeked into what he could now see was the master bedroom.

The television was on there as well, lots of screaming and grunting and blows. The two women had finished ministering to Gordo and were sharing a joint. The big man was naked, seemed inert. Bone waited until the girls passed out, too. His bladder ached, but he ignored it and edged toward the living room.

The other guard, a squat and muscular Latino with oily hair, was parked on a black leather couch, AK by his side, watching an old war movie with the sound way too high. *Almost too easy.* Bone got to his feet, stepped over quietly, choked and tied him up and grabbed the rifle.

Back to the bedroom. One of the girls, a hooker improbably named Angel, woke up to a hand over her mouth. The man standing over her had pantyhose over his face, and his features were mashed and distorted. He looked like something out of the film they'd all been watching; one of those bloody productions Gordo was famous for creating. The man held a finger to his lips and showed her the rifle. He motioned for her to wake up her friend, a cocaine whore more aptly named Candy.

"Be quiet," the stranger said in a menacing whisper. "I'm not going to hurt you. Gordo is the one I want."

Bone marched the two naked girls down the hall and locked them in the bathroom. Then he returned to the bedroom, found a chair and sat down. He watched the DVD for a while. A teen-aged girl who seemed genuinely terrified was being slapped around by two naked men wearing Halloween masks. She spoke Spanish. They burned her with a cigarette, then choked and raped her repeatedly. If it was faked, it was Oscar caliber work. Bone figured it for an actual video pirated from another country. His blood started to boil. He turned off the television, sat down near Gordo, aimed the rifle at the dealer and flicked on the light.

"What the . . . ?"

Bone once told me that nothing concentrates the mind as perfectly as the business end of a gun. Gordo shook off the drugs and booze slowly, but then sat up straight when he saw the man with the pantyhose face. His red eyes bulged wide. One palm came up in the classic vain gesture meant to ward off a bullet.

"Hey," Gordo said weakly. "Hey."

One of the Wicked

"It's about your money, motherfucker." The intruder spoke quietly, firmly. "And I want all of it."

Gordo tried the usual bobbing and weaving. Said he didn't keep it all at the house, the safe was locked and an employee kept the key, maybe tomorrow morning; I'll get you for this and you can run but you can't hide asshole. Bullshit like that, the things people say when they're bluffing. Meanwhile, the strange man just sat there with his face all twisted up.

Gordo probably got bolder then, made some threats without getting a response. Bigger threats. Maybe Gordo even eventually made the mistake of threatening Bone's family. I figure something like that must have happened, something that compounded having viewed the sadistic video. How do I know?

Because Bone tied Gordo to the chair, gagged him, and started in with the knife.

101

TEN

Flies already circled my dying cat, Wink. Her skinny sides heaved as she struggled for air. I didn't know what had happened; whether the little tabby had been hit by a car, eaten something bad, or maybe my stepfather had kicked her too hard. It was almost dark out and we were on the back porch. I was maybe eleven years old. The cat yowled and writhed for a second, then went silent again. I held Wink in my lap and did my best not to cry. Danny was drunk again, way too drunk to drive into Dry Wells. Besides, he said, "We ain't got money to waste on a vet. That animal don't do shit around here, except for killing rats. . . ."

I'd been fighting that day, and my elbows and knuckles were scraped raw. Danny had grudgingly cleaned me up and given me some of the money we'd won. I thought of offering to use that to pay Doc Langdon, but knew if I went to the phone Danny would beat me for sure. He had already said no, and Danny didn't brook sass, especially when he was drunk.

I decided that if the cat was still fighting for her life when my stepfather passed out, I'd collect my savings, put her in a sack around my neck, and ride one of the horses into town. With luck, I'd find Doc and be back before dawn.

Just then, the cat stopped breathing. My chest ached. I closed her eyes and cursed Danny, wished him dead along with the animal, but promptly felt a wave of guilt and shame. He'd given me a roof and food when my mother died. He was rough, but he was all I had. I reminded myself to be grateful.

My knuckles hurt. I put the cat down and tried to look at my hands but suddenly they weren't in front of me at all, they were behind my back, and I couldn't move. . . .

"When's he going to wake up?"

I was lying sideways on a seat that smelled like genuine leather. My hands were tied behind my back. I'd been gagged and blindfolded. The fight in my yard, the blow from the baseball bat. . . .

Everything was humming, vibrating. We were probably in the van, moving rapidly, maybe out on the highway. My head felt too large and I had what felt like a terminal hangover. My stepfather's memory spoke up from deep inside. *Danny chewed me out for having lost a fight. I felt a little sick, probably from blows to the head, but also from shame. When you get the chance, boy, you make them pay.*

"Who gives a shit when he wakes up?" Cowboy finally answered. "He stays quiet, it's an easier drive."

"What's this about, anyway? He's just some talk-show guy, for Chrissakes."

"That's none of your business."

This wasn't about revenge. They'd been sent to the strip bar, and had mistaken that first businessman they'd assaulted for Bud Stone. Apparently, I'd interfered with their plans to attack him, and then had been seen talking to Bone, so now they'd been told to pick me up. One of them turned up the radio. A repetitive pop hit assaulted my ears. I wriggled my hands and feet to restore circulation. They were bound by plastic police ties.

No James Bond shit tonight, I was just going to have to be patient.

Times like this, you suddenly think about dying. How easy it can be to get taken out. And anyone who claims they don't feel sick to their stomach and loose in the bowels when that happens is lying. Being helpless was the worst part. It was almost too much to bear on top of feeling scared. I'd woken up with my hands tied like this back in Dry Wells, and this wasn't any easier.

We drove on. I drifted in and out of consciousness for quite a while. The head and neck pain probably kept me from going under for good, a dangerous possibility with a concussion. I did sleep a bit; I don't know for how long, and when I focused again my stomach had settled. The drone of the tires changed pitch as the driver slowed down, maybe for a traffic light. It was light out. I fell asleep again.

"Wake up, Clyde," Cowboy said to Windbreaker. "We're here."

My heart kicked. After a few minutes we drove over bumpy ground and came to a stop. They rolled a window down, and suddenly I caught the scent of freshly turned earth and distant sage. It was dead quiet. We were probably in the desert, many hours from Los Angeles. The seatbelt warning pinged. I opened my eyes slowly, wanting them to have time to adjust, and winced. The sunlight hurt my eyes.

It was mid-morning.

"He's awake," the other one said. The one Cowboy had called Clyde. He rolled me over onto my back, leaned down and ripped the taped gag away. My face burned. Clyde looked down coolly. "Don't look like much now, does he?"

"He still looks like more than you could handle," Cowboy said. "Grab his feet, tough guy."

They hauled me out of the van and dumped me on my side in the dirt. The world got sharp and clear. The hills were beautiful and the morning was fragrant with sage flowers. The ground was rich and moist, as if someone had recently planted here and was tending a new garden. Were they going to shoot me now?

"Why?"

At first I didn't recognize my own voice. I'd asked the question aloud. Cowboy ignored me. He pulled out a switchblade knife and flicked it open. I swallowed. He rolled me over, bent down behind me and cut away the plastic bonds. He nicked my skin, but the rush of blood covered that pain with another.

"The fuck you doing?"

Clyde. He didn't seem to like the idea of me getting back on my feet. He backed towards the van and produced a small handgun. I caught a reflection, but not the make and model. I blinked and looked around. We were at some kind of building site. Tractors were moving in the distance, despite the heat. A construction crew was working busily. A new hotel?

"Sit up, Callahan."

I did. Cowboy cut my ankles free. I massaged them, and my wrists. I turned my head and saw a giant complex, a new hotel of some kind. The pieces started to come together. I squinted against the glare, made out a few markers here and there. Found one that said "The Valley of Fire Corporation."

"Can you stand?"

I rolled over, got up onto hands and knees, then to my feet. "I'm okay." I listed to port, and Cowboy caught me. "Maybe not so okay."

He examined my forehead. "You got popped pretty good. Sorry about that. Clyde gets a little carried away sometimes."

"Me?" Clyde was literally shaking in his boots. "The fuck you mean me?"

Cowboy didn't answer. He pushed me at the small of the back. We started walking. They led me across some black asphalt and bright white sand. We moved through a glass door still covered with crosses of beige masking tape and then into a deserted hallway. Rolls of thick, busily patterned carpet lay everywhere, not yet installed. Our footsteps boomed and echoed.

"Thirsty." I sounded like the possessed little girl in *The Exorcist.*

"In a minute," Cowboy said. He led me into a huge lobby that most resembled a gigantic brass tube. We crossed carpeting, passed a tall planter and some paintings still in their shipping cartons, and then walked over to a pair of glass elevators. Cowboy leaned me against the back wall, punched the top button. The damned thing shot upwards like a carnival ride. I nearly threw up. One hell of a lot of numbers pinged by.

Unlike the lobby, the top floor was finished. Recessed lighting, alcoves with art, thick carpet in a calmer pattern, fountains. We went down a long hall toward huge wooden doors that were partly open. Light came from beyond. The left side of the corridor was all glass. I could see the open desert and reddish mountains outside. As we walked, I stared like a redneck tourist at one stunning collection. Any one of those sculptures would have cost more money than I'd made in my entire career.

We got to the end of the hall, some kind of master suite, where the big boys always come to play.

"I'll wait out here," Clyde said. He was sweating. Cowboy opened the door and led me by the elbow. The room was huge, bright, and everything inside was clear glass or redwood. The effect was to take any light and refract and reflect it into a rich glow, thus the "Valley of Fire."

There was a long conference table, polished well beyond fingerprints. There were two men, one extremely tall, sitting half in shadow near the far end of the table. I could not see their features.

"Good morning, Mr. Callahan."

I didn't react quickly enough, so Cowboy turned me. For a minute, I thought he was going to force me to genuflect. I blinked away the brightness. A portly man in Armani was coming my way, right hand extended. I recognized the face from the file Jerry had sent me. In person, "Big Paul" Pesci was far more immense horizontally than vertically. I shook his hand.

Pesci peered up at me with concern. He glared at Cowboy. His face was pleasant, but the mood changed. "What happened?"

Cowboy cleared his throat. "Uh. . . ."

"Clyde, please come in here," Pesci said. A few seconds later, the big door opened and Clyde came into the room. His arm pits were dark with sweat. Big Paul motioned with a finger. Clyde came closer, stood next to Cowboy. It appeared my escorts had stepped in it.

"He has been injured. I'm not pleased."

"Boss. . . ."

"Shut up. Can I offer you some breakfast or a coffee, Mr. Callahan? Or some mineral water, perhaps?"

"Some water would be nice." The faux courtesy felt ridiculous, but seemed imminently better than being beaten and kicked, so I figured why not go along with it. "Thank you."

"Eric, get the man a drink."

So Cowboy's name was Eric. He glided away with the skill of an English butler and left Clyde to face the music. Pesci walked around Clyde, carving a tight circle like a farmer examining an animal up for auction. He was posturing for my benefit, demonstrating his virtually limitless power. This was his world, and he wanted me to know it.

"Clyde, did I not give you precise instructions regarding Mr. Callahan? That he was not to be harmed?"

Clyde was screwed either way. Either he was calling the boss a liar, or he'd fucked up. No wonder he was sweating. I glanced around, first over at Cowboy Eric, who was taking his sweet time with that bottled water.

On the other side of the conference table, the tall man was easing his chair back. He stood. I flinched. The bastard had to be six-eight or so. I could now see his chiseled face and hungry expression. The big man had a shaved head and the eyes of a junkyard dog. Meanwhile Pesci circled Clyde. That big guy didn't move closer, just stayed on his feet as if waiting for orders.

"I'm sorry, Mr. Pesci," Clyde whispered.

Pesci turned his look to Eric, who finally brought a glass with ice and a bottle of sparkling water. He poured me some and I drank it down. Pesci couldn't get a rise out of Eric. Cowboy was cool under fire. He kept his face pleasant and tried to wait things out. I moved out of the shadows and away from Clyde. The sun roared in the window and made my skin feel hot. *What the hell. . . .*

"It was my fault," I said, letting them off the hook. "I didn't give these guys a chance to explain. Thought I was being jumped and fought back."

At the end of the conference table, where the shades were drawn, cool shadows shifted. The huge man sat down again. He looked vaguely disappointed, and a bit bored. The balding younger man next to him had balled his hands into fists. I saw them relax again. My two new friends Eric and Clyde looked about ready to cry.

I turned back to Pesci. "I don't know where he is."

"Mr. Stone."

"I saw him at the club that night and he asked me for a favor. I haven't talked to him since."

Pesci waved me over to some easy chairs. We sat down to talk. Eric and Clyde decided to hold up the wall nearest the door. I'd be willing to bet their knees were shaking.

"We could have done this over the phone, you know," I said to Pesci with a frown. "Your guys have seen too many movies."

Pesci laughed. "Maybe, maybe. However, these days, with the government spying on everybody, it seemed more prudent to ask you to come in for a visit, a little bit of face time. And when we're done, there will be some chips for your favorite casino, a girl if you want. Believe me I'll make it up to you."

"No need. And like I said, I don't know where he is."

"Oh, I believe you."

My turn to be surprised. "Then why are we doing all this?"

"I'm going to go out on a limb here and trust you," Pesci said. "You'll understand why in a minute. Hear me out. Your friend Bud has made a very serious mistake, and then appears to have compounded it again while trying to make it right."

"I'm listening."

"As a result of these actions, he may now have something I need very badly, something which is of no value to him but of huge significance to me. And I do mean huge. If you help me, you keep your friend alive. It's that simple."

I finished the glass, poured another to buy time. "I'm still listening."

"Nicky, come here."

It took me a second to realize Pesci was calling the big man over from the conference table. The sun vanished. It was like watching Godzilla take Tokyo on television when I was a kid. The guy sat down a few feet away. He did not offer his hand. Our eyes met and I felt someone walk on my grave.

"Nikolaou Argetoianu," the giant said softly. "Some call me Little Nicky. You may call me Nick."

"Nick, meet Mick." Pesci giggled at the poor joke. We didn't.

Nicky continued smoothly, with only the slightest trace of an accent. Yugoslavian, maybe? Eastern Europe for sure. "I represent the people who have bankrolled Mr. Pesci in this casino endeavor, Mr. Callahan. I'm sure I don't need to tell you that these are very important people. At this point we are merely asking for your assistance in a business matter. If you fail to cooperate, at some other juncture, things could become . . . messy. You understand?"

I understood well enough to feel queasy again. *Oh, man. Bone, what have you gotten us into?*

"Mr. Stone borrowed a lot of money, one hundred thousand dollars with interest, to be precise. Therefore he owes Mr. Pesci almost one hundred and twenty thousand as of today. The clock keeps running. And then there is the matter of another of Paul's associates, one Mr. Rico Diaz."

"He's an associate?" Nicky was saying that poor Bone owed money to another arm of the Pesci syndicate without knowing it, all because of Faber and Toole and their shenanigans. Good news and bad news. You owe a lot of cash, but it's kind of all in the same place. Oh, and there's more going on than you think.

"Just so, thus unfortunately, your friend also owes Mr. Pesci another fifty thousand dollars for a missing shipment of quality marijuana." He pronounced the word perfectly, like a man also fluent in Spanish. This Nicky was smart, in addition to being genuinely scary. "Despite the shooting of the mule, Paul has indicated that he will forgive any interest owed in this instance. He just wants payment in full."

I turned to the mob boss. "Mr. Pesci, my understanding is that it was Toole and Joey Faber that took you down, not Bud Stone. In fact, they ripped him off for his original investment, stole that shipment of grass and skipped town with everything, leaving him holding the bag. So whatever it is you're looking for, they're the guys you want."

"Perhaps," Pesci said. "But there is more to the story. Tell him, Nicky."

In a voice devoid of emotion, Nicky told me that some tough bastard had just gone after a gang leader and violent porn maker named Gordo. Someone with military experience, who'd disarmed and disabled bodyguards and used torture to make Gordo talk. It had to be Bud, intending to score enough cash to buy his way out of trouble. I didn't ask how they knew all these specific details, didn't want to know.

I finished the water to buy time. "If it was Bud, and if he got away with a ton of cash, he'll contact you to pay you back. Be patient."

Pesci shook his head. "We can't take the risk. He could run."

"Bud doesn't care much for rules, but he's an honorable man. And he knows you'd have him followed to the ends of the earth just as a matter of principle." I thought about Brandi De-Lillo and hoped she and Jerry were safe. "He won't run. Bone won't put his family at risk that way. He wants this over. Frankly, so do I."

"Then listen carefully," Nicky said. He leaned closer. He had terrible breath, vaguely like fish food. "This Gordo person probably told your friend way too much for his own good. Not the entire picture, it was not entirely known by him, but possibly enough to endanger our operation. Believe me, Gordo was a fool to steal from us. We make your friend look like Mother Teresa. To make matters worse, Gordo talked, he gave your friend whatever he had hidden in the house, perhaps fifty thousand dollars in cash, some hard drugs. Most importantly, a package that was intended for me."

"This just keeps getting worse, doesn't it? This Gordo character sounds pretty low-rent. How did he get his hands on your property?"

Nick closed his eyes as if bored. "A bonded international courier was bringing in something from my associates, Mr. Callahan, something of tremendous importance. It was in a briefcase, rather like diamonds, and padlocked to her hand. She came to the United States on a private jet, and flew First Class from New York to Los Angeles. Someone intercepted her there and stole from us. Someone ruthless, who passed the item through Faber to Gordo."

"Ruthless?"

"My courier has not been found, just the empty briefcase and her hand. It had been severed at the wrist."

My stomach lurched at the image. "That someone plays rough."

"He deals in hard drugs and distributes snuff films."

Gordo. "Can you tell me what we're looking for?"

"I will tell you this much." Nicky held his hands apart as if to outline something the size of a compact disc. "The item in question is a small computer disc in a black plastic container. Mr. Callahan, see to this. I need it back, and at once."

His tone grated. "Write out a message. I'll tell him when he calls."

Nicky patted my hand. The touch made my skin wiggle. "Mr. Callahan, upon due consideration, I don't think I like you."

"Oh, that feeling is mutual."

He showed his feral teeth. "But of course."

"Mr. Callahan," Pesci said impatiently, "these are very substantial people, by that I mean Nicky's bosses, the guys that want that disc back. They are international players, okay? Very big-time. Give me a hand here, I'll make it worth your time."

Somebody else had already given a hand. I said, "I doubt that."

"This European cartel, for lack of a better term, represents ultra serious money, and I do mean the kind of loot that can wipe out a big bank or a small country at a moment's notice. They can buy and sell the rest of us with pocket change. That's why I'm in business with them. You understand."

"So." Nicky sat back in the chair and crossed his legs. "Think hard. Where could your friend go to hide?"

"Not his wife or son. Not me again. I'll have to poke around." I chewed some ice. "Gentlemen, Bud doesn't know what he's got, does he?"

"No," Pesci said, "he doesn't. And it is best for him that he never finds out."

"Then I don't want to know, either. I won't ask for any more details. Let me see what I can do."

"Fine." Pesci got to his feet. Nicky remained seated, a gesture that somehow oozed arrogance and scorn. Pesci said, "If you do not wish to tell us where he might be, locate him yourself. Just retrieve the item we need. And please know that you have very little time before matters come to a head."

I blinked. "Then get me home."

"Also, this must be said." Nicky slowly picked at his nails. "If you help, both you and your friend Mr. Stone shall remain breathing and above the ground. If you fail, or try to leave town, people will get hurt."

I got up, hoping my own size would serve to intimidate somebody. It didn't work. "What do you mean by that?"

"Let me make this easy. I shall be even more specific. We know about Jerry Jover, Señorita Hernandez, and your friend Hal Solomon, for example. You must find Bud Stone, Mr. Callahan, or someone you know and love will die."

I almost went for him. The big man just looked up at me with sleepy eyes and smiled. I sighed. "Know what, Nicky? Fuck you."

"Fuck *me?*" Nicky chuckled. "We shall see."

The air got thick. Pesci knew he'd lost control of the room. He blustered a bit, and then gave up. He waved to his men. "Eric, Clyde. Give Mr. Callahan a few hundred in cash and put him on the next plane."

ELEVEN

McCarran International. Chirping slot machines, winking lights, the stench of booze mixed with stale cigarette smoke. Old folks in wrinkled polyester yanked handles or pushed bright buttons mindlessly. Small, unobtrusive signs listed the number of Gambler's Anonymous. The Vegas airport was already mobbed with people heading back to the LA area. Clyde waited in the parking lot, but Eric the cowboy walked me to the escalator. He looked down at the carpet and screwed around with the toe of his boot.

"Guess I owe you one." He stuck out his hand. "We were kind of pissed about what happened the other night at the strip club and Clyde just got carried away. No hard feelings?"

"Sure."

I shook his hand without thinking. I'm a regular Gandhi sometimes.

Eric nodded, turned, and vanished into the crowd. I looked up at the board. The white letters made my eyes hurt. I located my plane, and discovered it was already boarding. I hurried for the gate. The flight was packed. The airline was the last one running without seat assignments, so getting aboard was something of a free for all. Standing on the aircraft waiting to snag a seat always makes me want to moo like a cow.

I didn't have a cell. I asked the blue-haired lady gabbing away in the next seat if I could borrow hers. She shot me a dirty look and turned sideways to look outside. The sun cut through the windows like a clear plastic razor. My head still ached. The flight attendants gave us their usual spiel, pretending we'd survive a real crash or a long float in the water, demonstrated the best way to buckle seatbelts we'd all used a million times before, and passed out stale peanuts and tiny plastic cups full of overpriced booze and flat soft drinks.

The ladies and one gent hurried to the front and back of the cabin and strapped themselves in. The old plane shuddered down the runway, groaned and lifted off to caustic applause. Booze service resumed.

I decided to use the brief flight to rest and think. I had to accomplish at least four different things. First, get in touch with Bud Stone and tell him what was going on. Second, run down Joey Faber and Toole as soon as possible. Third, protect Brandi as I'd originally promised. Finally, I had to pass the word to anyone who might be a target to be extra careful until this was over. My friends would not be pleased. Oh, and also find another job, assuming I'd even have the time to take one on.

Some days it's hardly worth getting out of bed.

I slept for twenty minutes or so during the flight, to my surprise, and my head felt a bit better, especially after I'd downed two small glasses of orange juice and some ice water. The landing was as noisy as the takeoff and the brakes sounded horrible. We taxied to a tall set of metal stairs and deplaned through the front. More cattle-in-a-chute stuff. Burbank airport is pretty efficient, and once out of the aircraft I was able to make pretty good time for the exit. I had no baggage other than a bad concussion, so I went straight to a cab and had it run me home. I tipped well because the money was dirty.

I searched the front yard and found my cell phone in the grass. It was still functioning. It said I had two messages. I let myself in, turned on the air-conditioning. I made some strong coffee, sat at the kitchen table, then punched in my code to listen. The first call was from Darlene, the phone had already announced that by showing her number, but it was a hang up.

The second was from Bone.

I flipped back while it played and read the area code: 310. He was still in Los Angeles. I couldn't make it out at first so I hit replay, sat up straight, punched up the volume. "Mick, it's me checking in. The wife is somewhere safe, and I already have most of what I need. I'll be in touch." *Click.*

"Damn it." I tried to dial the number my cell listed, and it rang three times. A machine announced I'd reached a room at the Sunset Inn Motel. My party wasn't in, and the recording said to hold on for the desk operator. I closed the phone and immediately dialed another number.

"Jerry? It's me."

"What up, bro?"

"How's the lady?"

"Lopez checks in every couple of hours. Last time we talked everything was cool."

"Tell Lopez someone raised the stakes, and to be extra careful the next few days."

"What's that supposed to mean?"

"It means watch your ass. That's all I can say for now. How are you?"

"Me? I'm fine." After a moment of reflection. "Okay, I've been meaning to tell you anyway. I bought a gun last week. It's a big old Taurus, just like yours."

I sighed. "Have you ever fired a gun, Jerry?"

"When I was a kid, and I'm going to the range today after what you just said." He got a bit defensive. "You still have yours, Mick. I've seen it up there in the closet."

"True," I said softly. I don't really like guns, they always escalate things, but right now having one in the house didn't seem like such a bad idea. "Jerry, let Lopez handle the surveillance stuff. You get back on Faber and Toole. Fast. I need to run them down, anything you can get, even guesswork. Where are they now? Get the files you've collected over to Darlene Hernandez through her personal E-mail service. I'm about to ask her for help."

"A likely story."

"Don't bust my balls, just move, okay?"

"Will do, Mick."

"Jerry, stay safe. I'll call you later."

I had to leave a message for Hal Solomon; he didn't answer at his hotel or via the computer. Since I was out of a job, I was going to need his money and resources if any serious expenses came along. I gathered myself, which took some doing, and called Darlene Hernandez.

"You are a dick, Callahan, know that?"

"Darlene. . . ."

"You call me up and say you didn't call me, and then push to get together when I asked for space. Then you call me last night and just hang the fuck up."

"I. . . ."

"Let me finish. You are just maddening to deal with, Mick Callahan. What the hell happened last night?"

"I want to fill you in, but you're not giving me the room. Darlene, I need to see you. And I mean now."

"No."

"Look, it's not about us this time."

That got her attention, but her next words also oozed disappointment, which surprised me. *Women.* "Then what the hell *is* it about? Are you in trouble again?"

"You might say that. Please check your personal E-mail; you should have something from Jerry."

"Hang on."

I looked at the clock. She was probably due for a meal break soon. Darlene also had recently transferred from Hollywood to the North Hollywood station on Oxnard. Her office was now just minutes away.

"What is this shit, Mick? Why these two ex-cons?"

"Don't ask. Let's get something to eat. I'll fill you in."

"No can do, Mick. I'm meeting Larry." Her cousin, who'd hired Lopez for me.

"Donato looks good when we talk. How's he doing these days?"

"He gets by without a walker most of the time," Darlene said coolly. Now and then she seemed to hold me responsible for his injuries. She sort of blew hot and cold on that one; I could be an angel or a schmuck on a moment's notice. I guess that was understandable. Larry had been shot down right here in my front yard, wearing my sweatshirt and thus taken for me by mistake.

"I'm glad to hear that." I meant it. "Okay. I have an errand to run anyway. Look at those files, and then how about I stop by the station in a couple of hours, just for a few minutes."

"Give me a hint?"

"I need to find two men. I'd rather not get into the rest."

"Never can tell who's listening?"

"Not these days. Five?"

"Five-thirty," Darlene said. "And you'd best make it quick."

I have such a way with the ladies.

I took Riverside Drive to Laurel Canyon, went south into the hills and over toward Sunset. There was no reason to call the motel back. Bud was unlikely to still be there, and I was certain he would have used a fake name and paid in cash. Traffic was light for the canyon, except for a brief construction bottleneck. Another slowdown happened because both sides of the road were lined with people in orange doing community service over traffic infractions and minor drug charges. I finally hit Sunset, but went the wrong way at first and had to find a place to turn around.

The motel was squeezed somewhat reluctantly in between two supposed LA landmarks; a decrepit drugstore with a famous soda fountain and a tacky bowling alley. It was bright and hot and the day-shift hookers were out in force, offering quickies to the passing drivers. I had a hell of a time finding a parking spot, so I went into the soda fountain and got an egg salad sandwich and cola to go, then left the bag on my front seat and locked the car.

The motel office was an ice box, meaning about that big and easily as cold. The guy behind the desk was pierced in silver and weird enough to resemble Pinhead from the Hellraiser movies. He sat back in a padded office chair, dozing, wearing a black tee with a death metal band logo, black jeans, and boots. His pale arms were crossed, hands folded. He looked recently embalmed. I showed him some money. One bloodshot eye opened.

"I'm looking for a friend of mine. It's kind of off the record."

"Him or you?"

"Both. A hundred bucks to *keep* it off the record."

One hand crawled the worn desk like an albino crab and the money vanished. I described Bud Stone. The clerk closed his eyes again. "You're in luck, 'cause I pulled a double. I checked him in last night. He got in late, paid cash, grabbed some instant coffee here in the lobby at around dawn and took off again."

"What name did he give you?"

"We get a John Smith in here damned near every night, for some strange reason. My boss should inform the *Guinness Book of Records.*"

"Did he say anything?"

"Just that LA needs a new football team. Oh, and Mr. Smith won't be back."

"Sure about that?"

The other hand dangled the key to 301. "Dropped this off on the way out, gave me fifty bucks and told me to forget him."

"Apparently that hundred I just gave you isn't going to buy much discretion."

"So I'm an asshole."

I leaned forward over the counter, looked left and right out the windows. A balding man wearing a blue and green aloha shirt was loading luggage into the trunk of a rental car while being assaulted by a distraught wife and two screaming little boys. When he bent over I could see his pate was pink and peeling. The guy glanced over at me as if looking for sympathy. I stood up straight again. *Too many witnesses.*

"One last question," I said. "Has that room been cleaned yet?"

The clerk yawned. "Probably not before three, man. Only two of the girls showed up for work today. It's like that sometimes."

I opened my palm. He gave me the key. "Don't slow them down. As you can see, we run a very tight ship, here. Up the stairs and to the right."

I jogged up to 301. The cleaning cart was four doors down and closing fast. Even though I felt silly and paranoid, I stepped to the side of the entrance and knocked twice. The sun burned down on my shoulders. A crow cawed raucously right above my head. Other than that, silence.

I opened the door and went in. The curtains were closed tight. The room was dark and stuffy. The bed was rumpled, the television cabinet wide open. I closed and locked the door, started by searching the bathroom. I had no law enforcement experience, but hoped to get lucky. Bud had taken a shower and left wet towels on the floor. The trash can held some used tissues, dental floss, and an empty book of paper matches from

GENTS, which seemed to be yet another strip club. The name had doodles through a few letters. I looked closer. The address said it was located out by the LA airport. I stuffed that in the pocket of my jeans.

The messy bed occupied most of the other room. I looked through the sheets, saw no evidence Bone had brought a girl to his room. I didn't really expect that he'd do that while on the run. He hadn't used any of the cheap stationery in the drawer.

The trash can by the right-hand bed held an empty half pint of cheap rum, one soft drink can, and a tissue with brownish stains. I lifted it out gingerly, sniffed. It smelled like gun oil. I flipped on the tube and it was set for the local news. It appeared Bud had cleaned weapons while watching television, probably looking to see if anyone had managed to finger him for the Gordo mess. He'd thrown out or taken the gun rag, but a bit of oil had gotten onto the bathroom tissue. That scared me. Lots of things seemed to be scaring me of late.

I went around the foot of the bed to look for the other trash can. It hadn't been used at all. I looked under the bed, in the dresser drawers, the closet. Clean as a fake tooth. Even the wooden coat hangers were straight. Of course, he'd be traveling light, maybe one change of clothes to wash in the sink or at a Laundromat.

I let myself back out and almost ran right into the cleaning cart. I smiled at an older Hispanic lady with a round, pretty face. She gestured to see if I was coming back, and I shook my head.

I stepped out of the way. When she went inside to clean up, I trotted back down the stairs and entered the motel office. The pale clerk was dozing again. I looked out both windows. The harried husband was gone and now the tiny parking lot was deserted.

I cleared my throat loudly and dropped the key on the desk.

The clerk opened one eye again. "You done?"

I nodded, waved a finger for him to sit up and move my way. "Let me tell you a little secret. What's your name?"

"Bob."

"Bob, come closer."

When he got near enough, I grabbed his neck and squeezed. His eyes bulged wide and the blood left his already pale face. He sputtered and writhed so I squeezed a little bit harder. He stopped moving.

"Bob, the secret is this. If you tell anyone else about my friend, in fact let them know that either one of us were here, I will come back and hurt you so bad your house plants will die."

"Okay, okay. . . ."

"Have we reached an understanding, Bob? You don't talk about this again, for any amount of money, not to anyone."

"Sure. Yeah."

I released him just as a toothy salesman entered with a thin hooker in tow. The tracks on her arms had healed, but they were both roaring drunk. They toasted to better days. Before I left, I gave Bob my last tainted hundred-dollar bill, smiled brightly and patted his very white cheek.

"Hey, and you have a really nice day."

TWELVE

Sergeant Bill Keller sat hunched over the front desk of the hyper-modern glass-walled North Hollywood station like a sleepy brown bear, listening patiently as an old woman with steel-wool hair whined on about a horde of rude middle school kids who cut across her lawn twice a day, damaging her petunias. I closed the door quietly but my boots made a racket on the polished tile. Keller looked up and immediately recognized me, not from my work but because I'd been dating Darlene Hernandez, a distinction that had earned me the nickname "That Lucky-Assed Civilian Son of a Bitch."

"Morning."

"Callahan." Keller scribbled my name on a press pass and slid it my way. The woman continued talking but dropped her voice, went paranoid and backed away without looking up. Keller rolled his eyes.

"Thanks, Bill."

"Ma'am," Keller said patiently, "someone will be here in a minute to help you fill out a complaint. Just wait over there."

The woman issued an exasperated sigh, spun around and trudged away in untied tennis shoes. She left an odd odor floating in the air; old lady dust and fertilizer. I pinned the guest badge on my shirt as Keller reached over, slid something wooden to one side, and buzzed me into the station proper.

The door slid open and I went into a perfectly air-conditioned area. Two wide corridors branched off into smaller lanes

containing brightly lit offices. The pristine walls were covered
with photographs and citations. I'd been here before, of course,
both for work reasons and to visit Darlene during happier times.
So the officers and plainclothes folks nodded politely.

At the end of the hall there stood a large elevator with faux
gold-plated doors. I have no idea why a Valley police station
would choose to look like a low-rent whore house, but it takes
all kinds. I pushed the button and chewed on a toothpick until
the car arrived. After a ping the doors slid open. Two female
patrol officers got out and walked off, whispering in low tones. I
went up one floor, paused for a moment to gather myself. I
hadn't seen the lady in a while.

I got off the elevator, went down six doors, turned right, and
found Darlene, wearing a beige blouse and dark pants. She was
facing away from me, rifling through a tall file cabinet. In the
short time since I'd last seen her, she'd lost weight, and her
brown hair was a bit longer. Darlene had stripped the office to
bare essentials, and I couldn't help but notice that my picture
was no longer on her desk.

Her shoulders tightened as if she sensed my presence, but the
woman didn't turn. I studied her from behind for a while, that
strong back and the way her brown hair whispered along the
nape of her neck. My heart melted at first, but when she faced
me Darlene Hernandez wasn't smiling.

"Close the door."

I did.

"Sit down."

I sat.

"Do you know how much trouble you can get me into by
sending me illegally obtained state and federal records? Jesus,
Mick, how the hell does Jerry get all this stuff?"

I shrugged and tried charming. "He's a genius."

Charming didn't work. Darlene had a sharp, red flame in her

eyes. They were damned pretty eyes, though. She checked to make sure the phone was on the hook and the speaker button was off. I waited, and managed to resist the urge to kiss her. Good way to get my nose broken again.

"Mick, don't you dare joke around. I had a look at those files, and if they got wind of what was in them, Internal Affairs would be up my ass in a heartbeat. I'd be racked just to find out where they came from."

"It's that bad?"

"Bad? Some of that stuff is from fucking Homeland Security! Don't you ever send me something like that again. You can delete the shit out of it and it will still be somewhere in the E-mail account and on the hard drive."

I stared back. "I'm sorry."

"Sorry my ass. Don't give me those puppy eyes. You knew better than to do that. You and Jerry are a couple of con artists. You just wanted my hands a little dirty so I'd have to do something to help you out."

My cheeks felt hot. I hadn't wanted to recognize it consciously, but Darlene was probably right. Jerry and I had trapped her into having this conversation. "I'm no expert, but knowing Jerry he probably burned the trail after he sent them. He can clean your computer, too."

"So I'd be receiving stolen property, breaking all kinds of known and unknown security laws, and then compounding the felonies by tampering with evidence. That's why you're a talk-show host instead of a cop. I'm better off playing stupid."

"What do you want me to say?"

"Mick, if I didn't love you, I swear. . . ."

I perked up a bit. Darlene frowned. "Forget I said that, damn it."

"But you did. You said you love me."

"Don't grin."

"Sorry."

"I mean it, wipe that smile off your face or I will."

"Yes, Sergeant."

Darlene eyed me with proverbial steam coming out of her ears. I looked down and away, back again. "Honey, I need your help."

"The last time I helped you my cousin Larry got shot and people died. I still have bad dreams about that."

"Me, too."

"Let's get the hell outside." Darlene was at the door before I hit my feet. She held it open and waited out in the corridor. I followed meekly. I must have masochism buried deep in my psyche, because her anger never failed to light my candle.

Darlene went charging on ahead of me, arms swinging. When she got upset it was like Olympic speed walking just trying to keep up with her. We went back out through the empty lobby. The old woman was gone and the desk job had rotated to a female officer I didn't know. I tossed the badge on the desk as I passed.

Out the doors, down the steps. A hot afternoon. Rows of cars packed onto narrow strips of concrete. Drivers on cell phones, sighing and swearing and honking their horns.

I followed Darlene nearly two long blocks down Oxnard. The air was thickening with afternoon smog and the heat announced an early summer. The news had just reported that the world now had the highest temperatures registered in over four centuries. Darlene stopped. Her head swivelled back and forth until she settled on a nearby taco stand. The place was nearly deserted. Darlene reached the window first and ordered two diet colas. We went to the furthest table and sat with our heads close together.

"Now what the hell is going on?"

I told her everything. About Bud Stone, the girl, my promise, the beating, all of it. Well, I left out the part about Brandi having a terrific ass. Darlene took some ice out of her cola and rubbed it on her neck. I wanted to volunteer for that duty but kept my mouth shut. Sometimes I'm smarter than I look.

"I don't believe you, Mick. We don't see each other for a few weeks and you're already up to your neck in alligators."

"And I just came here to drain the swamp."

"Let me get this straight. An old friend calls you up, and the next thing you know you're watching his lover, tangling with the mob, getting beat up in your own front yard, and threatened by some shadowy international organization that wants you to locate a mysterious package. Oh, and trying to find two ex-cons who took down a drug dealer and may be dangerous themselves. Did I leave anything out?"

"Well," I said weakly, "I got fired."

Her jaw dropped. "That's a joke, right?"

I told her about Judd Kramer and his betrayal. Darlene sagged and her face softened a bit. "That stinks, even for a Hollywood agent."

"Tell me about it. I know it's silly, but this feels kind of like being cheated on, although maybe by a very ugly woman."

Darlene flashed a grin. It was a very nice grin. "So, what now?"

"Well, I've got a bit of money saved, so that's good. And the house has gone up in value. There's no rush."

Her features tightened a bit. "Will you have to leave Los Angeles to get work?"

"I have no idea," I said honestly, "I might have to go. Hey, I do miss the desert. What I learned this time around is that I'm not really an LA kind of guy. If it wasn't for the work, to be honest, you'd be the only reason I'd stay here."

She stroked my arm, and a number of different emotions played across her features. Then her eyes hardened. "No. No promises, Mick."

"And I'm not asking for any. I was just saying."

"I know what you were saying."

"No you don't, you don't know what I was about to say, you know what you think I was about to say, and that's probably different from what I would have said."

"What the fuck?"

We laughed. Her eyes turned moist. So did mine. Darlene looked at me in a way that skinned flesh from my heart. She said, "I've missed you."

"I've missed you more."

"I doubt that, Callahan."

"And I love you." The bravery elicited no response. My stomach rolled sideways. I just swallowed my pride and continued on. "Darlene, why do we keep screwing this up?"

"You're the counselor, counselor."

"Because we're scared of what we're feeling, I suppose. Because we're so wounded. I know I'm scared. Aren't you scared?"

"No comment."

"I'm a mess." I stretched, shook my head. "Darlene, I wanted to be a player again, have another television show. I thought that was the most important thing to me, getting back in the game. Now I'm not so sure."

"You're too good to quit."

"I can always just stay in private practice. Never get rich that way, but it's rewarding."

Darlene shrugged. "You'll do whatever you have to do, same as me. You know something? Cops get a good retirement, that is, if they don't turn bitter, commit suicide, or get blown away on the job. But for just living day to day, I'd probably make more money typing memos at a movie studio."

"And you'd go completely insane."

"Not much doubt about that."

I leaned forward to touch her arm. She didn't pull back. "What do you really want from your life, honey?"

"Does anyone ever know the answer to that?"

"Probably not. I think we just consider and decide. Absolute certainty seems to be for the less intelligent. Not that I'm all that impressed with myself lately, either."

"Mick, you're a better man than you think. You deserve to be happy."

"So do you, with or without me." My voice trembled, so I blinked comically and sat back. "Good God, did I just say that?"

Her lip twitched. "A moment of true selflessness from the great Mick Callahan. Call the *Daily News.*"

I laughed. "It is so good to see you."

She nodded. "Likewise."

I bought some time, played with my straw. "I really am sorry to be here under these circumstances. I didn't ask to be a part of another drama. I owed an old friend a favor, and now it's turning into a train wreck. No good deed goes unpunished, and all that. I hate to ask, but can you help me out?"

A moment crawled by. "I'll see what I can do," Darlene said.

My shoulders sagged with relief. "I really appreciate that, believe me. If you can assist me in running these two guys down, I'll take it from there and leave you out of it, I promise."

"I can tell you this much. As of nine-thirty this morning there are APBs out for both Toole and Faber. LAPD is calling it something milder, but off the record, warrants are in the works."

"Warrants for stealing from a dealer?"

"For murder one."

I grunted. "Who got killed?"

"That drug dealer the Vegas dudes say your friend suppos-edly took down? Gordo? Faber and Toole are ex-cons, remember? They have jackets. And their fingerprints were all over that house."

I blinked. "I still don't get it."

"Gordo is dead, Mick. He was found cut to pieces early this morning."

It took me a minute to absorb that statement. Too many uncomfortable questions resulted. Did Bud Stone murder the guy, or Faber and Toole? And why would they be in the house of a dealer rumored to make snuff films? Were they there before or after Bone?

It couldn't have been all at the same time. Well, unless they were in it together, and Bone had lied to me from the start.

Oh, man, now that would be an ugly mess, wouldn't it?

"They were there, too," I said stupidly. "Faber and Toole. Before, after, maybe at the same time. Jesus."

"Yeah, and the brass likes Faber and Toole for the killing because of those aforementioned prints."

I whistled. "When I step in it, I really step in it."

"You sure do. And unfortunately, you also just told me about your pal Bud Stone. And that just put me in the position of either betraying the man I love or willfully withholding evidence in a murder investigation."

"I don't know what to say."

"Don't say anything." Darlene shook her head and sighed. "But please tell Jerry to stop sending me shit. Let me come to your house."

THIRTEEN

No good deed goes unpunished, all right.

Now, Robert Burns wrote "the best laid schemes o' mice and men gang aft a-gley." That's in a lovely, though nearly incomprehensible Scottish poem my stepfather claimed was one of my mother's favorites. I can't vouch for that, I don't remember her, but it stuck in my mind. I take it to mean that just when you figure you've got the bases covered and have a sense of how to dig yourself out of the poop, the other damned shoe drops.

We have to back up a few hours, to earlier that same morning, when I was being dragged to the Vegas airport for the flight back to Burbank. Here's what happened, as best I can reconstruct it. Off-duty cop Dave Lopez was guarding Bone's ex-girlfriend Brandi DeLillo from a discreet distance, just as I'd requested. Lopez had been working almost round the clock for a couple of days. In short, he was beat.

Dave Lopez was a good-looking guy gone to seed, a divorced cop hanging on by his fingernails for that holy twenty-year pension. He was a chain smoker, a quiet man given to stress headaches, a nice guy but completely burned out. He didn't know that his pals were already covering for him, looking the other way about his increased drinking and absent-minded mistakes. That made him the wrong guy for any really dangerous job.

Lopez had four months to go, and had no intention of signing up for more, but nobody wanted him to wash out. He'd been delighted to get the referral from Larry Donato to hang back and bodyguard. Hell, why not? Just follow a pretty girl around for twenty bucks an hour, with a shot at playing the hero one last time. How bad could that be?

Oh, man.

Jerry got bored with the enterprise after two shifts and handed it all back to Lopez, who had just come out of a four on, three off rotation. He'd already announced he was free to work through the start of next week, and needed money for that imminent retirement. He'd purchased some cheap land in a remote part of Mexico, near where his parents had been born, and wanted to build a small house. The construction expenses, not to mention the bribes, were breaking his back.

Brandi DeLillo had been in her apartment complex all night. That morning Lopez was nodding off a bit when the metal parking gate suddenly screeched and rolled back. Brandi drove up and out onto the street, rap music blaring. Lopez dropped sideways onto the seat and vanished from view just before she looked his way. He stared at the dashboard and waited for her engine to fade away, sat up and started his own car.

Brandi drove fast, but Lopez caught up with her near Wilshire and dropped back into traffic. She changed lanes a lot and took sharp turns, almost like someone who didn't want to be followed, but surveillance was one of the few job skills Lopez still possessed. He stayed with her every step of the way, and felt confident he hadn't been made. The day was turning hot, making Lopez grateful he wasn't stuck on the other side of the hill in the sweltering San Fernando Valley.

The girl moved down Wilshire, either heading for the San Diego Freeway or possibly the beach. Lopez was careful not to lose her near the freeway ramp, for fear of being left behind, but she sailed on by, maybe heading for Brentwood or Santa Monica. The traffic snarled and coiled and hissed.

Some high school boys in a new Ford Explorer honked and waved. Brandi did not respond, and that somehow made them bolder. They pulled up alongside her car and shouted something. She smiled brightly as one slender hand rose with the middle finger extended. They hooted and drove away with the rowdy faux courage of the desperately lonely adolescent.

Lopez trailed the girl all the way to Second Street in Santa Monica. When she pulled into one of the parking garages, he stopped with the turn signal blinking and pretended to search for something. Listened to her tires squeal up the ramp, then collected a ticket and entered the garage. Lopez lucked out just as someone was pulling out on a lower level. He beat an angry old man to the spot, locked his car, and jogged to the elevator. Then rode it in silence, wishing he'd brought sun lotion.

Brandi came out onto the sidewalk wearing a white sundress and a baseball cap. She paused and looked both ways. Lopez was already at the corner ordering a greasy hot dog from a street vendor.

The pretty girl donned an overlarge pair of black plastic sunglasses, spun around and marched east. She moved briskly, straw purse swinging, heading straight for the busy Third Street Promenade. Dave Lopez saw this new development as a decidedly mixed blessing. On the plus side, it would be easier to stay hidden in a large crowd. On the other hand, Lopez knew he could easily lose her there.

The Promenade is generally packed with street hustlers, trained pets, jugglers, musicians, rappers, hip hop dancers, caricature artists, poets, and oddball vendors. It's a fun spot for the beach crowd, tourists, and kids out on a cheap date. Brandi slowed down when she hit the back of the crowd, found an opening and slid into a group of couples watching an old man sing live opera accompanied by a scratchy cassette recording of an energetic orchestra.

She walked. Lopez moved a bit ahead of her, and stayed on the other side of the street. He ordered shaved ice and faced the window of a Greek restaurant. He could see Brandi reflected in the dusty glass.

The girl checked her watch and slid sideways out of the mob. She moved further east. Lopez stayed ahead of her for a while. When it felt right to change up again he stopped by a man selling liberal bumper stickers and allowed her to pass him by, so that he was behind her. Lopez was kind of enjoying himself by this point, feeling on top of his game.

Brandi enjoyed a kid doing magic tricks with helium balloons and left him a decent tip in his coffee can. She had to freeze out a couple of men who approached her. The cats doing circus tricks made her laugh out loud. Eventually the girl chose a restaurant, sat down at a glass table, and ordered a light salad and coffee. Relieved, Lopez went into an alley a bit west of her and smoked a cigarette. He opened his cell phone and called Jerry.

"It's me. We're in Santa Monica at the Promenade, doing the tourist thing all by our lonesome."

"Oh," Jerry answered. He sounded like he'd been napping. "Want me to pick it up again this afternoon?"

"I'll keep going, unless you're running out of budget. No problem."

"We have the cash. Enjoy the view, Dave."

"Later."

Lopez closed his cell phone, glanced up and saw two cops coming so he stomped out the cigarette. The cops hurried into a coffee place without spotting him. Lopez peeked around the corner.

Brandi was gone.

Lopez felt his heart jump. He looked again. The chair and food were still there, half the salad uneaten. He told himself that she'd gone to the ladies' room, but his instincts were saying something else. *Damn. Damn.*

Lopez sighed, stepped out into the sunlight and risked walking directly by the restaurant. He peered through the glass, and saw a woman exiting the small toilet. No one else seemed to be inside.

He swivelled, eyes darting here and there. Where could she have gone? He glanced back at the table. The waiter was cleaning up with a very sour expression. Brandi had apparently walked out on her check. She'd been generous with the street vendors, and had flashed an okay roll, so why stiff the waiter? Was she forced to leave? Had someone gotten by him?

Continuing on, Lopez swept the street as efficiently as he could. Brandi was not in any of the shops, and there was no way she'd returned to the parking garage. She would have had to have been in plain view for a lot longer if she'd tried. Lopez was certain he hadn't been spotted. Someone must have taken her. *Christ, one lousy cigarette and it all comes crashing down. What the fuck do I do now? What if she gets killed? How am I going to explain this?*

He considered going back to the restaurant and asking the cops for help, but on what basis? He wasn't on the job, and had no specific evidence.

Lopez was packing a .38, but knew if he shot a man while moonlighting his pension would be gravely endangered. Still, he fingered the weapon as he spun in a circle. The question was, did she shake him, or was she kidnapped? He had to bet on the worst alternative, that someone had snatched the girl. Who or how or why, Lopez hadn't a clue.

One thing he was reasonably confident about. Whoever did it was unlikely to know Brandi was being tailed by someone else, so if he could find her in time, Lopez figured he still had a decent shot at saving the day. But where should he start looking? Which way should he go?

He had no choice but to gamble, so Lopez chose the most likely exit route, a wide alley behind a Starbucks. He slipped past a bearded homeless guy who stood muttering to a cigar butt like it was his therapist. Lopez went into the alley. The reeking trash containers offered some cover. If the girl was taken by force, there was a very private parking lot at the end that was cool, dark, and likely to be deserted unless someone from the high-end company just happened to be coming or going. He palmed the weapon, feeling rather foolish, and slipped along the brick wall. He knelt down, looked at the alley floor, and saw what appeared to be drag marks. He pictured her being dragged by the shoulders, legs limp.

Yeah, or someone just dragged a trash sack through the dirt. Don't be a rookie and cap some security guard by mistake.

Lopez got to the end of the alley and paused where the drag marks stopped to examine the large metal door to the private parking area. It was closed. Lopez tried the handle. It wasn't locked. The door swung open and he stepped into the cool, shadowy cement garage. Everything seemed too loud, even his breathing. He closed the door to keep the sunlight from giving him away and moved into the gloom. Lopez paused to listen and thought he heard muffled voices down below. His palms were wet.

A rustle of clothing, feet crossing cement. Lopez jumped back. A portly man in jeans wheezed by, searching for his keys. He went off into the shadows and started trudging up to the next floor.

Where was Brandi?

A woman said something in what seemed to be an angry voice. A man barked a response. Two car doors slammed shut. Someone gunned an engine.

Lopez broke into a jog. He moved hunched over with the

gun pointing straight ahead. He had cement above and below. Lopez knew he'd likely kill himself if the weapon accidentally discharged a round that went anywhere but toward the far off staircase. He moved down into the lower part of the garage.

The ramp split, and through metal bars painted a sickening green he spotted a silver Lexus backing out of a parking spot. Lopez caught the flash of blonde hair, perhaps from a woman thrashing about in the backseat. He aimed his gun, knowing he'd be a fool to shoot. The car backed up, Lopez knelt on the cold cement and aimed for the driver, but didn't know if he could pull the trigger.

Just then a tall woman in a red dress and florid costume jewelry got out of the elevator and beeped her car. Lopez grunted. He couldn't safely fire a round anyway but that really tore it.

Shit. Shit.

The car was coming. Lopez ducked. He didn't want to be spotted. He got most of the license number of the Lexus, hunched forward and repeated it to himself as he backed into the stairwell.

The big car came around the corner with a harsh squeal of tires and sped up the ramp. Lopez watched as it went to the mouth of the garage and drove out into the sunlight.

There were two men in the front seat, Caucasians wearing sunglasses. If Brandi was in there with them, she was lying down on the seat or locked away in the trunk.

FOURTEEN

Bone was also on that side of the hill that morning. Not at the Promenade, but outside of Brandi's apartment. He pulled up before dawn and parked a ways off. He had some old military binoculars and used those rather than get too close. Bud knew I'd have someone on her and it didn't take long for him to spot Lopez. He was pleased, and found the man's presence reassuring. He kept those glasses handy for hours, staying way down the block, hoping for a glimpse of Brandi. Bud was exhausted and hungry and more than a little hung over.

He had spent most of his time in the car, his third vehicle in as many days. He didn't want to talk to Brandi; he was just making sure she was okay.

When she came out of the apartment building, his face lit up.

He watched how Lopez stayed back and got to work and mentally thanked me for knowing people who know people. She appeared to be in safe hands, and his wife was out of the state, so despite the complications, maybe things were working out okay. Brandi disappeared, Lopez a safe distance behind, and Bone started his own car and eased down the street.

When the light changed Bone turned left and drove away. The air-conditioning didn't work and the heat was rising as he found Coldwater and headed back over the hill. Traffic was bad but lightened up after Sunset.

As he came down into the valley, Bud turned on the news for the first time that day. What he heard made him stomp on the gas and almost rear-end the car in front of him. He yanked the wheel, passed on the right, and sped up, feeling both furious and more than a little scared. Gordo. Damn. The fucker was dead?

Traffic was light along Ventura. Bud moved up north of Victory, turned left. He drove north rapidly, up into Van Nuys, and cruised through a barrio neighborhood. Eventually he found an old car up on blocks out behind a bar that sported a CLOSED sign. He got out and rapidly switched plates with his own vehicle, just to be on the safe side. No one saw him.

Bone drove away and found a convenience store a couple of miles west. He stopped there to grab some coffee, a donut, hair dye, and some paper toweling. He sipped brew and carefully read the directions twice.

Finally he went to a full-serve gas station, grabbed his travel kit, and got the key to the men's room. Inside, he managed to clean up. Bud shaved but kept the burgeoning moustache, dyed the grey out of his hair and shortened it a bit. He straightened up the mess, wrapped the dye package in paper towels and stuffed them down into the oversized trash container. He let himself out, left the key in the lock, walked briskly to his car and drove away.

He parked on a side street and listened for the news again as he finished the coffee. It took a while, but the story popped up again. Bone pondered the mess he was in, a mess he'd now dragged me into as well.

A few minutes later he called me on my cell phone but didn't get a reply. That's because I was working out for the first time in a week. Seeing Darlene had stirred up one hell of a lot of already unruly emotions and I wanted to blow off some adrenaline. I generally circuit train, working my way up from the legs, and try to get in about an hour of cardio at the same time. It's not the most efficient way to do things, but I don't need to bulk up, just stay toned.

After weight training, I ran two miles then jogged at an angle before slowing down to a walk. I had a thing for Darlene that wouldn't quit, and I knew it. She was the most amazing mix of smart and tough I'd ever run across. I was more of a problem to her than any normal boyfriend. I resolved to get out of this mess as soon as possible and make it my last. Yeah, I know. I didn't believe me, either.

Bone's first call must have come in when I was doing the bench press, because I'd been at Golden Gym for maybe an hour. After that I did flies, side lats, the overhead shoulder press, upright rows; the whole gamut. Finally, I finished up with another light jog on the treadmill and went to my locker. This time I heard the phone and noticed it was the second call.

"Where are you?"

"Never mind where I am. What the hell is going on?"

"I was hoping you could tell me."

"We need to talk, but not over the phone. Not anymore. It may not be safe."

"You're here in town."

"I'll come to you right now."

"We talked about exercise in the bar, remember? You said you knew the place. Well, there is a juice bar in that strip mall."

"Twenty minutes."

I took a quick shower, got dressed, tossed my stuff in the trunk of my car, and walked over to the health food store. They have a small patio with screens around it that's reasonably private. I ordered a couple of protein shakes and took them outside. The day was growing heavy as the bad air thickened. LA heat in the summer can feel like a wet quilt.

Bone drove up a few minutes late, made a slow circle of the parking lot like a man suffering from justifiable paranoia. He finally parked a short distance from the store. Every time I saw him he had a new piece of crap ride. Bone arrived and sat down. He looked a bit different. It took me a minute to realize why. He had darker hair and a new, rather feeble moustache.

"Any luck?"

He shook his head. "You?"

"Faber and Toole were last known to be in Vegas, at least according to their credit card records. My guys lost the trail there."

"I assume you've heard the news?"

"Which news?"

"It seems a drug dealer and porn maker named Gordo, a real badass from all accounts, was found dead yesterday. Somebody really sliced and diced him."

"Yes, I heard." And I gave Bud a short version of my experience with Big Paul in Vegas and did a very spooky impression of the man called Nicky, who I described as a meat locker with eyebrows. I caught the accent pretty well. Bud listened carefully. He shook his head back and forth like a robot with a short circuit. I told him what Nicky had said about Gordo and the missing courier. The briefcase and the hand. Telling it made my skin crawl.

"Now, I'm not saying I know anything about this shit, you understand."

I leaned back in the chair and downed some of the protein drink. It tasted like strawberry chalk. "Of course not, but if you did?"

"Well, if I did, I'd tell you the sorry bastard was alive and well. That he wimped out after a couple of small cuts on his arm and would have surrendered his grandmother to Bin Laden. I'd tell you that somebody else must have gone in there and finished the job in a really messy way."

"Because it wasn't you." I wanted to believe my friend, I really did, but I also sensed how deep the ditch would be if I was wrong.

"Mick, I didn't kill him." Bone leaned forward. "For some reason I'm being framed. I made him piss his pants, but I didn't take him out."

"As far as I know, no one is after you for this yet." I decided not to let him know I'd told Darlene the whole truth. That seemed like a great way to screw up two of my friends at the same time. "Maybe we can keep this quiet."

He shook his head. "Want to bet? My name is going to come out soon. There's only one possible explanation, Callahan. These guys want me running scared, with nowhere to hide, so I'll get them what they want. And they're going to keep turning up the pressure until I do."

"So give it to them."

Bud barked a short laugh. "Jesus, don't you think I'd love to?"

For some reason I didn't know if I believed him. Again. That troubled me. "What's stopping you?"

"I don't have any computer disc, Mick. All I have is a bunch of cash and a lot of blow in plastic bags."

He seemed sincere. "Bone, that is not what I wanted to hear."

"Tell me about it."

We stared at each other for a long moment. Started to talk again, but broke it off when a pair of girls in sweats went into the juice bar to order. Some pigeons found a bit of trail mix scattered by the curb and went to war over it. Bone spent the next couple of minutes finishing the shake. I spent them thinking hard. The girls finally left.

"Okay, so what do we do now?"

"You forget you talked to me, stall for time."

"Bone, these guys aren't screwing around. They threatened to hurt my friends. That is just not going to happen."

Bone chewed his lower lip. "The disc has to be somewhere, Callahan."

"Yeah."

"Someone was there before or after me, right? So, maybe Faber and Toole took off with it. It was their goal all along. They set me up to take the rap all the way around, not just over the missing money."

"How would they know you'd hit Gordo?"

He laughed bitterly. "Shit, now that I look at it the right way, Faber damned near drew me a map to the gang's big Friday night party. He told me all about Gordo; how he was raking in the bucks, even what a prick he was and how someone ought to take him down. It looks like they really played me for a fool from day one, Mick."

"We have to do more than stall."

"Look, I'll work on it my way, you go yours." Bone got to his feet. "I'll dump the drugs, screw selling them, it would only make me easier to find. I have a lot of cash to spread around. I'm going hunting. The less you know the better."

I got up, too. "What about 'Gents,' Bone?"

His jaw dropped, and then he smiled. "I left stuff behind, didn't I? Getting old. You always were a smart son of a bitch. The matchbook?"

I held it up. He shook his head. "Oops."

"I assume you've been there?"

"This may be hard to believe, but I've never darkened their door. Actually, Joey Faber left that behind the last time I met him. I found it in the pocket of my jeans, used up the matches and remembered where they came from. I had planned on stopping by tonight."

Again, I had no choice but to believe him. "I'll do it, you may be about to get too hot. Have any other ideas?"

"One or two, but I'll keep them to myself for now." He cracked his knuckles. "Okay, that bar is yours. I'll be in touch."

"Watch yourself."

"You, too. And Mick? I'm sorry about all this."

We hugged clumsily, two men uncomfortable with physical affection. I watched my friend cross the lot, start his engine, and leave in a hurry. I went back to my own car, where I sat for a while, worrying about my friends and missing Darlene. I was wondering how I was going to make enough of a living this year, and what it was in me that could not seem to stay out of trouble. Finally, I checked my watch, started the car, and drove to my office for an appointment.

FIFTEEN

I got to my office with time to spare, so entered through the parking garage, picked up my mail, and went upstairs via the elevator. I let myself in to the small waiting room, put some soft jazz on the stereo and turned on the light near the magazine rack. Took my mail into the main office and closed the door. I had two checks sent in partial payment, one magazine, and a reminder from my landlord that those of us working into the evenings had to lock up more carefully. Some vagrant had been sleeping in the lobby and using the men's room to freshen up.

The magazine had an interesting article on the lead up to the disastrous war in Iraq, so I sat down to read until the new client came in. There was a small switch on the waiting room wall that turned on a red light above the door, so I'd know when she arrived.

All I knew about this woman was that her name was Mary. Her message said she'd overheard a young couple discussing me at lunch and the conversation prompted her to listen to my show. Eventually she'd decided to call and make an appointment for an individual session. The presenting issue had something to do with her childhood. No surprise there.

A little after the hour I head footsteps coming down the hall. I peeked out through the curtains and caught a glimpse of a tall, dark-haired young woman wearing blue jeans and a long-sleeved brown blouse. I closed the magazine and took a quick look around the office, fluffed the pillows, and sipped a bit of water. I gave her a couple of minutes to settle in and then I opened the door.

"Hi, I'm Mick Callahan."

I find most people sitting on the couch, but Mary was still standing. She was a big woman, maybe five-foot-ten, obviously very athletic. Her hair was shoulder length, but currently tied back into a ponytail. She met my gaze with even brown eyes and shook my hand with a firm grip.

"Mr. Callahan, I'm pleased to meet you. Do we go in there?"

Interesting the way she took charge right away, standing and almost giving directions.

"Yes, go right on in and have a seat on the couch. And no, you don't have to lie down."

The joke sailed over her head. Mary walked briskly into my office and gave herself a quick tour of the bookshelves and my collection of knickknacks. "Pretty spiritual office," she said. "A lot of this is from Eastern thought, right?"

"Just a hobby of mine, Mary. I don't follow any particular belief system. Have you studied comparative religion?"

She ran her fingers along a glass shelf, flicked away a bit of dust. "No, but I'm a recovering Catholic."

We shared a smile. I motioned toward the couch. "As I said, have a seat and tell me why you called. Perhaps I can help."

"I'm not sure you can," Mary said. Her voice cracked a bit on the last word and she immediately knew she'd left me an emotional opening. The realization clearly made her uncomfortable. I just looked at her and left some dead air. Mary cleared her throat and looked down.

"I've never done this before," she said. "You'll have to guide me along."

"I'll do my best."

Mary busied herself, removed the band that kept her hair in a ponytail. She shook out her brown hair and combed through it with her fingers before looking up again. She had fascinating eyes. There was something familiar about her. I found my mind wandering a bit too much. She was still standing and we shared an awkward moment. Finally, I went around the table and parked in my easy chair, forcing her to sit in response.

"Okay, so where the fuck do we start?" The profanity came easily but seemed forced and a bit out of place. Mary sat back and crossed her long legs. For the first time I noticed a couple of small tattoos, a green shamrock on the inside of her right wrist and a red heart low on her exposed right ankle. Her skin looked weathered and her eyes said she'd lived some.

"Start by calling me Mick. There are no rules, okay? Except for confidentiality, and the fact that once this relationship becomes formal, we should have little or no contact outside of this room."

"Ever?"

"There have been some situations, but for the most part, they're very rare occurrences, like weddings and funerals."

"Oh, I didn't know that."

Did that statement disturb her? I watched Mary carefully, but it was as if she'd slipped a new mask into place. Same features, different soul. "It's in your best interest," I said. "It's so you'll have a zone of privacy, a safe place to open up without consequences that spill over into your personal life."

"Can I ask you some questions before we begin?"

"Of course. It's your fifty minutes."

"Only fifty?"

I shrugged. "That's an expression, at least as far as I'm concerned. The ten minutes of down time are to give a counselor a brief break between sessions. I have a bad habit of running over, especially since people often wait to the end to reveal what's really on their mind. I'd suggest you avoid that trap."

"I'll try."

Mary searched her purse, found a scrap of paper and looked at some questions she'd scribbled down. I studied her body language and tried to absorb her essence. Mary had the kind of voice that sounded familiar, a celebrity's voice, and an odd, quite potent charisma. She was a very attractive female, yet wasn't particularly sexual and definitely not girlie. She displayed the kind of confidence and power generally radiated by a successful businesswoman or perhaps a professional athlete. I liked her. She also carried a sadness that sat on her shoulders like a black shawl.

Mary went on to ask me several standard questions, like where I'd gone to college, how long I'd been in practice, what modality I tended to favor, if I'd ever been sued by a client and so on. They were all good, logical questions. Most people don't bother to do that, just assume the recommendation of a friend is guarantee enough. Sometimes they're right, sometimes they get burned.

Satisfied, she put the notes away. "I read your bio on the station Web site before they took it down."

I winced. *They took it down already? Damn, that's cold.* "I'm moving on to greener pastures."

"It said you grew up in Nevada."

"Yes, I did. My stepfather had a small ranch a few miles south of a little town called Dry Wells."

"Do your folks still live there?"

I shook my head. "They're both gone. Actually, I never really knew either one. My biological father abandoned us. And I can't remember much about my mother. She died when I was a small boy."

"That's sad. Did you know her name?"

"Katherine." Saying my mother's name aloud still makes me sad, and it probably showed. "I think Callahan was her married name, but I'm not even certain of that. I could never be sure if my stepfather was lying. I think he genuinely loved Katherine, I remember him sobbing when she died, but it ate him up inside that she'd had a child by someone else."

"Wow." Her face softened. Mary smiled. "You should probably talk to a shrink about that."

"Believe me, I have." I leaned forward. "You're more comfortable running things, aren't you, Mary? Maybe you have a few trust issues of your own."

She crunched ice. "You could say that."

"Where are you from, Mary?" I used her first name again, hoping to bring us a bit closer. She was a strange one.

"I was born in Utah," she said. "We're almost neighbors."

"Whereabouts?"

"Salt Lake City."

"How old are you?"

"Oh, I'm going to be twenty-nine indefinitely."

We both grinned this time. "Not a bad idea. I intend to implement a plan like that just as soon as I turn forty. Let's just stop time in its tracks. And are your parents alive?"

Her head dropped. "My mother is in a convalescent home in Oregon somewhere. We haven't spoken in a long time. She was abusive as hell and never wanted to cop to it. It's too late now. She has wet brain from boozing."

"And your father?"

Mary looked up. "Another thing we have in common. He left us when I was a girl, although I was old enough to remember a few things."

"Like what?"

She sighed. Drifted far away. "He smelled like cigarettes and sweat, you know? And there was usually a bit of whiskey on his breath when he kissed me goodnight. He was huge, or maybe that's because I was so little. Such a wide chest, those big hands.

He had a really low voice."

"You loved him."

Her eyes went damp. She didn't respond. I tried to get into her head space. "You waited by the window for him to come home," I said softly. "For his headlights in the driveway. You loved the way his beard scratched against your face, even though it hurt. You wanted to be his special one forever."

Mary wiped her eyes. "What are you trying to do to me?"

"Every little girl wants to be Daddy's little girl, Mary. It's as normal and healthy as breathing. It's part of how we grow up. It must have hurt like hell when he didn't come home."

"He beat her," Mary said. "Not all the time, but often enough."

"Your father hit your mom."

"And yeah, he knocked me around a little, too, but only if he was really, really smashed. And that was usually because I tried to get in the middle."

"They both drank."

"Lots of people drink. Lots of people fight." Mary shrugged. "And lots of kids grow up that way. I've been known to take a drink now and again myself. You got sober, though, right?"

"Yes."

Her eyes flickered with something that looked an awful lot like scorn. "Are you one of those Bible-thumping AA demagogues, Mick? Are you going to save my immoral soul from the fires of hell?"

It seemed wise not to respond. I just let her sit with what she'd said. Mary had the good grace to blush, although she offered no apology. The kid had a real temper. After a long beat, I decided to respond to the subtext of what she'd just said.

"AA isn't perfect, Mary. It's not for everyone. And it certainly has the same percentage of assholes as any other group. There are dogma freaks who speak in bumper stickers and there are sociopaths and whiners, but a lot of reasonable healthy people, too. There are a lot of different kinds of drunks, and there are different kinds of recovery."

"So you did the bit, then? You got a sponsor and everything. Wow."

"My sponsor, Hal, has become my best friend. I don't know if it's like that for other men, but it worked that way for me."

Mary was doing some kind of a slow burn. The question was whether or not to add fuel to the fire. We could also just change the subject and come back to alcoholism and AA later. I split the difference. "Did one or both of your parents try the program? Have you been to meetings?"

A hit, a palpable hit. Mary got redder. "Let's just say I'm not fond of the whole twelve-step thing and leave it at that."

"Okay, fine with me. As I said, it's not for everybody." There was now a large elephant in the room neither one of us wanted to talk about. *Screw it.* "Did you come here to talk about alcohol and drugs, or do you have something else on your mind?"

Mary said, "How much do you charge?"

Damn, can this girl tap dance. "My stated fee is a hundred and fifty dollars an hour, but we can negotiate if that becomes a hardship."

"It became a hardship the second you said it. You must be pretty rich."

"Actually, far from it. However, what I make or don't make shouldn't really concern you beyond whether or not you can personally afford my services. Or do you kind of resent people who make serious money? I'm just curious."

She closed her purse and composed herself. "I've taken up a half an hour of your time, and I have maybe sixty dollars in cash on me. Let's call it even."

I weighed her nervousness. She was definitely on the way out. "No, in that case keep your money. We're already here now, so let's just talk. If I can't help, maybe I can refer you to someone else."

"Why?" She studied me suspiciously. "You ever hit on a client, Mick? You seem like the type who would."

What a button pusher. "No, that's a line I won't cross. Some day you'll have to explain why I seem like the type."

"You don't. I lied. I just wanted to hurt you back."

"Hurt me back? What have I done that caused you pain?"

"You got born."

"Excuse me?" She got up. So did I. Normally I would have given up on her, but for some reason I couldn't let go. "Don't leave yet, Mary, let's finish up the hour."

She moved hurriedly to the door but then paused and turned with one hand on the knob. "I'll make you a deal, Mick Callahan. We'll finish the hour under one condition."

"What?"

"We go for a walk, you and me. There's a bar down the street. You can drink cola or whatever the hell you want, but right now, I need a cold beer and a shot."

"I won't do that."

"Afraid you'll drink, too?"

"Actually, no. It's just not appropriate."

She turned the knob a few times as if hoping to change her destination to somewhere more acceptable. "Mick, was your father named Michael?"

"So I was told. Why?"

"When I tell you, believe me, we'll both need a drink."

"Mary, what the hell is going on? Let me level with you. It took me a while, but I recognize you now."

Her brown eyes widened. "You do?"

"You've followed me around. I've noticed you a couple of different times. Like you wanted to approach me but felt too shy. You've gone to a lot of trouble to be here if it's just for an autograph and a hug. You may as well get something more out of this."

"Man, you are *slow.*"

She opened the door and went out into the waiting room. I followed, honestly bewildered. Mary went to the stereo, turned it off, turned off the light, and moved back to the middle of the room. Either I was to dutifully lock up and follow or she was now hitting on me. She closed the distance and looked deep into my eyes. I wanted to say something but suddenly couldn't move or speak. Suddenly she gave me a hug.

I patted her back but kept my head turned away. I used both arms to re-state the proper distance. "Look, let's not do that, at least not just yet."

My shoulder felt damp. Mary was openly sobbing. She stepped back, and I could tell she was both surprised and angry to be so emotional..

"I'm no client, Mick. My name is Mary Kate Callahan."

Suddenly I got it, and the room tilted sideways for a moment. "My God."

"Yeah. I'm your goddamn kid sister."

SIXTEEN

"I've been watching you for a couple of weeks. For some reason, I just couldn't walk up and start talking. Then I just called your show."

"I think I remember. You asked a family question."

"Anyway, that suddenly seemed like the wrong place and time."

"You hung up."

"Finally, I just called you for an appointment. I figured I could bring it up if I wanted, or just see what you were like and leave without rocking your boat."

"Consider it rocked."

"Sorry."

"No, that's okay, but I'm still trying to catch up because of how this got started, setting up an appointment and everything."

"I apologize for lying so much just now. I just sold you a load of crap, but now we'll straighten things out."

"Give me a hint to get started?"

"Wipe the slate. The only part that was true is that I heard some people talking about you in a bar. I'd wondered if you were related, but never followed through with finding out."

"Until now."

"Up until that moment, it hadn't crossed my mind that you'd be in Los Angeles. I knew it could all be coincidence, but Mick can be short for Michael and the last name was the same."

"So you wondered, and got bothered just enough to start digging."

"I read an article in the paper that talked about you, and it gave me chills, but I wasn't certain. Next, I listened to your show, and your voice sounded like something I'd been hearing in the back of my own head all my life."

"Now that I know what to look for, I hear that in your voice, too."

"So I went to a library and looked at your picture on the Internet, and that's when I knew for sure."

"Where are you staying?"

"Woodland Hills."

"Wow."

"Yeah, wow. Anyway, I came to LA to see the sights and plan on leaving within the week."

"Where is home these days?"

"Nowhere set. I wander, you know?"

"I've been there. Damn. I don't know what to say."

"Me, neither. I read your bio, and it says you grew up in Dry Wells, Nevada. Isn't that up near Utah?"

"The boonies, on the way to Wendover."

"Yeah, I kind of remember. So you never knew your mom?"

"Katherine died when I was just a boy."

"Who raised you?"

"My stepfather. He was a rancher name of Danny Bell."

"So it was just the two of you? Is he still alive?"

"Danny died a long time ago."

"I'm sorry. Were you close?"

"Not really. He was a very difficult man. Hot tempered, a drinker. Viet Nam did a number on his head. Hell, he used to make me fight other kids for money. Thought he was toughening me up, I suppose. A tortured soul."

"Jesus."

"He died and I left to join the SEALs. I made it all the way through boot and won the trident but got tossed out right after training because of boozing, brawling, and messing with an officer's wife. I got some help, but didn't sober up, and eventually went back to school and became a therapist."

"You got a television show, right?"

"I drifted into that kind of by accident. It did pretty well, but eventually the partying caught up with me, and now I'm finding out just how difficult it can be to start your life over."

"You seem to be doing okay."

"Yes and no. Compared to before, not really, but I'm better off than one hell of a lot of folks, too. That's enough about me, though. As you can imagine, I'm curious as hell to hear your story."

"So. . . ."

"Hey, my manners. Want some water, or tea or something?"

"Some water would be nice, Mick."

"Here. Now fill me in. Where were you born?"

"In Washoe County, outside of Reno. My mom worked as a casino waitress and bounced around town. She caught our father's eye and got pregnant with me. They lived together for a few years, then had a quickie marriage that lasted until I was maybe seven or eight. That's when he up and left for good."

"Ouch, bad time for a girl to lose her dad."

"Hell, he'd already come and gone a few times by then."

"This feels so strange to me. I've wondered all my life, as you can imagine. What was he like?"

"You never knew where you stood with him. He could roughhouse and play one minute and fly into a rage the next. Dad was pretty cool when he was drunk, but even as a little girl I knew there was something strange about that. He had badness in him that was always fighting with the other part, you know?"

"Yeah, I think I do. Wow, you actually remember him."

"Just bits and pieces, and most of those not so great."

"Still, I envy that. I have always wondered what happened to my father. Why he left. Who he was. Do you have any idea where he went?"

"Texas, I think, but maybe that was just Mom talking."

"Did he ever try to contact you?"

"If he did, or sent us any money, she never told me. She hated his sorry ass for leaving like that."

"Did you ask about him?"

"Sometimes, but she always shut me down fast. Like I said, I was seven or eight when he split, so I took it hard. She hated that, and finally she just told me he left because he just didn't love us anymore."

"She was pretty hostile."

"You know it. And the way I figure it, that's why he left. Anyway, pretty soon I was busy dealing with a long line of bad boyfriends and stepfathers of my own. Finally, I just forgot to give a shit."

"I can't get my head around it. This feels like looking in a mirror."

"Yeah. Me, too."

"How old are you?"

"I'm almost thirty now."

"Your mom still alive?"

"She died of lung cancer when I was fresh out of high school."

"Did she keep anything of his? Anything I can see?"

"She might have had some stuff packed away, pictures or letters or something, but I doubt it. And whatever there is has been in a cousin's garage since then."

"If it's not too much trouble, someday I'd like to look through whatever you can find."

"Because it's starting to matter now, right?"

"Yeah, it is. I put the past away for a long, long time, but as I get closer to forty it's growing in importance for some reason. Like a map that would show me where I've really been all this time, you know?"

"That's why I had to meet you."

"I can understand that."

"I'd love to do some drinking with you, Mick. Unfortunately, you're one of those sanctimonious, sober AA dudes now."

"I don't think I'm all that sanctimonious, but I'm staying sober."

"I'm not. I drink and I've been known to stick up for myself in a fight."

"That's your business, not mine."

"Damned straight. And if we become friends or something, you'd best not start telling me what's up and how to live."

"Mary, I don't have the time or inclination."

"Mary sounds odd."

"You prefer both names?"

"Most people call me Katie, but to be honest, I've never much cared for that."

"How would you like to be called?"

"You're going to think this is weird."

"Try me."

"Let's have secret names, just between you and me, as if we'd had the chance to be kids together."

"If you ever call me Mickey I'll have to flatten your ass and start calling you Virgin Mary."

"Ha! Now we both have a secret weapon."

"What names shall we use?"

"Be patient, we'll pick them down the line somewhere, once we know each other better. Deal?"

"Deal. You know something?"

"What?"

"I say 'deal' a lot, too. Call the genetic engineers."

"Shit, we're both from Nevada, the land of the gambler."

"True enough. Mary?"

"Yeah?"

"I'm glad you found me. I don't know what else to say right now, because this is all so damned bizarre, but that much I'm sure about. I'm really, really happy you tracked me down."

SEVENTEEN

There must be a factory somewhere where they churn out the boob bars the owners euphemistically refer to as Gentlemen's Clubs. They all look like the dump where I met Bone. The same neon lights with garish lettering, dumb names, and watery drinks at stratospheric prices. The one called Gents was down an industrial side street, and right under a noisy flight path to LAX. It squatted behind the wire gate and tall chain-link fence like a pale green toad. I had stopped by my house to print out the grainy photos of Faber and Toole, and they were folded up in the back pocket of my jeans.

I pulled into the driveway and followed three businessmen in a taxi up to the front door. The joint actually had valet parking. The snotty kid who came to take my car had the veined, pink eyes of a stoner. He gave me an impudent sneer and enough 'tude to boil my blood, though the night was still young. I handed him the keys.

My nerves were a mess. I'd been unable to reach Hal, and suddenly wished I'd taken in a meeting instead of driving straight over the hill. My mind was spinning like a Frisbee in a hurricane. It began to dawn on me that not only had I let my AA program slip, but I'd slacked off on regular meditation as well. As a result this shock had thrown me completely out of whack. In some strange way I could not have explained, meeting Mary Kate had lifted my spirits at first, but then brought them crashing down again. I now felt stunned and almost unbearably sad. I wasn't sure why.

My father had at least one other child. Amazing. We'd lost so much time, could we manage to build a genuine relationship at this late date, or would we drift apart once the novelty wore off? And what if there were others? If so, what had their lives been like? How many, how old, what gender were they, where did they live? I honestly couldn't remember dreaming about having other family members. I'm sure I did as a child, but not once I hit my teens. My life with my stepfather, Danny, was so consistently miserable that I'd buried the idea.

And yet now one protracted conversation had thrown an entirely new world into my face and left me stupid with possibility.

When the kid came back from parking my car, I was still standing in the doorway with my hands in the pockets of my jeans. I'd gone into a fugue state of sorts, and was just staring at the planter. Something about my expression brought out the latent Homo sapiens in him. "You okay, dude?"

Adrenaline filled my system. I came to and almost took his head off, but snapped out of it just in time. "Yeah, thanks. I've just got a lot on my mind."

"Hey, go have a drink. Some pussy will do the trick."

The arrogant wisdom of youth.

I opened the door and went inside. The music was fainter than expected because the girls were working the floor instead of strutting on stage. A thin redhead was shaking it for a pair of guys in uniform. A tiny blonde was headed for the ladies' room. They both looked fifteen and were painted up like dolls from a horror film. I suddenly wondered if my sister had ever been reduced to stripping. For some reason that thought made me angry. A faint voice in the back of my head warned me to calm down and try to stay out of trouble. No confrontations. I was running on anxiety with a hair trigger and starting to see a red-tinged haze coloring my little corner of the universe.

The cover charge was the defense budget of some small African countries. I crossed the room quickly and found a stool. The bartender was a peroxide blonde with capped teeth, a plastic LA nose, and the kind of fake breasts that would be standing at attention after a nuclear war. When she asked me what I wanted, I froze and licked my lips. *It's been years*, my addiction said. *You could probably handle a drink or two now. Just have a couple to relax and go on home, no big deal.*

No doubt about it, I needed to get back to the meetings.

"Honey, it's a two-drink minimum."

I blinked, stepped back, and ordered a five-dollar cola. I took my drink as far away from the action as possible, found a dark corner and sat down to hide. The grief had taken me totally by surprise. I felt excited, both melancholy and bittersweet.

I'm not accustomed to feeling truly connected to others, by blood or in any other manner. I have friends like Hal and Jerry, but usually tend to move through life the tiniest bit schizoid, detached in a nonmalignant way, generally just doing my best to be the kind of man I'd respect. If you don't count on other folks you're seldom disappointed. Danny Bell taught me violence and alcoholism, but some self-reliance as well. It had taken me a long time and a lot of false starts to get close to Hal, then Jerry, and eventually Darlene. I'd first had to experience and discard the false gods of machismo, alcohol and drugs, sex, money and power. Other than that, I was generally a pretty good guy.

Now meeting Mary Kate had changed everything. Here was a relationship automatic, born in blood. It felt inevitable. I nursed the cola and considered why. Certainly the resemblance was a factor; looking into eyes almost identical to my own. I'd never known that feeling, at least not as an adult. It was something I'd been missing without even being aware of an absence.

Now I could see that I'd only been a fragment of something larger, thus always incomplete. The moment Mary Kate had revealed her identity in my office, those pieces had come together with a force that weakened my knees. The feeling of attraction that wasn't sexual; the way I'd noticed her briefly by the radio station, watching me from her car, and found her so striking; the way she had a feminine version of my hands, a bit small for her body but strong, and the same kind of long, powerful legs. Her voice and other mannerisms made a powerful argument for genetics.

My gut told me Mary Kate could also drink most men under the table. And throw a punch. No surprise there, either.

So, now what?

Mary really had needed and wanted to drink, and when I continued to refuse, she left to get one on her own. We'd traded cell numbers and promised to meet again. Frankly, I don't think either one of us knew what to say, or even do, beyond that one simple act. We just ran out of words and ideas. Hell, it never even crossed my mind to ask for an E-mail address. We both needed time to regroup.

Physician, heal thyself. . . .

Now I chewed on some ice and looked around the dump called Gents, wondering what the hell to do next. I had the printed head shots of Joey Faber and Frank Toole and some cash in my pocket. Walking back to the bar and offering a bribe for information seemed like something out of a bad TV series, but at the moment it seemed like my only option. I took out the matchbook and played with it. Held it up to the light of the candle. The doodles were actually straight lines drawn through the G, N, and S of the name of the bar, leaving only the initials ET.

"Another?"

I looked up, startled. The waitress was a cute redhead. I had to get past her perfect breasts to see the blue eyes and freckles. "No rush, it's just cola."

"Smart."

"Why's that?"

She grinned. "Because the booze is watered down anyway, and the drunker you get the more money you'll spend."

"Wow," I said mildly. "I have found an honest woman, and in the most unlikely of places. Alert Diogenes."

"Excuse me?"

"Never mind. How much do I have to pay for you to sit down for a while?"

"First, I can't until I go on break in a few minutes and second, that depends on what you're after."

"I just want to talk, maybe ask a few questions."

"Twenty nets me fifteen. Fifty makes me look like a hero."

"Fifty it is."

"Then the second cola is on me."

"Deal. What's your name?"

"The one I use here? Tiffany. See you in a few."

I watched halfheartedly as she walked away, knowing management would expect me to act lascivious. I looked at the matchbook again, couldn't find anything else worth noting. I tore it into small pieces as if to pass the time, made one trip to the bathroom and dumped the scraps in the trash can under some wet towels. Threw some water on my face and stared at myself in the mirror above the sink.

Damn, Mary Kate really did look like a pretty version of me. Well, except for that perfect Irish nose. Hers wasn't broken.

A Hispanic man came into the men's room. He was shorter than me, but with a thicker chest and buff arms. He had a large scar on the left cheek and a shaved, bowling ball of a head. The guy looked right through me, went into a stall and fired up a joint. White dragons filled the air as he gasped and coughed. I waved the smoke away and went back into the bar.

Three inebriated businessmen came out of the VIP room grinning like sideways zippers. The dancers remained behind, and as the door eased shut I saw them toweling off with weary faces. Another wave of sadness came over me, an odd mix of disgust and pity. I'd been one of these customers only a few years before, a brash kid in search of the next high, on an eternal quest for distraction. I'd been so terrified, so alone. Avoiding one's life, and the reality of death, can rapidly become a soul sickness. In AA they say, "One's too many and a thousand's not enough."

This was no longer my element. The men, the girls, the loud music, the drugs and alcohol were collaborating to shake me up.

I pondered the initials ET and the meaning of life. Cleaned my fingernails, rubbed my neck. The waitress called Tiffany came back topless, perhaps fifteen minutes later, carrying my second soft drink. I made a show of handing her fifty dollars. She tucked the bills in her scant bikini bottom and sat down.

"You married, gay, or looking for your sweetheart?"

I smiled. "Guess I'm not fitting in as well as I'd hoped."

"You look bored. That stands out here."

"Thanks for the warning. I wouldn't want to get you in trouble."

"We'll be fine, long as you remember to stare at my boobs while you're talking. Well, at least some of the time, anyway."

I stared. "Wow. They're nice."

"Thank you."

"Okay, here we go. I have a couple of photographs to show you, Tiffany. I'm looking for two men."

She kept a smile frozen in place but shook her head. "Don't.

Do anything like that and we'll both be in trouble. You a cop?"

"Nope. Look, I have two pieces of paper. How about I slip them to you and you take a peek when it's safe?"

She considered. Remembered the fifty bucks. "Slip them under the table, man."

"Mick."

"Don't get me fired, Mick. Do it nice and easy."

I kept talking, shifted my chair, all the while moving the folded papers from my back pocket to her hand. My body now screened her from the rest of the club. Tiffany took a quick peek at each page and slipped the papers back to me.

"Do you know either of these men?"

"Try to touch my tits."

It took me a second to catch on. I reached partway across the table as if to caress her. Tiffany backed her chair away and wagged a finger as if I were a naughty child. The charade must have satisfied whoever was watching, because Tiffany moved closer again. She kept a silly grin frozen on her face the whole time, although her tone was serious. I kept thinking of that old movie about an exorcist. The effect was pretty disconcerting.

"I've seen them around, but not in the last week or so. The first one calls himself Joey, can't remember much about the other one except that he's an asshole. Gropes the girls, tries to get out of paying for private dances, that kind of crap."

"Take your time. Anything will help."

"Out of curiosity, do I want to know why you're here, Mr. Mick?"

"No, you probably don't."

"I get that." She shrugged, still grinning. "That's why I'm not asking. And I never saw those pictures, you never asked me shit except for my home phone number, are we going to be square on that?"

"I promise."

"In a couple of minutes we'll have the part where I'm supposed to get up and walk away to try and get some more money out of you. You don't want to go for that, just looked pissed."

"This is what we get for fifty bucks? It should be easy to look pissed. But I have one more question to ask you, Tiffany."

She eased her chair back, held up her breasts with both hands. I felt like a physician looking for cysts. "Shoot."

"Somebody scratched out three letters of the club's name and left just ET. Would those initials mean anything to you?"

People try to hide things from each other all the time. Most aren't very good at it, once you know what to look for. The initials decked her. Her pupils contracted and all the color left her face. "Not really, no."

"That's the first time you've lied to me tonight, Tiffany."

"So sue me."

"Who is it? What is it? Hell, just tell me if this ET thing means a place or a somebody."

She licked her lips, dropped her breasts. The lack of bounce told me they were as fake as her smile. "Look, it's a somebody, and he's trouble."

The smile vanished. Tiffany got to her feet. "And you didn't hear that from me. Now I got to go, and don't follow."

"Christ!" I looked pissed and raised my voice. "That's all I get for fifty bucks? What a rip off."

Tiffany walked away, swinging her hips, and slowly flipped me the bird. I made a show of downing the rest of the watery cola and got to my feet. I scowled like a man about to make a scene and took two steps forward. The huge Hispanic stoner arrived at my right elbow at exactly the same time.

"What up? You have a good time here tonight, right, *ese?*"

Close in, I was looking down at him, but the bouncer was so damned wide my height wasn't much of an advantage. Besides, I had to stay out of trouble. "Fifty bucks for some skin and a bad drink?"

He smiled. One tooth was gold. "It's only twenty-five a titty, bro. That's fair enough, you think about it. The girl's got to make a living."

My elbow felt like it was in a steel vise. I looked down at where he gripped me. It hurt. My blood rose. My nerves were blown. I resented being handled and wanted to blow off steam. The anger felt good. My vision turned black and then tinged with red. The guy came into incredible focus.

The bouncer sensed something and shifted his weight. Seeing that, another large guy detached from the crowd at the bar and headed our way. I reminded myself that if I made a scene and lost the fight, someone might get their hands on the photos in my back pocket. I was beyond caring about myself, but knew that Tiffany could end up in serious trouble. I let myself go loose again.

"Peace," I said. "I'm out of here, okay?"

That gold tooth. "That's right, you are out of here. And next time don't get so jacked up before you come in. Take it easy. It's only money."

"Yeah, my money."

"You got to learn to kick it. This ain't the real world, bro. It's playtime."

About then, the second bouncer arrived. He was a real gym rat, juiced and oiled up, and probably a hundred percent bluff. I let him believe that he'd intimidated me, walked up the steps and left the club without a fuss. I even tipped the kid when he brought my car. ET was a man. And at least now I had some idea of what to do next.

EIGHTEEN

"That's not much to go on." Jerry was being a bit melodramatic, probably to impress Dave Lopez. We all knew he'd come through with something about ET. He rubbed his burn scar with two fingers. The baseball cap had reappeared and was sitting sideways on his buzz-cut head.

"Jerry, we have the utmost confidence in you," Hal said, without a hint of condescension. He leaned closer to the camera. "Mick, speaking for myself, I am eager to hear more about this Mary Kate person. Will you promise to call me in the morning with more information?"

"There's not much more to tell, Hal," I said. "At least not yet. I'm hoping we can become friends."

I'd mentioned my sister to Hal, but hadn't said a word to anyone else. I don't know why exactly. Guess I was reluctant to talk about it until I'd processed it further. Anyway, Jerry and Lopez were both still in the dark. They exchanged puzzled glances. Hal picked up the slack, returned to business.

"Mr. Lopez, can we go back to the disappearance of Ms. De-Lillo for just a moment?"

Dave Lopez shifted his weight in the chair, yawned and rubbed reddening eyes. "Sure, I guess."

"When did you notify the police?"

"I called SMPD maybe ten minutes after it happened, almost as soon as I was out of the area."

"And what exactly did you say?"

169

"I changed my voice a bit and made an anonymous report about a young woman being abducted from the parking garage by two or more men. I gave them what I could remember of the make and model of the car and the license number and got off the line. The whole thing took maybe twenty seconds."

"Smart move," I said. "That allows us to play it both ways. The cops are working on it, too, but without knowing we're involved."

"I'm running a program designed to locate a car by a partial license number," Jerry said, "but I don't think we got enough to make an exact match. The cops probably won't be able to do that, either. We'll narrow it down as far as possible and then make the rounds, I guess."

Hal said, "Detective Lopez, have you ever been hypnotized?"

"Tried once," Lopez replied. "They said I was too neurotic, or something. I wouldn't go under properly."

"Pity. We might have gotten you to remember something you missed."

"I doubt that," Lopez said. He seemed uncomfortable, off balance. "There wasn't much to miss."

"That's what's bothering me," I said. "Everything sounds so well organized, so smooth. Not that I'm an expert on this stuff, but from what I've heard you wouldn't figure mob guys for that kind of snatch in broad daylight."

"I'll bite," Jerry said. "Who *would* you figure, then?"

I shook my head. "Beats the hell out of me."

The doorbell rang. We all knew who it would be, but that didn't stop my heart from fluttering. I resisted an urge to scurry around the living room to straighten things up. Again. Jerry beat me to the door, opened it, and there she was. Darlene wore torn shorts and a tee shirt and still managed to look wonderful.

"Sorry I'm late," she said. "Did I miss anything?"

"I was just asking Mick who he figured took the girl, if it

wasn't the mob."

Darlene kissed my cheek. "And?"

I didn't answer, took her hands. "Thank you for coming."

"In for a penny, in for a pound. I can't let you clowns go off by yourselves. You'd go down in flames without me."

"Good evening, Miss Hernandez," Hal said. "It's nice to see you again. Well, in a manner of speaking."

I moved away from the computer so everyone could see Hal's face, and the camera could catch us all. Lopez, Jerry, and Darlene sat and leaned forward.

"Let's get started." I parked on the edge of the desk and crossed my arms. "First, I want to go over everything we know, start from the very top, and I do mean everything."

"Good," Jerry said. "This one is getting pretty confusing."

"Okay, first Bud Stone contacts me about looking after his old mistress. He's borrowed money from Pesci to finance a drug deal for two guys named Faber and Toole. As of now, it looks like they probably scammed him, because they've vanished with both the money and the drugs. Jerry?"

"Not a sign of them, Mick. Well, except for that one Range Rover rental from Enterprise. No other credit card runs, parking tickets, personal sightings, E-mails, large cash purchases; nothing. Either they're damned smart or they're out of the country entirely and using different names. Otherwise I'd have turned up something new for us to go on."

"What makes you say that?"

"Well, Mr. Solomon," Jerry continued, "they have a lot of cash, of course, but you'd be surprised how tough it is to move around without leaving a trail of any kind. Now, that black Range Rover was returned in Vegas, then rented for a second time and brought back here to LA. It's got to be somewhere. That's the angle I've got my computer working on, anyway."

"Good. Stay on it." I paced a bit. "All right, so next, I get bonked on the head by two men. These are guys Bone and I had a run-in with. They turn out to be working for Pesci and some thug named Nikolaou Argetoianu, also known as Little Nicky. He's from Eastern Europe and appears connected to the sleazy side of international banking."

"My contacts say he's representing a consortium of new money from oligarches and eastern European crime syndicates," Hal said. "He may just be high-class muscle, but he's certainly no fool."

I leaned back on the computer desk. "These guys want me to help them out. They say Bud has stumbled into something bigger than he realizes. If he does locate Faber, Toole, and those stolen goods, Bone may also find himself in possession of a mysterious computer disc. Pesci and Nicky make it clear that what's on that disc could get us all killed. I say 'us,' because they've researched me well enough to know who my friends are, and motivate me by threatening your collective welfare."

"Delightful." Hal smiled thinly. "Oh, did I remember to thank you for dragging me into this one?"

"Me, I'm just sitting here steaming," Darlene said. "It frosts my brown ass to hear that and not be able to do anything about it."

"We are going to do something about it," I said. "I'm just not sure what, yet. Anyway, Bud Stone goes looking for another source of cash. Darlene, since you're up anyway?"

"Okay." Darlene crossed her long legs in those tight shorts and severely impaired my breathing. "It seems Stone rips off a serious badass drug dealer named Gordo, leaves him alive, but apparently gets set up for a murder charge. Turns out the place is littered with prints belonging to Faber and Toole. Now APBs go out. LAPD also finds the prints of one other 'as of yet unidentified' male."

I said, "So anyone want to guess who that will turn out to

be? I'm betting the setup will end up going one step further."

"Well, we can't know that for certain yet." Hal shuffled some papers. "Damn it, I had something here about this Nicky fellow, but now I can't find it, due to an influx of senior moments."

"Believe me, it'll probably be Bud Stone's prints," I said, "even though he most likely wore gloves. Someone wants to place him at the scene."

Hal frowned. "Can you really be so sure he didn't kill this Gordo fellow?"

"Maybe, but I agree with Mick," Darlene said. "This Bud *hombre* seems to be one of the good guys. Whoever is pulling the strings here is very organized and efficient. I say we go on the assumption that the computer will eventually spit out a match for Mr. Stone's military prints."

"Trust me, Hal," I said. "They're going to set him up."

"To pressure him," Lopez offered.

"Hell, this is to tighten the screws on everyone," Darlene said. "Looks like they want that property back. Anyone smart enough to do all of this could easily lift some items Mr. Stone had handled and leave them behind for CSI."

"The question is, why drag a celebrity like Mick into this?" Hal asked. "Wouldn't that complicate things? Why don't they just go after the disc on their own?"

Jerry said, "They probably started improvising after the fight with Mick. They saw him with Mr. Stone and decided to use him to pressure the guy. As Darlene said, it seems to me everything that's going on is designed to turn up the heat."

I shook my head. "I still don't get why they don't just do it themselves. It seems way too complicated to drag so many people into the situation. We must be missing something."

Hal sighed. "Sometimes the simple answer is the right one."

Jerry played with the bill of his baseball cap. "If Bud goes down or gets killed, there's nothing to trace this situation back to them. Maybe they don't want a trail. So they use Bud to go after the disc, and use Mick to pressure Bud. Meanwhile, they have some distance from it all, and some plausible deniability."

"We need to figure out what they're so afraid of," I said. "Then we'll be able to understand the rest of the picture."

"I'll tell you one thing," Lopez said. "This disc must be worth a fortune to somebody."

Hal cleared his throat. "If the disc even exists."

Darlene blinked. "Explain."

"Well, it is also possible to look at this as a setup in another way. Mick, you told us that this cowboy character and his partner ambushed Mr. Stone and yourself at the strip bar. That means they were already looking for him. Perhaps Mr. Stone is just a pawn, dragged into it by the very people who are now demanding that he solve their little problem. The question is why."

Jerry was scratching his scar. "Yeah, why would they go to so much trouble? Wind him up, set him up, and then turn him loose?"

"Hal's saying it's a possibility that Bud has been worked by them from the very start," I said. "Perhaps they're setting him up to take the fall for something far bigger than a little drug deal gone bad, or even the murder. As you said before, this way nothing traces back to them."

Jerry seemed dazed. "What's bigger than murder?"

Hal sighed. "Perhaps the corruption that goes on between governments."

"Or look at it this way, Jerry," I said. "What if they already have the damned disc, and have had it in their possession all along?"

"Huh?"

"It could all be smoke and mirrors. In that case, they'd need some kind of a fall guy to get the international syndicate off their backs, someone who supposedly stole it, or found it and ran off. So they use Faber and Toole to con Bone, as if they came to him on their own, but actually they were just setting him up from the start."

"And you?" Hal suggested. "Setting you up as well?"

"I don't think so, Hal. Like Jerry said, I probably just blundered into it."

Darlene raised an eyebrow. "Again."

"What can I say? It's a talent."

"Let us take the potential machinations to another level, then," Hal said. "Bud Stone called you for help. Perhaps he had ulterior motives of his own."

Jerry snorted. "Okay. This is all starting to sound pretty paranoid."

I ignored him. "Maybe, but I still think I just happened to step in the cow patty. They were planning on bracing Bud at that club, and picked the wrong drunk. I took them on by surprise, and turned out to be meeting Bud, so now I was on their radar. They probably didn't know he'd arranged for me to meet him there. Suddenly they had to adjust their plans to include me. And now, by extension, you guys."

"Look, let's assume all that's true," Darlene said. "But once again, why pick your friend Bud in the first place? What the hell is so special about him, his SEAL training?"

"Could be, or maybe it's nothing. If they just wanted a fall guy, all they needed was someone dumb enough to cough up serious money and get suckered in. Well, and maybe just wild enough to pin a murder on."

Darlene rubbed her temples. "Or it's the girl, this Brandi, who's the link. What do we really know about her?"

Smart woman. "Not much, not enough. I left a message on Bud's cell that we'd lost track of her. If I read him right, he's going to have smoke coming out of his ears over that one."

"By the way," Darlene said, "I narrowed the partial plate Lopez gave us down to six possible owners. Jerry and Dave were hitting the pavement. Guys, do you have anything yet?"

"Working on it," Jerry replied. "We should have something firm later tonight or tomorrow."

"I want to go back to something you just said." Lopez eyed Hal on the monitor. "Another idea is that this disc may not even exist?"

"We have no way of knowing, obviously," Hal said. "I just don't think we should assume it's real merely because they told Mick about it. As a matter of fact, we should probably keep an open mind about anything and everything associated with this rather confusing enterprise."

"True." Darlene sighed. "However, the people who threatened Mick are real, and quite powerful, so we have to take their threats seriously. After all, Gordo was murdered a couple of days ago. That much we know for certain."

"So let's catch the rest of the way up," I said. "Bud is out searching for Faber and Toole and a way to solve his problem. When he gets my message, he's going to know that Brandi is missing, too. I'm trying to get out from under this for everyone's sake, including my own. Lopez here was watching Brandi DeLillo."

"Who gets snatched from under my nose in broad daylight by some very freaking professional people." Lopez glanced over at Darlene. "And so she may or may not be a key."

"Last, but not least, Bud gets his hands on a matchbook from Gents that leads us to some mysterious guy named ET." I got up and went to the kitchen to make some coffee, called back over my shoulder. "Anybody hungry?"

No's all around. Darlene said, "Mick, I could get in deep trouble just for being here, you know that, right?"

"Understood and appreciated."

"If your friend was there the night Gordo was murdered, he is a material witness at minimum, and here I am just sitting on that knowledge. If anything goes wrong, my career is toast."

Lopez sighed and cupped his face in his palms. He looked like a beagle puppy. "That goes for me, too, Darlene."

"For what it's worth," Hal said, "I promise to cover any legal expenses that may arise should there be such a catastrophic conclusion."

I stopped what I was doing and looked back over my shoulder for the second time. Darlene stared at the computer screen. Her features were blank, but I was surprised her eyes didn't scramble pixels and melt down wiring. "Mr. Solomon, I'm just going to pretend I didn't hear that."

"Heavens, I still can't find those papers," Hal said, to cover his reaction. "I need to jump off now, people. It is way past my bedtime. You are all valued."

Jerry studied the carpet. Lopez had a strange expression on his face, a mix of irritation, embarrassment, and gratitude. He glanced at Darlene, who was steaming with offended pride, and wisely opted to remain silent.

Damn, Darlene was amazing looking when she was pissed.

"Shalom, Hal," I said. "You're valued, too."

"Mick, call me tomorrow, as discussed. We need to talk."

"Will do."

The screen went dark. I came back into the room with some coffee and cups on a tray, put them on the coffee table, and sat down. "Guys, I appreciate everything you've all done, and the risks being taken. Anyone can jump out at any time and I would understand completely. I brought you here because I honestly don't know what to do next, and I need your input."

"Playing devil's advocate," Lopez said, "why don't you just go to the department with everything you've got so far?" His cheeks reddened. "Well, assuming you could just leave me and

Darlene out of it."

"Exactly."

"Well, why not?"

"That's pretty tempting, except for a couple of other complications. First, the one who is clearly in the most danger is Bud Stone. Well, and apparently this girl Brandi. We don't know what these people would do if they knew the law had been brought into it. They were pretty specific about not wanting that to happen. Would they kill the girl? Come after you guys to get back at me? We don't know."

Jerry poured himself a cup of coffee, dumped in enough sugar to poison a diabetic rhino. "And would that help, or make matters worse? The way things are right now, we don't have to play by the rules, because what we're doing doesn't officially exist. If you bring in the cops, give them the whole picture, that all changes."

"And you'd have to finesse me out of things as well," Darlene said. She was still angry at Hal for offering to pay for legal fees. I wasn't sure I understood why, maybe just at the thought of needing an attorney. I wasn't about to ask for clarification. I like my gonads attached to my body. "Leaving me out isn't that easy a thing to pull off this late in the game, Mick. You've been down to the station, we talked."

"We have a relationship," I replied. "Why wouldn't we talk?"

"Had, not have," Darlene said abruptly. Ouch. Jerry and Lopez examined their fingernails. The silence went warm and rubbery. I looked away and looked back and when I did, Darlene was looking my way and her eyes were moist. You always hurt the one you love.

Jerry said, "Mick, by the way, this guy Nikolaou Argetoianu? Little Nicky? I think I know what Hal was trying to remember. Hal's folks opened the door for me, and now I'm getting a ton of data on him. This is one nasty son of a bitch. Interpol record, lots of charges including murder, but no convictions. And the guy shouldn't even be here. He's on a watch list with Homeland Security."

"He's here, and he didn't look scared."

"Like Hal said, Nicky is definitely connected to some version of the Russian oligarches, a kind of banking mob, but it's still hazy. He may be the cause of all of this. I should have a lot more on him tomorrow."

"Thanks." *And thanks for changing the subject.* "Logic dictates we keep our eye on Pesci, though. He's at the center, and the likely player behind the scenes. He'd easily have the contacts and cash to pull off a large scam and set Bone up to be the fall guy."

"I'll keep digging on him as well," Jerry said. He drained his coffee, got up. "I'll e-mail you in the morning, Mick, and I promise I won't ever put anything in writing for anyone else, that's between you guys."

Lopez got up as well. He stared at the carpet.

"Dave?"

"Maybe I need to get out," Lopez said finally. "You guys go to the mat on this, I could lose my pension, you know? I hate to be a flake, but. . . ."

"You want out, you're out," I said.

"Thanks, Mick. I appreciate that."

I didn't look at Darlene. Lopez worked for her cousin, but if he turned yellow and went to Internal Affairs, she was sunk. "Just think on it some tonight, and we'll talk in the morning."

"Okay." He said it with the tone of a man who'd already made his decision but wanted to be polite. He walked out quickly and quietly, just two quick steps behind Jerry.

I followed Darlene out onto my front lawn. She moved a few feet away from me as if making a statement. Jerry drove away and Lopez followed. Then the street went silent. The stars were out and there was a light breeze. Darlene stared at me. Her brown eyes reflected the skeletal moon.

"They're both empty," I said finally.

She cocked her head. "Excuse me?"

"My heart, my bed. Both of them."

"Oh, Mick. . . ."

"I don't know why we fight, and I'm supposed to understand these things. Gender. Pride. Fear. Sometimes I think intimacy is like trying to hold together the wrong ends of two magnets, you know? Some kind of force field gets in the way and won't allow it to happen, won't let them touch."

"I should go."

"Yes, you probably should."

Darlene turned around and took three steps. I followed, spun her around and kissed her lips.

"Don't," she said. "Please don't."

I didn't listen.

NINETEEN

We made love on the living room floor, without speaking and still partially clothed. Afterwards, I placed small candles in the bathroom. I lit them and bathed Darlene before joining her in the tub. We rubbed each other down with towels, stretched out on the bed and listened to an old Ella Fitzgerald recording, a personal favorite of mine. I'd missed her so much, my skin felt hungry.

"Sometimes I'm sure there is a God."

Darlene touched my broken nose. "Only sometimes?"

"When it's a sometimes like this." I sat up in the gloom and found the red numbers on the digital clock. It was only a bit after nine. I found my underwear, stepped into my jeans. "I'm hungry. How about we drive down to Ventura Boulevard for some pasta?"

"Do you have anything to nibble on?" Darlene patted her trim stomach. "I'm watching my waistline."

"So am I," I said. "It looks wonderful from here."

"Thanks, but no thanks on the pasta."

"No sweat. I probably have some salad stuff, let's have a look."

I left her getting dressed, flipped some lights back on as I journeyed down the hall and out into the kitchen. I opened the fridge, knelt down in the pool of light and poked around the plastic drawers. "There's not a lot here, bread and cheese, some lettuce and tomatoes."

"Sounds fine."

I picked some browning leaves from a small head of lettuce, grabbed the last tomatoes and other makings and got busy. I might have tried to sing; hadn't felt this good in months. Whipped up a pretty good salad in a wooden bowl, prepared it with some fresh cheese slices and a little bread, made us a pitcher of fresh iced tea.

I turned to see Darlene standing in the kitchen doorway with a look of almost unbearable sadness on her face.

"What's wrong?"

"We shouldn't be doing this, Mick."

My heart sank. "Doing what, eating salad? It's good for you."

Darlene moved closer, took the bowls from my hands. I got the cheese and bread and followed her to the living room. She busied herself setting the table. I trailed back and forth like a hungry hound dog, got the iced tea and glasses. I tried to lower the lights again, but Darlene found the dimmer switch and turned them back up. We sat down at the table, stared at each other.

"Darlene," I said again, finally, "what?"

She nibbled on a piece of cheese without looking up. "We've already tried a couple of times."

"Maybe the third time's the charm."

"Or maybe we end up not even being able to stay friends." Darlene looked up, eyes shining. "I would really hate that."

My mind spun. What was she trying to tell me? Was Darlene already seeing somebody else? I didn't dare ask, because I didn't really want to know. We got lost in each other's eyes for a moment. Suddenly I heard someone coming up my front steps. Darlene frowned, asked me with a look if I was expecting anyone. I shook my head, got up. My pulse quickened.

Whoever it was stopped at the door without knocking and didn't ring the bell. Seconds passed. Considering the events of recent days, that served to make me even more nervous. Darlene felt the tension. I held a finger to my lips and eased away from the table. She padded down the hall in bare feet, came back with her 9mm; held it down beside her right leg, pointed at the floor.

Finally, someone tapped halfheartedly on the metal security door. I stepped to the side and called out. "Who's there?"

A woman's voice mumbled something. She sobbed. Darlene stepped into the kitchen, puzzled and wary.

"Hello? Who is it?"

I turned the handle, eased the front door open. The porch light was off. Another sob, higher pitched. Someone stood there, shoulders hunched forward, half leaning on the metal screen. I had to step out in front of her to find the switch. When the yellow light came on, I saw a tall brunette with smudged makeup and some splatters of dried blood.

"Mary?"

She mumbled something, sobbed again. I opened the lock and she fell into my arms. She reeked of alcohol and cigarettes. As I carried her into the living room it became clear she'd also been in a fight. She was pretty banged up. Her blouse was torn. Darlene backed away rapidly, out into the kitchen, I assumed to get some ice and a towel.

"Relax, Mary. You're okay, now."

I eased my sister down into a sitting position and went down on one knee. I checked her out. It wasn't too bad, despite the blood. She had a small scalp wound that had dried up after staining her white blouse and smearing her face. Her cheek was bruised and her lower lip puffy.

"What the hell happened?"

She looked up at me but wasn't able to focus her eyes. Her breath was strong enough to kill flesh eating bacteria.

"Mick?"

Mary Kate, looking up over my shoulder, finally registered Darlene's presence. She offered a halfhearted smile and said, "Hi."

Darlene was not amused. Then Mary Kate frowned and said, "Uh oh, I think I'm gonna puke." I took her into the bathroom, put her by the toilet and left her there. She didn't vomit. I backed out, closed the door.

Darlene pushed by me, carrying her purse and keys. She'd put the gun away. Her eyes were red. I finally caught up. "Wait, no. Darlene, I need to explain this, give me a second. . . ."

"You don't need to tell me anything, Mick," she said. "Your personal life is none of my business."

"Darlene, damn it. . . ."

The woman did a lot of upper body work. She shoved me out of the way and opened the door. Stopped abruptly. "Shit."

Now a man was standing on the steps.

I think we both went stupid for a moment. For one thing, my house is not usually Grand Central Station. I've seldom had so many people there in one night. As for Darlene, I think her circuits had already shut down because of what appeared to be another woman. In any event, we were both caught flat-footed for a time, and nobody moved. At least I had the presence of mind to check for weapons. None were visible, anyway.

The stranger glowered at me. He was almost my height, slim with a dark tan and a five o'clock shadow. He wore a blue sweat-shirt and jeans. He raised his right hand and pointed a finger. "Get out of my way."

I blinked, laughed involuntarily. "Excuse me?"

"I said get the fuck out of my way, before I kick your sorry ass, motherfucker. I'm here for Mary."

"I've got a better idea, bozo." Darlene stepped in between us, headed out the door. "How about you get the fuck out of my way first?"

Man, she was really steaming. To Darlene, I was not only fooling around, but had been seeing someone else's woman. She probably figured I deserved what I got. "Mick, it's been real, but now I think it's time I went home."

The stranger stuck out his hand. The gesture caught Darlene by surprise. Incredulous, she looked down at his offer to shake. Finally gave in.

"Name is Ed Talbot," the man said. "Bet you didn't know your boyfriend was screwing around with my woman."

"No, I didn't."

"Me neither, until now." Talbot hitched up his jeans, glared my way. "But now I plan on giving him a proper ass whipping."

Darlene looked up at me, shook her head sadly. "Yeah, well, maybe he has one coming, Mr. Talbot."

I moaned. "Now wait just a damned minute."

Things can always get worse. Mary Kate finally heard us through the bathroom window. She wailed, "Mick, don't hurt him. Please."

"Mick," Ed Talbot said quietly, as if memorizing my name. He brightened and grinned, then pretended to beg. "Please don't hurt me, okay?" This guy Talbot was starting to piss me off.

"Ed, just go away," Mary Kate called. "You've done enough for one night. Leave me alone."

Darlene finally absorbed the sound of Mary Kate's misery, remembered her battered face. It awakened something in her. She looked back at the stranger and produced her ID. My lady was herself again, and rapidly losing patience with this whole charade. "Perhaps I should mention, Mr. Talbot, that I'm a police officer. Now, the young lady in question seems to have a few cuts and bruises. I don't suppose the two of you had a little disagreement tonight?"

His mouth opened and closed. Darlene stepped forward,

searched his eyes. "And don't tell me she started it, or that she hit you, too. That won't wash. Striking her would be a clear case of assault and battery. And since I don't see a mark on you, under the law, you'd be the one going to jail."

He lost color. "Ma'am, I. . . ."

Darlene smiled coldly. "I should also warn you that the man whose ass you came here to kick has a pretty fair temper of his own. As of now, you're about to attack him on his own property in front of a witness. I wouldn't recommend that, either. Of course, you could wait until I leave, but then you may wish you had a police officer here to save you from a trip to the ER."

I still hadn't said anything. Why bother? *Damn, what a woman.*

Darlene walked down the steps. Talbot backed away from her, following the cement path. I let them go. He seemed far more afraid of Darlene than me, anyway. And he was probably right.

Darlene paused. "If I were you, Mr. Talbot, I'd think very carefully about the next thing you say or do. An awful lot might depend on it."

Talbot shot me a foul look. He backed up all the way to the wooden gate, clearly struggling for a way to save face. He pointed that damned finger at me again. I really wanted to run over and break it, but refrained.

"I'll see you some other time."

I waved, smiled brightly. "Looking forward to it."

I didn't mention that I was Mary Kate's brother because I just didn't figure Talbot deserved to know. We watched him jog down the sidewalk to his car, gun the engine and squeal away. I turned back to Darlene and one look at her expression wiped the smile off my face. "Honey, listen. . . ."

She closed the distance and shoved me back against the wall of my house. "As of right now, Mick, lose my number."

"Darlene. . . ."

"Shut up."

She turned to go. Her anger barely masked tears. I touched her arm and said, "Mary Kate is my sister. Well, half sister. I only met her yesterday."

"Excuse me?"

I pulled her close, hugged her. "Hal is the only one I've mentioned this to. You got here late and I hadn't told the other guys." I filled her in. Darlene finally relaxed. Then she grabbed my shirt, shook me.

"Why the hell didn't you say something?"

I shrugged. "I was about to, but then dickhead showed up. Part of me wanted him to twist in the wind thinking I was a boyfriend, so maybe he'd leave her alone."

Darlene looked away into the darkness. "He won't leave her alone, Mick. His kind never do."

As if on cue, Mary Kate wailed again. "Ah, God!"

This time we heard the sound of vomiting. Darlene beat me to the doorway, tossed her purse on the living-room table. "Get some ice."

I've handled a few drunks in my time, but Darlene made me feel like I was an amateur. She held Mary Kate's hair back, flushed the toilet, wiped her mouth, sat with her and mopped her brow with a towel full of ice chips. They hugged like old friends. Women never cease to amaze me. I watched from the hall for a while, then wandered out into the living room and sat alone in the dark.

"Alcohol and drugs are the number one cause of death in the United States." I remember an instructor saying that, back when I was working on my certification in chemical dependency counseling. Most of us doubted the veracity of his statement, until he went on to add, "just throw in drunk driving, spousal abuse, murder, assault, lung cancer, strokes, and myriad other health and societal problems related to the use of alcohol, nicotine, and both legal and illegal drugs. Use your imagination. I'm not up here arguing that everything should be against the law. I'm just observing one disturbing fact. Alcohol and drugs are involved in most violent crimes and many terminal illnesses. But they are also big business, and worth billions of dollars in profit and tax revenue. You can forget banning them. Prohibition failed in the twentieth century, and is not likely to be attempted again, so get used to it. People want the right to get high and destroy themselves, even if the collateral damage is mind boggling."

I grew up knowing my father had abandoned us because of alcoholism. My stepfather also had a bad drinking problem. Naturally, I followed in their wake. Seeing it everywhere, having experienced it myself, and struggling to help my clients sometimes depressed the hell out of me. Generation after generation thinks it is exempt from the percentages, and spawns a new group of drunks and addicts before coming to its senses. And now my sister was a drunk. Alcohol is significantly harder on a woman's body than a man's, so Mary Kate was on her way to serious health problems.

I realized it had been quiet for a time. "You guys okay in there?"

I heard muffled laughter, and then Mary Kate called out, "We're better now." The nursing "we." More laughter. Women have such a mysterious ability to bond, become gal pals within moments. That impresses me, although it's also disconcerting, this time because I had a sneaky feeling some of the laughter was at my expense. Of course, it's also very crowded here at the center of the universe.

Eventually, Darlene came out of the bathroom. She looked around, saw me sitting there in the dark. "Okay, help me get her into bed."

"We can put her in the office, the couch folds out."

"Whatever. She needs sleep."

I crossed the room, looked down into her eyes. "Forgive me?"

"Actually, I can't help but wonder if you wanted *me* twisting in the wind over this. If so, I'm not sure I can."

"This wasn't about you," I protested. We were both speaking in low tones. "I just didn't want to take this Talbot character off the hook."

"So you let him think you were her new boyfriend."

"Exactly."

"And what if he was carrying a concealed weapon?"

A weak smile gave me away. I hadn't thought of that.

Darlene sighed. "Doesn't it ever occur to you that people can handle things without fighting?"

"I'll go find some sheets."

Mary Kate had passed out. Moments later, we each took an arm, hauled my sister into the office and dumped her on the guest bed. I left the room while Darlene undressed Mary Kate and covered her with a sheet. I went into the kitchen and hit the fridge again. A few minutes later, Darlene joined me at the kitchen table. She took the diet cola from my hand, stole a sip. I told her a bit more about the conversation with my sister.

"And what are you feeling now, counselor?"

"Numb."

Darlene wrinkled her eyes. "Isn't that an evasive answer coming from a therapist?"

I shoved my chair back and stretched. "Maybe, but the truth is that I'm sleepy and completely overloaded, not up for getting into a big discussion tonight. Honestly, I don't know what to make of this, Darlene. Part of me is glad to have found a living relative, and part of me is . . . scared."

"Of?"

"I don't know, getting entangled, being in over my head somehow."

"And feeling something you've never felt?"

"Yeah, a bit of that." I yawned. "And no kidding, I really am sleepy."

"Okay, I should go."

"Not yet." I touched her hand. "I don't want you to leave."

"I don't have a change of clothes, Mick. I have an early shift tomorrow."

"What the hell am I supposed to do with her come morning?"

Darlene just looked at me. "Treat her like any other alcoholic, Mick. If she wants to get sober, help her. If not. . . ."

I stared back. My eyes gave me away.

She leaned over, kissed my cheek. "Okay, I'll leave when you're asleep."

Like I said, what a woman.

TWENTY

One day earlier, Bud Stone left our daytime meeting near my gym, went back to the dump he was staying in and forced himself to sleep for a few hours. He waited until well after rush hour before packing up and hitting the Hollywood Freeway. That was probably at about the time I was checking out Gents. He drove carefully.

There was a bad wreck near Universal Studios and traffic was snarled for several miles because people slowed down to rubberneck. Bud's blood pressure skyrocketed and didn't return to normal until he was safely past the thick cluster of police cars and a line of emergency vehicles. He went through Hollywood to catch the split towards Santa Ana and then San Bernardino. A Highway Patrol car followed him for a bit, probably out of curiosity, but then dropped away to chase after some screaming kids in a new Ford pickup truck.

Bone was driving his third battered wreck, and his luck ran out near the small town of Upland. He blew a radiator hose. Bone didn't want to risk calling Auto Club or attracting attention, so he shoved the car to the side of the road. He hiked to a service station, paid cash for a replacement, walked back and installed it himself.

That one diversion threw him off by a couple of hours. Bud didn't pull into Vegas until after two in the morning. Even at that hour, and from miles away, the strip was still a demented neon rainbow. The new "family-friendly" streets still had plenty of nighttime action, most of it hardcore. Some things never change.

All my friend had to go on was names and places Faber and Toole had dropped along the way. He hit two bars and a twenty-four-hour buffet, asking questions. He went to the newest Wynn casino, mostly just to eyeball the surroundings, and then poked around until he got information on a high-stakes poker game near an upscale barbeque restaurant called The Boneyard Bistro. Joey Faber had once bragged to him about taking down some black guy named Taylor in that game. It could have been a bunch of bullshit, but Bone figured it was worth a look.

The restaurant was closing when he got there. It was a beautiful place, well appointed, and seemed an unlikely place for that kind of event. Eventually Bone drove around the block and discovered another building behind the restaurant. It looked like a small industrial storage facility with high fencing. A number of people were standing around smoking and talking in the dimly lit parking lot as the grim night pressed down.

Bone checked and got my message that Brandi had disappeared. He didn't know what to think about that, so he drove about a quarter mile down Sagebrush, parked near an empty lot, and tried to decide what to do next. His emotions told him to drive back to Los Angeles, but Bone decided to just keep going. He went back to the poker game, parked down the alley, and strolled toward the small crowd. A tall businessman with a bald spot and a ring of white hair was chatting up a quiet Latino man whose slanted posture announced his criminal background as clearly as arms roped with jailhouse tattoos.

"How do you get a seat at the table?"

The ex-con cupped his cigarette and turned away without answering, but the businessman had downed a few drinks. He laughed too long, too loud. "Get in line, pal, and you'd better have a wad of cash." He gestured over his shoulder.

Now that he was closer, Bud could see at least fifteen men were waiting for a chance to play. He whistled. "Best get here early, huh?"

The ex-con spoke in a guttural whisper. "You got that right."

"Any advice?"

"Be ready by six, game usually breaks up around two. Everybody in town wants a piece of Ernie Taylor."

Bone felt a little starburst of excitement. Ernie Taylor. Pay dirt. "Taylor? That black dude?"

"He's the man, homes. ET. That dude has played on TV." The convict used his cigarette as a pointer. Bone squinted. Through a small space in the thick curtains he could see the poker table, a crowd watching. There were only four men left playing. The huge, largely empty room was thick with cigar smoke. Only one of the men was black. Ernie Taylor was handsome, a man well into his forties, with gym-rat muscles and a thick moustache.

Bone shrugged. "He doesn't look like much."

"Hey, he wins." The businessman belched. "Mr. Taylor also owns most of the Wagon Wheel. The rumor is he won that right here, maybe four years ago."

Bud feigned boredom. "Ah, fuck it. I don't want to have to stand around."

The convict said, "ET, he got the hottest hand in town. You want in, got to maybe try next Friday."

"Maybe I'll come back."

"Good luck if you do," the businessman laughed. "It's five grand just to sit."

Bone drove straight to the Wagon Wheel, one of the newest businesses on the strip. It was a faux wood building, round, and a mere ten stories tall; known more for hosting small concerts than gaming. He parked in the lot, eyeballed the area, and strolled in through the main entrance.

The casino was not crowded. The décor was Western, and the walls were decorated with paraphernalia gathered from Nashville, Bakersfield, and a few other locales connected with country music. Some artifacts referenced old twentieth-century black-and-white Western serials featuring actors like Tom Mix and The Cisco Kid. It was cheese, but good cheese. Other than that, the place was typical, with loud colors, bright lights, big tits, short skirts, jangling noises, and free booze.

Bone made one circuit of the main room, to check out the location of the security cameras and guards, just to be on the safe side. Then he left and went several doors down to a chain coffee shop for a stack of wheat pancakes and some strong coffee. He lost a few dollars on their slot machines before wandering away.

By now my friend was bored and feeling tired. He walked the strip for a while, trying to make sense of what he'd learned so far. So the fabled ET was a card pro, a casino owner, and somehow affiliated with Big Paul Pesci. Everything led back to Pesci, sooner or later. Maybe Pesci had ordered Brandi kidnapped, in order to have one more tool to apply pressure.

Bud, like the rest of us, had a nagging feeling that he was missing something important. He walked and pondered. All around him tourists paced, sinned, lost money, went home satisfied or in disgrace. What happens in Vegas stays in Vegas—especially your money.

At around two in the morning, Bud Stone was sitting up the block from the Wagon Wheel, watching the place through military binoculars. He'd parked at the top of the hill, where he could see both entrances. Bone figured Ernie Taylor would come back to his casino to look at the receipts and check things out before retiring. It also seemed likely he'd use the back, where the private parking spaces were marked by a low concrete divider, but Bone didn't want to take any chances.

Time passed slowly. The crowd thinned even further. Two o'clock came and went. No ET

Bone got out of the car to stretch his legs. He had another look while standing. He blinked and refocused the glasses. A Lincoln Town Car had appeared and was parked in the back, near the private entrance. Two men got out of the car. One was huge, the other of average height and weight. Neither one was black. No Ernie Taylor. Disappointed, Bone almost looked away, but did a double take and zeroed in on the smaller man. He brought the sweaty features into focus then grunted.

"Well, I'll be damned."

Down below, the taller dude got back into the backseat of the big car. It drove away. Bone watched the younger, smaller man as he walked across the empty parking lot. The kid's shoulders were slumped forward, and he looked up only to zero in on his vehicle. He appeared thoroughly miserable.

Bone tossed the glasses onto the passenger seat and cruised down the slope with the lights off. Hissing tires, the crackling of pebbles. He passed the casino without being noticed by the sleepy security guard and eased into the back of the Wagon Wheel's parking lot.

Meanwhile, the young man had found his car, a shiny red BMW. He raised a remote and the alarm chirped. Bone pulled the binoculars again, focused. The guy got in the Beemer and fired up what could have been a small cigar.

Bone dropped the glasses, opened the door and eased out. He left his vehicle and jogged along the back, near the bushes, then crept up to the parked BMW. The driver's window was cracked and the skunk odor of top-quality marijuana permeated the cool evening air. Bone leaned close and spoke through the opening.

"Juicy fruit?"

"Ah!" The young man in the car jumped, coals went flying.

He slapped at his expensive pants and shirt. "Jesus!"

"Actually, it's Bud Stone. How're they hanging, Jacob?"

Jacob Mandel swallowed and waved his hands around. "Uncle Bud? What the hell are you doing here?"

"Oh, you know. Vacation."

They looked at one another. What was left unsaid hung in the air like thick syrup. Bone heard a burst of wild laughter from the back entrance as a group of revelers left the casino. Finally, he rapped his knuckles on the glass. Mandel reluctantly lowered the window the rest of the way.

"Uncle Bud, you scared the shit out of me."

"Lawyers are too full of shit to have any scared out of them. No, I ain't on vacation. Now, I know why I'm here, but what are you doing in Vegas, slumming, gambling, or getting your dick sucked? Last time I saw you, it was going to be Beverly Hills or bust. This town is beneath you."

"Nice of you to think so."

"And by the way, how's Jack?"

Mandel licked his lips. "Better. He's still got a little speech impediment from the stroke, but he's up and around again."

"Shitty thing to happen to such a young man."

"You know it."

"You tell him I send my best. The Chief was always a damned good man. We were bro's, your dad and me."

"Tell me something I don't know. I grew up hearing those stories, Bud. Sometimes I felt like I was in Iraq with you guys."

"Yeah, well, soldiers do like to reminisce. So why are you in Vegas?"

"I have a small office here, just for the time being. I'm sort of concentrating on this one special client."

"Who's that, Jacob?"

"A new outfit called The Valley of Fire Corporation." Mandel cringed as he said it. Bud noticed.

"Just the one client?"

"It's kind of hard to explain."

Something crouching between the lines again. Bone probed a bit. "Hey, try me."

"You want to go get a drink or something, Bud? Maybe catch up?" Mandel was clearly trying to change the subject. He opened the door as if to get out, but by now he was too stoned to stand properly.

Bud motioned for Mandel to stay in the car. "I've had enough booze for one lifetime." He slid into the passenger seat. "Jacob, I need you to do me a favor. I'm only here for a few days, and it's kind of on the quiet, so keep it to yourself if you run into someone we know, okay?"

"Sure."

"Actually, keep it quiet period."

"Uh, okay."

"It would be good to catch up with you. Hey, you got a business card or something, Jacob?"

Mandel patted the pocket of his jacket, handed over an embossed card. He was pretty faded, but Bud's caution finally registered. "You okay, Uncle Bud?"

"Yes and no. I might need a way to speak to you in confidence."

Mandel focused those bleary eyes. "Are you in some kind of trouble?"

"Actually, I am. And you're in some kind of trouble, too, aren't you, Jacob?"

Mandel's eyes filled. He turned his head away and studied the night sky. "Oh, man. You don't want to know."

"Yes, I do."

"I can't talk about my clients."

"Not to put too fine a point on it, Jacob, but of course you can. We just have to make certain you don't get caught."

Bud watched Mandel closely, saw wheels turning in his head. They heard high heels on pavement, some laughter. Several young women came their way, probably dancers getting off work. The two men fell silent. Bud Stone slid down in the front seat. The women turned to the right several cars off and their voices faded away.

Mandel sighed. "You know who Paul Pesci is?"

Bud nodded in the gloom. *Bingo.* "Sure, I've heard of Pesci."

"Well, he's behind this new company. And they have some people working for them that give new meaning to the term mob."

"Go on."

Mandel sobbed quietly. "Jesus, Uncle Bud, I'm in way over my head. I've seen some things, bad shit. I don't know what the fuck to do."

"Maybe we can help each other out."

Mandel wiped his eyes. "How's that?"

"I'm in a box of my own," Bud said. He gave Mandel bits and pieces of the story, just enough to score points. Said he owed Pesci money, and that he was being squeezed to find some stolen property, that it was spiraling out of control. "So you can't tell them I'm here, okay?"

"Of course not," Mandel said. "Man, it sounds like we're both fucked."

"Not really. Maybe we can help each other."

"I don't see what either one of us can do."

"You will." Bud opened the door and stepped out onto the pavement. He looked around. The coast was clear. "Hang in there, kid. I'll be in touch."

"Uncle Bud," Mandel said quietly, "these people play rough."

"That's okay," Bone said. "So do I."

TWENTY-ONE

I'm dreaming, can't wake up. . . . *A big kid with a runny nose is circling me in the dirt ring, fists raised. His right eye is swelling. He's been crying. The men around us are hooting, laughing, cursing, and mocking him for being afraid. My heart swells with pride because Daddy Danny is pleased and we're going to make a nice piece of change on this one. Everyone thought Scott would put me down. He kicks at my crotch, I twist and give him a hip, then an uppercut that straightens him up like a board and drops him in the dust on his back. Scott cries "Uncle" and quits. I give it some theater, spit at his feet. The crowd cheers. Some part of me has the decency to feel ashamed. That's the first night Daddy Danny offers me booze to celebrate.*

I am eleven years old.

I woke up to the roar of a leaf blower and some shouting as the next-door neighbor's gardener browbeat his Latino employees in what sounded like Japanese.

The bed was empty. Darlene was long gone.

I rolled out of bed, disturbed by the dream, heart kicking against my rib cage. I went flat on the floor, stretched, and did one hundred push-ups and enough stomach crunches to create a nasty burn. Went off to the kitchen, started a pot of strong coffee. To the bathroom for a long, cool shower.

I came out of the bathroom wrapped in a towel and found Mary Kate waiting in the hall. She was wearing the same clothes, and looked a whole lot better than she smelled. Darlene had patched her up pretty well. Except for a major hangover, some minor swelling, and a small bandage on her scalp, she seemed okay. Turns out my sister was a pretty woman.

"I'm sorry."

"You should be."

"Fuck you."

"Fuck me? Fuck *you.*"

We glared at each other for a long beat, and then burst into laughter. Mary Kate hugged herself. "Well, I don't suppose you keep a hair of the dog around?"

"No booze in this house."

She shrugged. "I'll get something later, just to take the edge off."

"That will start it all up again."

"I know that whole speech," Mary Kate said. Her voice dropped to a whispered mixture of defiance and remorse. "I don't want to hear it again."

"Well, then, what I'd suggest is a mug of hot coffee with honey, some plain wheat toast, and a few aspirins."

She brightened a bit. "You could talk me into that."

I led her back to the kitchen. "If you're feeling better later on this morning, I'll whip up a protein shake with fruit. You'll need to get something decent into your system pretty soon."

Mary Kate planted herself at the kitchen table. A beam of sunlight cut through the plaid curtains and blinded her. She blinked rapidly and changed positions. The chair squeaked on the linoleum. My sister winced and rubbed her temples. "Oh, man. This one is brutal."

"Lots of honey for the blood sugar? I'd advise it."

"Yeah. Sure."

I knew better than to lecture, but it was hard to watch her suffer and just keep my mouth shut. AA has an old saying about being "a program of attraction, rather than promotion." Of course, I hadn't been a very good AA member lately. That's why Hal had been on me about getting back into regular meetings. I made her sweet coffee and some toast, poured myself a cup and sat across the table. Mary Kate licked her lips. "Damn, I'm really thirsty."

I got her a glass of ice water. A plane crossed west to east on the way to the Burbank airport. My other neighbor came outside whistling, started watering his yard. Mary Kate ate most of the toast and finished the coffee. We talked around things, rather than about. Shared how we missed the desert sometimes, how the city smelled bad and felt crowded. We both agreed that country music was in the toilet except for the Dixie Chicks and that they had brass ovaries for speaking out against the war a few years back.

"Don't you have a show to do?"

I told her I was out of work again. Said I hoped to find something soon, but didn't know where I'd end up. Mary Kate expressed sympathy, and it seemed sincere. We agreed we'd have to make an effort to stay in touch.

Finally, I poured a second cup. "Let's talk about dickhead. How long have you known the guy?"

She sighed. "A couple of years and change."

"It's serious?"

"As a heart attack. We were engaged once. I broke it off because all we did was fight all the time." Mary Kate looked up. "He won't forget about this, Mick. You should have told him you're my brother."

I laughed. "Okay, you can tell him if you want. Personally, I didn't think he deserved to know."

"He's not so bad. Usually."

"Mary Kate, he beats you up. I know I don't have to explain how low it is, you're smarter than that."

"I bring it on myself sometimes," she said, and then blushed.

"I can be pretty hard to get along with."

"I can't believe I'm hearing this crap from you."

Her eyes flashed, but she didn't argue. The blush deepened to purple. Mary Kate picked at her fingernails. "You know, we still have to make up some nicknames for each other one of these days. You been thinking on that?"

"Not really, not yet, but I will."

"Okay."

"Mary Kate, I'm biting my lip to keep from going off on you. Have you ever tried the program? For real?"

"AA ain't for everybody," she said defiantly, repeating my own sentiments. And, of course, she was right. It was there for everyone, but only worked for a fortunate few.

"You gave the program a shot?"

"I went to meetings in Reno for a time and even got a sponsor, but I can't handle all the God crap. It's too much like a cult."

"It can be. It can also save your life. A lot depends on how you approach it, and who you choose to hang out with. You ever change your mind, want to give it another try, I'll introduce you to some women who have it together."

She met my eyes. "Not likely, big brother."

I shrugged. "Standing offer, kid sister."

"Fuck you," she said, but not unkindly.

I touched her arm. "Hey, and fuck you, too."

The wall clock seemed to get louder. Our eyes went moist and drifted sideways. Mary Kate and Mick Callahan, sentimental Irish fools. We both looked out the window as if suddenly fascinated by the shadows caressing the leaves. A couple of awkward kids.

My telephone rang, almost on cue. I left her at the table and went to answer it in the living room.

"Callahan."

"Good morning, sunshine," Jerry barked. "This is your lucky day."

I took the portable phone out onto the back porch, lowered my voice. "What have you got?"

"We found the car Faber and Toole rented. It's sitting unclaimed in a parking lot out by LAX."

"Did you call Donato?"

"Yeah, and he suggested we stick with Lopez. Like, why bring someone new into it, right?"

"Makes sense, but Dave said he was out."

"Five hundred bucks in cash changed his mind. Anyway, late last night Dave and I had a look. We were careful, believe me."

"And. . . . ?"

"And nothing. Zip. Nada. That ride was wiped clean of prints, Mick. It didn't have so much as one cigarette butt in the ashtray. Maybe a police forensics team could turn something up, but one thing I can tell you for sure is that Faber and Toole really don't want to be found, not any time soon."

"That's a lot of trouble for a couple of drug dealers to go through, since as far as they know, the only one after them is Bud. That is, unless they do know something serious about Gordo and the murder. Or maybe killed him themselves?"

"That's what I was thinking."

"Good job, Jerry. What about the other vehicle, the one that nabbed Brandi?"

"Lopez is doing some legwork. He says we have it down to a few more cars in the LA area that might fit the bill. I'll keep you posted."

"Okay. Thanks."

I cut the connection, sat down on my back porch and considered this new development. The pieces had to fit together somehow, but the pattern eluded me, the next piece tantalizingly out of reach. I finally decided to take Mary Kate to the

Hungry Fox for some home cooking, just to take my mind off a steadily increasing state of confusion. I put the phone back.

"Sis, you up for some breakfast?"

No answer. I went into the kitchen. Her plate and cup were in the sink. I went back down the hall to the bedroom then checked the guest bathroom. No one. I looked everywhere. The house was empty. I walked out into the front yard and went to the curb, stared both ways. No sign of her. Mary Kate was gone. Hell, I don't know how, maybe she just hitched a ride with the neighbor's gardener.

"Nice knowing you."

I walked back inside, feeling weighted down. I locked the door and went into the office to fire up my computer. I had three E-mails, one from Judd Kramer. I opened it and discovered a paragraph describing a job offer at a small station in New Mexico. I'd have to do some local news, but the money was decent, and the company would pay any moving expenses. Would I be interested? I did a search on the call letters and called up some photos of the locale. Nice. It pissed me off that Judd hadn't had the testicles to just call me, but then I'd been pretty rough on his sorry ass. Should I even call him back?

Maybe, but not yet. The idea I'd be allowing Judd to collect a commission from me ever again gave me serious pause. Besides, I'd have to sell the house and leave town. I didn't know what it would mean for my relationship with Darlene, if I could still call it that.

Eventually I took the easy way out and e-mailed back that I'd think about it for a couple of days.

The next missive was from Darlene, asking me to call her as soon as I had some privacy. The third was from Hal. I called him first, tracked him down and pulled him up on video chat.

"Where are you?"

Hal held up a glass full of what appeared to be iced coffee.

"I'll give you a hint. It's very hot."

"So? It's hot as hell here in Los Angeles."

"Drive to the coast, young stallion. Enjoy the sea breeze and the clear air. Then you'll have a better idea."

"Hal, it's too early in the morning for this. Hawaii?"

"You think like such a plebeian." He sipped the drink, slowly turned the computer and camera to show me an expanse of white sand and clear water. His face appeared again. He was rubbing on sun screen. "I am ensconced on the beach near San Juan, sir. The people are pleasant, the prices outrageous, and the ladies scantily clad."

"Hey, I am so happy for you, old man."

"You would be if you loved me. Oh, Callahan, I can personally assure you that the thong bikini is the best invention since sliced bread."

"Sliced bread is such an apt metaphor. Can you spare a few minutes, or have you already taken the Viagra?"

"Don't get snippy with me." Hal leaned back, took another sip of his coffee drink. "It is times like these that almost make a man wish he weren't over twenty-five years clean and sober."

"If you weren't, you'd go to sleep in Puerto Rico and wake up in Cleveland."

"Hey, I said almost."

I told him about Mary Kate having shown up and just as suddenly disappeared. Hal shook his head. "This must break your heart."

"What was left. It really is a shame. And I know there's not a damned thing I can say or do to make it better, Hal. Mary Kate has already been to meetings, and she's easily as stubborn as me."

"Perhaps she'll be back, Mick. This is a program of attraction."

"Rather than promotion. I know."

"Any news from Jerry on our project?"

"We're closing in. The car Faber and Toole were driving is out by the LA airport, but it was picked clean. There's nothing for us to go on, except that it was a rental. Hopefully we'll have something more to work with soon."

"Hopefully."

Hal leaned back in his chair. Sun reflected from his forehead and confused the camera for a moment. I looked down at the keyboard. "Kramer relayed a job offer. It's in New Mexico."

"Oh, excrement."

"Exactly. Good news, bad news."

"I have begun to ponder the notion that you may be in the wrong business anyway, stallion. Imagine the money you could make if you started getting paid for all of this . . . extra-curricular activity."

"Just imagine." I stared at the screen, my face letting him know I considered that a terrible idea.

"It was just a thought."

"Believe me, Hal, sometimes I do think about changing careers, but I suppose I enjoy it enough to keep going."

"Really?"

"Well, the therapy part, anyway."

"Consider carefully. Mick Callahan, Private Eye."

"Sounds like bad television."

"And your point would be. . . . ?"

"Up yours, old man."

We both grinned. Hal said, "I just have to ask you one question, Mick. It is a very serious question. Do you love this young policewoman? Love her enough to seal the bargain?"

"If I knew the answer to that, I wouldn't have to come to you for advice."

"That seems slippery, and perhaps beneath you."

I leaned forward. "I love Darlene, Hal. How much and in

exactly what way is the question. And to be honest with you, if I proposed I don't think she'd accept, for a lot of different reasons."

"Give me two."

"We fight way too often. My work makes me travel. Finally, she is dedicated to her own career."

Hal pursed his lips. "Unfortunately, those are very good reasons."

"I know."

"I feel like a stroll along the sand," Hal said. "May I check back with you later this morning?"

"Sure, or I'll call you."

"How are the finances, do you need anything?"

I shook my head. "You're very generous, as usual. Jerry has plenty of cash for what he's doing, Lopez is caught up, and our other expenses have been covered."

"Do you require a loan whilst unemployed?"

"I'm fine. Go study butt cheeks."

"I shall, I assure you. I shall indeed."

We broke the connection. I sat back in the chair and rolled backwards, away from the computer just as my fax machine whirred and began printing. Two pages of text arrived; a cover sheet from a public machine and a one-page fax from Darlene. As I studied it, my stomach sank to the hardwood floor and even did a bit of mopping. *When it rains, it freaking pours. . . .*

It took me a good five minutes to work up the gumption to dial her on the cell. She picked me up from caller ID. "First, I want you to know I just put in for some personal time. I get the distinct feeling you're going to need all the help you can get. I'm on leave when I wrap up my shift this afternoon."

"I don't know what to say."

"Try you're beautiful, sexy, and I love you more than life itself."

"You're beautiful and sexy and I love you more than life itself."

"Once more with feeling."

"Later. I'll work on it, I promise."

The humor was a bit forced. We both knew it. Finally, Darlene said, "Did you get my fax? I sent it from an office supply on Vineland in North Hollywood."

"Yes, it just arrived."

"And?"

I sighed. "To be honest with you, Darlene, I'm feeling pretty strange right now."

"Me, too."

"Because I don't know how to take this."

"What do you mean?"

"Well," I said quite carefully, "last night you were complaining about being dragged into a bunch of new problems and having your career endangered. Today you say you're taking time off to watch my back, and you dig into Mary Kate's past and fax me her jacket."

"No good deed goes unpunished."

"What possessed you to take the risk of running her through the system?"

"Did it ever occur to you to thank me?"

"I sincerely thank you for being in my life, Darlene."

"Mick, I'm trying to help."

"And I appreciate that. But this is my sister we're talking about, not some lowlife we just stumbled across. Suddenly reading about her past problems with the law sort of gives me the creeps."

Uh oh. Darlene was steaming again. "Mick, just in case you need glasses, Mary Callahan, your newly discovered sister, has used the alias Mary Catherine Carter. She has an open warrant in Texas for failing to show up for sentencing on a DWI. She's also been busted for kiting checks, case dismissed for lack of evidence. Oh, and she was once charged with prostitution but charges were dropped when she turned State's on the escort service."

"Okay. Okay."

"Look, nothing personal, but she doesn't seem like the kind of girl that should have the spare keys to your car or access to any of your finances, and I thought you should know."

"Okay, now I know."

Darlene took a deep breath. I heard voices approaching her. "I have to go," she said. "And, Mick? It gets worse. We were right. According to CSI they found some of Bud Stone's prints at the Gordo murder scene. There's a warrant and an APB on your friend as of this morning. I'm sorry."

The phone went dead. I closed my eyes. "Yeah, I'm sorry, too."

TWENTY-TWO

"You've got mail."

I opened my eyes again, checked the screen. The E-mail said "may have found that Range Rover for you." I deleted the obsolete message and stared at my hands for a long beat. Wondered if it was really time to put up or shut up with Darlene. I couldn't fathom the idea of being married. I had enough trouble trying to get along with any woman for more than a couple of months.

Something caught my eye. A second E-mail had been caught by the spam filter. I didn't recognize the E-mail address. Almost on a whim, I opened it up. It was a text message. It read: ITS ME. PESCI BEHIND MESS. MORE SOON W/C L8R BONE. I had the palpable sense that things were finally breaking our way. My heart began to pick up speed.

I suddenly realized I hadn't given the radio job in New Mexico another thought. That awareness didn't please me. More violence. What if Hal was right? Maybe I was born for pain and chaos, but part of me hoped not. It clashed badly with the man I'd intended to become. In school they showed us something called the Johari Window, a sketch that showed how little a man can actually see of his own, true personality. The human capacity for self-deception never ceases to amaze. Including my own.

Someone tried the front door. Had I locked it? I was on my feet in a half second, and headed down the hall. The person stepped into the living room.

Mary Kate and I stared at each other for a long beat. Then we surprised ourselves by melting into a hug. I rapped two fingers on the top of her head. "You scared me. I thought you'd taken off."

She'd been crying. "I meant to." Mary Kate reached into the pocket of her jeans, took out two twenty-dollar bills, put them in my hand and forced my fist closed. "I stole this from the coffee can in the kitchen."

I didn't say anything, but kept the money. Waited, watched. "I went to the liquor store down the street," she said, "the one with the Mexican name. I was going to get some beer. There was an old guy out front, passed out. His pants were soaked with piss. I don't know why, but that really upset me."

I stepped back. "Go on."

"So I go into the store and over to the booze, you know? I find the beer section, and open the glass door but just stand there. And the icy air feels so cool, so nice. I can taste a cold bottle of beer like it's already on my lips, but I don't reach for the six-pack. I just stand there in the breeze. My arms get all bumpy and the sweat dries on my clothes. Finally the guy behind the counter, he clears his throat real loud, it's like someone clapping their hands, meaning it really startles me, snaps me out if it."

"What did you do?"

Mary Kate was still there, in that funky liquor store. "I let the door close. Step back. And suddenly I don't want a drink. I just want a good cry." She looked up at me. "Does that make sense?"

"You want me to take you to a meeting?"

"Now?"

I shrugged. "I haven't been to one myself in quite a while. Now seems as good a time as any."

"Can I think about it?"

My gut told me this was not a good time to push. I smiled

and nodded instead. "If you don't go wandering off."

Mary Kate brightened and smiled back. "Any more coffee?"

"I'll put some on." I wandered into the kitchen and made another pot. "Do you want me to whip up a protein shake?"

She made a face. "Sounds gross."

"It's not, really. Chocolate or strawberry with half a banana and some fresh fruit. I've gotten used to them."

"Yeah, well you seem to work out a lot. Okay, guess I can give it a shot."

I brought out the fixings. "Mary Kate, if you're going to stay glued to me today, be advised I have to do a lot of running around. Some of it might seem a little weird, and discretion will be necessary."

"Discretion?"

"Fancy way of saying you'll have to keep your mouth shut."

A big smile. "Why, Mick Callahan, are you breaking the law?"

"Let's just say I have been known to bend the rules." I went to the counter and dug a sharp knife out of the drawer. Laid it to one side and washed some fruit. "And I'm dead serious. I need your word."

"Sure. What's this all about?" Mary Kate moved next to me and started cutting up the strawberries.

"It's kind of complicated, but I'm helping out an old friend. He's in trouble with some very shady people."

"What kind of trouble, if you don't mind me asking?"

"The kind that starts small and turns out big."

Mary Kate cupped her hands around the strawberries and dropped them into the blender. Her shoulders slumped a bit. "I know something about that kind," she said sadly. "Does he have the law on his ass, too?"

"As of this morning."

"Well, then I'll have to be kind of careful," Mary Kate said. "I have a live warrant in another state. I can't afford to get nailed for anything. That's one of the reasons I didn't want to call the cops when Talbot beat me up, you know? Something would have turned up, and then where'd I be?"

She'd told me the truth, and almost casually. That felt good. Still, I couldn't help but wonder. Did Mary Kate have any ulterior motives for looking me up, like maybe thinking I had serious money? Darlene had planted the thought in my mind, and it had a surprising amount of traction. And what if we stumbled across the missing drug money Bud needed to pay off Pesci? Would some cash grow legs and walk away?

Mary Kate was looking at me. I hadn't responded. "We should be able to keep you away from the cops."

"Then let me give you a hand."

I considered. My sister sighed. "Look, I can't go anywhere without money or friends. I'm scared of being alone and terrified of Talbot, mostly because I will probably have to shoot his sorry ass if he touches me again, you know? And I sure as hell don't want to sit around your house climbing the walls, wanting to drink. Let me make myself useful."

"I'll think on it."

The cell phone rang. I left my sister in the kitchen and jogged around the house trying to remember where I'd left it. It was on the stereo. Another text message. Jerry wanted to talk and was online. I went to the computer and his face appeared on the screen. His burn scar was suffused with blood, probably due to excitement.

"I think I figured out how they fooled us. It started with the rental of that Range Rover Faber and Toole drove to Vegas and back. We didn't find any other credit card records because somebody mirrored them off Faber's history."

"Mirrored?"

Jerry held up a piece of paper with some numbers and a sketch of what seemed like computer screens. "They used some damned fine tricks to switch the charges to another account and then another, just kind of bounced them around, so that stuff appeared paid for but it was always a bitch tracing the costs back to the original account numbers. You can get away with that for a while sometimes before the card people catch on and stop it. They did that a couple of hours ago, shut down Faber's account."

My pulse quickened again. "So? Do we know where he is?"

"That girl you talked to at the rental company gave us the records, but they were useless. Well, that's because it was only what now turns out to be a mirrored address, okay? So what I had to do was trace it back through the scam to the original. The one they were trying to hide."

"You've got it?"

"I've got it." Jerry focused on something behind me and stopped talking at once. I spun my chair.

Mary Kate was in the doorway. She'd heard every word. I turned back to the screen. "Jerry, meet Mary Kate Callahan. My half sister."

"Howdy. Where did she come from?"

"It's a long story, Jerry. Anyway, go on."

"The house is paid off, no mortgage. The guy on the title is some old fart name of Anderson. He lives in San Diego. In other words, it's a rental property. My guess is Faber and Toole paid someone to lease it in a different name. I got it off an old application for a gas card. They've been hiding in plain sight, Mick. In fact, right under our noses."

Jerry gave me the address. It was maybe four or five miles south and east of me, in a decent area called Valley Village. I whistled. "You really figure this is where they're staying?"

"If it ain't they sure went to a hell of a lot of trouble to hide it, *comprende?* I mean, why bother unless you plan on hanging out by the pool and don't want to be bothered any time soon."

We heard the vague screech of tires as someone had a fender bender up the block. "Brilliant work, Jerry. Way to go. I really owe you one." I smiled and began to turn off the computer.

"Wait. Don't."

I stopped. "Don't what?"

"Don't move on this. Let me ask Donato to turn us on to somebody that plays rough. A pro that can check this out."

"Why risk another man's skin? I'll do it myself."

"Think it through, Mick. Maybe you don't want any of this to have your scent on it. For starters, you can't tell Darlene. She would need to immediately report it to her bosses, or IAD would toast her buns for good. It's a Murder One warrant, my man."

"Sit on this for me, Jerry. I'll get back to you."

Jerry frowned. "You'll think about what I just said?"

"I promise." I signed off, turned to Mary Kate.

"That poor boy," she said. "What happened to his face?" I told her the whole story. "His foster mother burned him with an iron? God, that's awful." Mary Kate's eyebrows arched in query. "You said you were going to think about what he said. Well?"

I grinned. "I did. And I'm going."

She laughed with a mix of excitement and surprise. "Then I'm going with you."

"Not this time. He's right, it could be dangerous."

"You can die on the freeway," Mary Kate said, "or up at the end of your block, from the sound of it." She crossed her arms. She looked ten years old and cute as hell. "I'm not letting you go alone."

I didn't want to leave her in the house by herself. I sighed. "We'll just have a look, and beat feet after, okay? If they seem to be there, or there's any real possibility of trouble, we'll take off and get reinforcements. Fair enough?"

I put the address in a search engine and got directions. We went out into the harsh sunlight just in time to hear an ambulance arrive. I watched my sister take a quick and nervous look around. The accident up the block had gathered a crowd of pedestrians, and now neighbors' cars were coming and going as well. That made it impossible to know if Ed Talbot was nearby.

Although it was clear that the house was quite near the Hollywood Freeway exit, I took surface streets and a few deliberate wrong turns. I thought one brown Ford stayed on our tail for a while, but it was hard to be certain.

"What's your ex-boyfriend driving, MK?"

"Talbot hot-wires a lot of his rides, but as of last night it was a brown Taurus."

"Think he's skilled enough to tail us without being spotted?"

Mary Kate hugged herself and cracked a thin smile. "Ed is good at a lot of things people shouldn't be good at."

"I may have seen him a couple of minutes ago, can't be sure. If it was him, seems to be gone now."

"Shit, I hope not."

"Me, too."

Mary Kate laughed softly. I raised an eyebrow in query. "You just gave me my nickname," she said. "You called me MK."

"So I did."

"I kind of like it."

We drove down Colfax and had to pause to let a stream of adolescents saunter through the crosswalk. This was a nice, middle-class LA neighborhood, meaning the home prices were through the roof because it was close to a decent public school. We got to Moorpark, turned, went a couple of blocks east and turned north again.

The street came to a dead end. The day was hot and many houses were closed up tight. Air conditioners hummed like purring lions. Large fans spun rapidly in prefab windows. Most of the cars were gone, and those that were left bristled with sunlight reflected from hubcaps and fenders like shards of broken mirrors. I parked several doors down, left the keys in the ignition and the engine and air-conditioning running. Mary Kate's eyes were wide.

"You don't even have a gun, do you?"

"Not with me." I shrugged. "I don't much like them, they tend to escalate things. Besides, I don't plan on being here long or attracting much attention. Just want to see if anyone is living there, and if so, could it be Faber or Toole."

"That's it?"

"That's all." I patted her hand, gave her my cell phone. "Get over in the driver's seat and wait for me. If anyone else shows up, and it looks like trouble, honk the horn twice, wave at one of the other houses like you're saying goodbye to somebody and just drive away."

"Drive where?"

I thought for a second. "Did you notice that coffee shop a ways back, the one by the freeway? Go and get something cold to drink. I'll meet you there."

Mary Kate nodded. "Okay. Watch your ass."

I got out, slammed the door and rapped my knuckles once on the windshield. Turned my back on the car, looked around carefully. It was too damned hot for anyone to be hanging around their front yard. I figured we'd have some time. I jogged closer. The house we wanted was compact, most likely a two-bedroom with one bath. It was painted green and white and had a small backyard. I walked by and took a quick look. Closed up tight, but so was every other place in the neighborhood. Couple of warning stickers in the windows, but probably fake. No sign of a real alarm system.

A few yards past the side gate, I stepped into someone's front yard, strolled along the hedge and had a look at the back: five-

217

foot chain-link fence, lots of undergrowth, and a browning, uncut lawn; some rampant ivy that looked carnivorous and a covered spa that probably hadn't been used in years. No swimming pool. The air conditioner was on. All the window shades were pulled, and someone had placed tin foil on the panes facing east to reflect away a bit of the relentless heat. I had to shade my eyes. I glanced back at the street, saw no one, and went into the backyard.

As I passed the back bedroom, I smelled something foul either in or under the house. My skin rippled. *Probably just a dead rat, Callahan . . .* I saw no sign of an alarm system in the roof eaves, no notice on the windowpanes or doors. I flattened against the house and eased along the wall, squatted down under the back window just to play it safe. Caught that smell again, rancid even over the air-conditioning.

What came next really shook me. The phone lines had been cut.

Now what? I considered going back to the car, calling Darlene and turning this one over to the cops. Something or someone was dead. But what if Faber and Toole had somehow killed one another in a fit of greed, and the cash and drugs Bone needed were still inside? Should I try to get them?

I went to the back door. It was glass-paned. I bent over, took my shirt off, and wrapped it around a rock, then got prepared to run like hell if an alarm went off. I knocked out the small pane nearest the knob. Nothing happened. I used my covered hand to open the back door, then shook out my tee shirt and slipped back into it. Stepped inside what turned out to be the kitchen.

Something hissed and rushed at me. I gasped, backed away and threw up my hands just as a large orange feline bounded past my feet and raced off into the yard. *Well, whatever's dead, it wasn't the cat.*

The house was freezing cold. The kitchen was filled with empty pizza boxes and plastic garbage sacks full of beer cans and other fast-food containers. I saw several piles of trash, but not enough to account for the stink that was now unmistakable. I didn't need a police background to recognize the stench of rotting meat.

I moved into the dark hallway. The thermostat had been set to the lowest possible point, cold air on round the clock, probably an attempt to hide the evidence for as long as possible. I gagged, could barely breathe. I heard flies buzzing, feasting.

A naked man was in the living room, hands and feet bound behind his back with some kind of thin wire. I coughed and pinched my nostrils, then stepped closer. I recognized the face. It was Frank Toole. He had been cut repeatedly, and some red patches of skin were bubbled and burned. Two of the front teeth had been knocked back into his mouth. This had been an ugly death. *So much blood.* Had his partner killed him and left with the goods?

I backed away, nearly knocked over a stack of newspapers; moved into the bedroom, still breathing through my mouth. Still no sign of the loot or even a sack big enough to hold that much cash. I found two suitcases on the floor, both unlatched. I opened them with my tennis shoe. Each held pants and shirts of different sizes. Were both men still here? I moved back into the hall, nearly vomited but kept myself going. An invisible clock was ticking. I needed to get the hell out.

I entered the pantry, shivering. Almost stepped in what appeared to be a puddle of urine and feces. Then I saw something stretched out on the tiled floor, near the washing machine. It was a second corpse, bound in the same fashion, thin wire, hand and foot.

Joey Faber had managed to stay alive for a while. He'd crawled and rolled into the pantry to get at and consume the dry cat food and water left behind in two plastic dispensers. His body was faceup, mouth wide open, eyes closed. My gorge rose again, but I went down on one knee, touched his neck to search for a pulse. When Faber twitched in response, I almost fell over backwards. His eyes opened.

"Help," Faber said weakly. *"Help."*

"Easy. I'm going to call for an ambulance."

He coughed blood, licked cracked lips. "Fuck him. Fucking fuck."

"Who, Joey? Pesci?"

Faber reacted to the use of his own name. He appeared confused. Was I a friend? "Listen, just don't let the asshole get there first."

"Okay," I said, trying to ignore the amorality of questioning him further. "Tell me where it is, so I can get there before he does."

"Salt Lick," Faber whispered. "Old house, bomb shelter. ET owns it. Fuck must have told them."

My skin rippled again. "Told ET, or Nicky?"

Faber shook his head. Spat. He tried to move around but the pain made him moan. "My hands."

I patted his arm, forgot and took a deep breath. Gagged. *God, that stench.* "I'll call for help."

I heard something behind me and whirled around in a crouch. Mary Kate stood in the doorway, eyes wide with horror. She was a child again, this time really spooked and chewing on her fingers. I barked at her without thinking, something like, "Don't touch anything, damn it!"

Joey Faber snapped out of it. He looked carefully at my face, and at that moment finally realized that I was a complete stranger. He tried to say something defiant, but grimaced instead. His eyes widened in horror. His body shuddered and went into a spasm. Bound feet drummed the floor, and his bowels loosened, adding to the odor. He was dead.

"Back out of here carefully, Mary. Don't touch anything, don't step in anything that will hold a footprint. When we get back to my house we're dumping these shoes."

"I hear you. Mick, come on. Let's get the hell out of here."

"I'm coming." We eased into the hall, crossed the kitchen, and backed out into the yard. The heat hit us like a fist. I touched her face and whispered. "Whatever you do, don't throw up."

"Who could cut someone up like that?"

I swallowed my own stomach acid. *Good question.* "You'd be surprised what people are capable of when there's a lot of money at stake. Damn it to hell. The question is what do we do now?"

"We run," my sister said softly. "You can't possibly be thinking of doing anything else, right? I mean, come on, Mick. That was bind, torture, kill shit. I don't know about you, but I don't want to meet whoever did it."

"I probably already have met him. Did you leave the car running?"

She nodded. "I was just going to take a peek inside. You were taking so long."

"Let's go."

I left the back door open, figuring one of the neighbors would come looking sooner or later. We made it down the side of the house without being seen. My heart was in my throat all the way across the street, but we got into the car safely. It was all I could do to drive slowly, calmly, instead of gunning the engine. We were at the intersection near the coffee shop before I remembered to check for familiar cars. No brown Taurus in sight, but that didn't prove anything. *Jesus, what a mess.*

I pulled out my cell, checked for messages. Bud Stone had called from an unfamiliar number. I hit redial and reached him.

"Bud, we got trouble." I filled him on what happened to Faber and Toole and told him about the old ranch with a bomb shelter. "The stuff is supposed to be there, bro. Don't go it alone."

"Salt Lick is a dump maybe forty minutes outside of Vegas," Bud said coolly. He didn't seem surprised or upset, not even by the extremity of the violence I'd described, and that puzzled me. "Can't be but six spreads out there. I'll find the place."

"Wait, I'm coming along."

"Don't be an idiot, Callahan. I got a warrant out, remember?"

I glanced at Mary Kate. "Lot of that going around."

"So don't go hanging with a lowlife like me. It could be the death of you."

"Does appear that way, doesn't it?"

Mary Kate had her eyes closed as if working to erase a memory. We passed the south end of North Hollywood Park on Riverside. I took Tujunga up to the freeway this time, headed for home. Being in such dense traffic made me claustrophobic. My cell phone cracked and popped.

"Listen," Bud said, "there's a young lawyer in Vegas name of Jacob Mandel. Turns out he's been handling stuff for the bad guys, but I've known him since he was a kid. I told him about you. From now on, contact me through him."

"Why?"

"I'm losing cell phones for a while. I won't be leaving messages, either. You should get extra lines yourself, or at least dump this one. Hell, in fact just promise me you'll have your pal Jerry burn my electrons out of your life, get it like I haven't seen you in years, pretty much the way it was before. That would make my country ass smile."

"You're starting to worry me, Bone."

I gunned the engine and went into freeway traffic. The reception drifted.

"Hey?"

"I'm here."

"Bone, what are you going to do?"

"Get the money back, Mick. I'm tired of being manipulated. I'm taking the fight to them for a change."

He cut out again. "Hello?"

"Be good."

Bone broke the connection. Just then, Mary Kate rolled her window down and put her face out like a collie, most likely to keep from throwing up. I closed my phone and drove home in silence. By the time I pulled up in front of my house, I was on the same page as my friend about taking the fight to them for a change.

Hell, yes. . . . Why not?

TWENTY-THREE

Late that same afternoon, The Valley of Fire was living up to its name. The concrete grounds and blacktop driveways of the new resort were blistering hot, almost bubbling after a week of record temperatures. The centerpiece of the central project, the hotel itself, stood nearly complete. Virtually all of the construction crew had vanished for a week's break before resuming work on the resort, except for three panting electricians finishing up one of the lampposts located at the outer rim of the vast, empty parking lot.

Twelve long limousines were parked in a row before the entrance. Their drivers had gathered in the lobby to relax in lightly misted air that streamed over tall, potted ferns and a huge pond filled with koi. One of the drivers wandered too close to the security guard stationed by the gold-plated elevators. The man raised a night stick and ordered the intruder to step back.

The big opening party began with afternoon cocktails on the twentieth floor, near a glass-enclosed office designed for Big Paul Pesci. The floor-to-ceiling windows had been specially treated to darken on demand, and a computer continually adjusted the tint according to the angle of the afternoon sun. Classical music whispered from hidden speakers. Elegant call girls in scant evening gowns circulated carrying trays of champagne and hors d'oeuvres.

Eric, the Pesci goon I'd once dubbed Cowboy, was planted

near the sealed fire doors with his dim sidekick, Clyde. Their assignment was to watch out for the girls, follow them to the rooms and back again. Someone had to make sure the politicians didn't get carried away and slap the girls around. Well, and to get as many compromising photographs as possible. Never can tell when a few shots of the Mayor with a hooker bobbing his Johnson might come in handy.

Big Paul was standing up straight, still holding forth at the long, wooden conference table. He'd already downed enough vodka to redden his cheeks and paint a thin sheen on his piggy eyes. His mistress, a slender blonde coke whore named Michelle, stayed anchored to his arm and even managed to look enthralled by his discourse. Cowboy watched with detached disdain as Pesci droned on and on about how expensive everything around them was, like some kind of drunken Donald Trump.

"Edie is taking Senator Wenk to four-eleven," Clyde whispered excitedly. "You want I should check on the cameras?"

Cowboy yawned. "By all means, Clyde. Go on down to four-eighteen and be sure the equipment is working properly. Hell, stay and make sure you get both of their faces in the same shot."

Clyde left a happy puppy. *Porn freak.* Cowboy massaged his temples and tried to zone out. He could just see the elevators from an angle, and when they opened it caught his eyes. Little Nicky stepped out. Eric swallowed. There was something about the big man that made his skin crawl.

Nicky moved slowly through the assembled guests like an aircraft carrier, only pausing to respond to a "Hello," and a handshake. His cold, grey eyes remained fixed on Big Paul Pesci. When Michelle saw Nicky coming, the blood left her face and she sat down with a thump. Nicky had that effect on people. Pesci stopped talking, looked at her. "You okay, sweet thing?"

"We need to talk, Paul," Nicky said.

"No business this afternoon, Nicky," Pesci protested, "we're having a party!"

"It's important."

Pesci spread his hands to the assembled politicos and businessmen as if to say, "Hey, what can you do." Relieved to be released from verbal bondage, the men wandered away. Pesci searched the table, found his glass of iced vodka. Nicky promptly pried it from his fingers, set the glass back on a coaster. Sensing the mood, Michelle slid further under the conference table.

"Come with me."

Pesci glowered, glanced over at Eric the Cowboy, who prayed he wouldn't be asked to intervene. Pesci was annoyed, but chose not to make a scene. He followed Nicky through the crowd, across the room and into the next hall. They entered a small, soundproofed room regularly swept for electronic listening devices.

"What's so damned important?"

Nicky knew that was the liquor. He let the impertinence go. "Both Faber and Toole are dead."

Pesci found a padded chair. He sat down heavily. "Any sign of the disc, or my money?"

"No," Nicky said. He slid another plush chair directly across from Big Paul, but remained standing, with one foot on the cushion. The position allowed him to look down, a fact not lost on Pesci. "They were in a rental house near Los Angeles. The police came to investigate a possible burglary and discovered the bodies. A cop we paid off to track the Gordo case saw the report and passed the information on to me."

Pesci shook his head. "Shit. What the hell happened?"

"Happened? They were tortured," Nicky said calmly. "Thus, we can deduce whoever did it must now have the disc."

"We're going to need a new perspective," Pesci said. "We have to think outside the box. Our current plan isn't working. Maybe we should kill Stone and Callahan and go back to square one."

Nicky leaned closer. "We will give you twenty-four hours to resolve this, Paul. And then I'm going to have to handle things my way."

"What does that mean?"

Nicky smiled that smile. "It means exactly what it sounds like, no more, no less. We will simply do whatever seems necessary to recover the disc, regardless of the consequences to you or your organization."

"I don't care for the sound of that," Pesci said. He forced a smile. "I'll give Mr. Stone one more night to find and bring us the disc, Nicky. If we don't hear by tomorrow noon, I'll pull the plug on that version of the operation. We'll get our own people on finding it, even at the risk that something may be traced back to us. That's what lawyers are for, right?"

Nicky sat down abruptly and rolled his chair backwards. "You have one of your own. Young Jacob Mandel. Consult with him on how to best muddy the waters, as you say. But get this job done, Paul. Bring us the disc. My superiors are gravely concerned."

"I will," Pesci promised. "I have something for you, my friend. I'd planned on saving it for later tonight, but there's no time like the present." He spun his chair, picked up a remote control and punched two buttons. A wooden panel on the soundproofed wall slid away with a faint hiss, revealing a giant screen television set. The picture came into focus. Two gorgeous young Asian women lay naked on satin sheets. They noticed the camera had come on, smiled and waved. One began to fondle herself. Nicky grunted with desire. The women were magnificent.

"Room two-eleven," Pesci said. "They are waiting for you."

"The camera?"

"Keep this." Pesci used the remote, handed it to Nicky. "The code is the room number in reverse, one-twelve. When you're done, come back here and pop out the one DVD copy, and hit erase. Or just turn it off now if you don't want to record the experience. It's your choice, but somehow I think you're going to want to have something to remember them by."

Nicky got up, touched the screen. He was already erect. "They are indeed beautiful. Thank you, Paul."

Pesci had taken a small mirror, a straw, and some cocaine out of his pocket. They did two lines each. Nicky rubbed his nose. "Very good shit."

"The twins are fifteen hundred apiece for the night," Pesci said. "So please, don't leave any marks."

The two men shook hands. "No hard feelings, Paul," Nicky said. Both knew he was lying. "Twenty-four hours, or I must take over the recovery operation."

"Understood."

They went out into the hall. Pesci slapped Nicky on the back, locked the room, and headed back to the party. "Enjoy."

Nicky stood for a moment, examining the remote control, his natural caution momentarily overcome by lust. He left the recorder on, put the remote in his coat pocket, and took the hallway to the small private elevator. It felt like a padded coffin. He rode down to the fourth floor. The girls met him at the door, saw his size, giggled and began to rip at his clothes. Nicky double-locked the hotel suite, placed his 9mm under the pillow and watched them hump and stroke one another until he couldn't stand it anymore.

The next few hours dissolved into shadows and sexual heat. Nicky carefully positioned the twins so that the secret video would be exceptional. They rubbed top-grade cocaine on his penis and sucked him in tandem, one on his scrotum and one on his shaft, then traded places. After ejaculating for the first time, Nicky returned the favor with a generous tongue. When the cocaine took him a bit too high and created jitters, he smoked a bowl with the twins and licked vodka off their pert breasts. Three orgasms followed the first. Exhausted, Nicky ordered the women to turn on the Jacuzzi tub. A tiny electronic ringing tone kept him from dozing. He opened his cell phone.

"Nikolaou."

One of the twins, he'd never bothered to learn their names, was squatting on the bidet, far too close to the bathroom door for comfort, so the conversation that ensued was entirely in Nicky's native language. She glanced his way, saw his features darken with rage and shot her sister a concerned look. When the tub was ready, the twins padded back into the bedroom with forced smiles, each to one side of the oversized bed. They reached for his arms, but paused. Little Nicky had fallen asleep. His mouth opened in a snore, thick lips bubbled with saliva.

The two women locked eyes. The one on the left side of the bed trembled with fear and shook her head. She raised her hands, palms up, and mouthed the word "no." The female on the right ignored her plea and tiptoed over to her purse. This one had a feral glint in her eyes, and clearly a different kind of soul than her sister, who had already slipped back into her evening gown and was heading for the door.

They shared another long look. The first girl wept, crossed herself, and left. The door closed silently behind her.

The second twin knelt on the carpet, opened a secret pocket in her purse and produced a syringe already loaded with a clear fluid. She was not about to pass up one million dollars. She studied Nicky, whose snores were deep and evenly paced, knowing his was the last cock she was ever going to have to suck. She eased closer, the needle hidden in her palm and partly behind her back. She paused at the side of the bed, legs slightly parted.

Another long wait. There could be no mistakes.

Finally, she went down to one knee, leaned in close and located the carotid artery. The girl had been on and off heroin for two years. She knew how to work with needles. She brought the syringe up and did a practice run, stopping just short of injection. She'd been told the contents of the syringe were obscure poisons mixed with insulin. They would induce an immediate heart attack and leave no trace evidence.

In less than a minute, this would all be over. She mentally rehearsed the act and then the aftermath. She would smash and scatter the syringe. She was to leave immediately. Her sister was already in a car, headed for Reno. The second the death was verified, a call would be made. Her sister would go to a bank, open a safe deposit box, and leave with a bearer bond for one million dollars. The plan was to meet in San Francisco the next day for an overnight flight to Berlin. And then they would disappear forever.

The girl took a deep breath, released it, then a shallow one. Nicky continued to snore. She brought the needle down, and stabbed for his neck.

The world went white and she found herself on her back, legs splayed. She could not get a breath. Her hands clutched at her throat. Nicky was now pacing the room like a Bengal tiger; his hairy, heavily muscled body rigid with rage. The girl heard wheezing sounds. *His right hand. . . .* It had come up in a flash, flat as a board, and caught her flush across the neck. Her throat had been crushed. She writhed in agony, whimpered and struggled as she slowly strangled to death.

Nicky went down on his knees. "Having fun?" He slapped her face, held up the syringe. "You could take an hour to die, bitch. Or I could help you out with a dose of your own medicine."

"P-p-please," she managed to gasp, "h-h-help."

"Oh. You wish me to call the physician who is downstairs at the party, to see if there is something he can do?"

Her eyes begged. Nicky fondled her nipple absently. "You have given me great pleasure tonight, so I shall consider your request."

The girl gagged, wheezed, whispered promises of things he'd never dreamed about, things she'd never done for anyone, all the while slowly gasping for breath. Her world was going dark and cold and she did not want to die. Not here, not this way, naked on a carpet and still a whore. . . .

"But, of course, I have a condition," Nicky said, leaning closer. He stroked her forehead in an obscene parody of affection. "First, you will tell me who sent you, yes?"

Moments later, Nicky did two more lines on the edge of the spa tub. He went into the water and ran the jets. After a short bath, he freshened up and returned to the bedroom to get dressed. The second twin was barely moving by now. Her face had blackened. Her eyes were wide with terror. She had wet herself. Nicky slipped into his Armani suit and stood over her. He held up the syringe.

"Ready?"

By this time the woman could no longer bear the pain. She nodded vigorously, gratefully . . . *please get it over with, please.* . . .

Nicky dropped the syringe on the carpet. The girl tried to scream but could only manage a vague hissing noise. "Do it yourself, if you want death so badly. I'll see you in hell."

He walked out without looking back.

Out in the hallway, Nicky checked his 9mm and a second gun, a small Firestar, he kept strapped to his ankle. He made a mental note to be sure to get that DVD. The sex had been outrageous—replaying it, followed by the death of the hooker, would provide many intense climaxes in the years to come. He glanced at his Rolex. It was only ten o'clock, but the party had been going on since the late afternoon.

Nicky rode the private elevator up to the top level. He returned to the celebration as if nothing happened. The glass room was dimly lit, classic rock music blaring from hidden speakers. The night outside was bright with a summer moon and speckled with crystal stars. People were dozing with joints in their fingers, burning holes in the expensive leather couches. The catering bar was officially closed, but open bottles were everywhere, enough to keep the event running until morning. Nicky surveyed the room. A State senator was getting lap-danced. Some local businessman had begun playing strip poker with some of the call girls. Nicky left and locked the doors behind him.

Meanwhile, Big Paul Pesci was in the Presidential Suite, sprawled on the bed in his boxer shorts with a drink balanced on his fat belly. Paul was watching his favorite hooker dance around the room in high heels. Finally, Michelle went to the closet, bent over to give him a great view. She brought out a hat box, opened it up and produced sex toys. Pesci laughed drunkenly as she strapped on a huge, black dildo and walked around in a circle, jiggling.

"Sorry to interrupt."

"The fuck?" Pesci sat up suddenly, spilling his drink. Michelle screamed, lost her balance and fell backwards, crushing the hat box. Paul shaded his eyes. A huge man stood in the doorway.

"We need to talk, Paul." Little Nicky moved into the room, waved for Michelle to get out. She ran for the bathroom without bothering to remove the dildo. "Someone just tried to off me."

"Off you? What happened?"

"The twins, Paul," Nicky said. "They were great in bed, as you promised, but it did not end there." He sat on the edge of the bed. Paul saw that he was smiling. That only made things worse. "One of them tried to inject me with something, which got me thinking. Why inject? There is only one reason. A gunshot wound would attract attention, but an injection of something that could not be traced. . . . But who, then? Who gave this order?"

Pesci swallowed. "Ask the girls. Make them talk."

"One got away while I was sleeping, unfortunately. The other is dead."

"That's too bad," Pesci said. "Now we'll never know who hired them." He leaned back against the wall.

"Wait." Nicky showed his teeth and produced a small handgun, the Firestar. "Let me see your left hand, Paul."

Pesci blinked. "My hand?"

Nicky grabbed it, wrapped it in a pillow, pressed the gun against the fabric and fired. Big Paul shrieked and gibbered and clutched his bleeding hand. Nicky gave him the edge of the bedspread. "Quiet. Bite down on this. If Michelle walks back in here, I'll kill her on the spot. It's your call."

"What are you doing? Why did you do that? I don't know anything about this! Please, listen to me!"

Nicky studied him. "This is beneath you, Paul. You fucked up. Take the consequences like a man."

"I didn't do anything, Goddamn it! Nicky, it wasn't me!" His other hand crept to the side of the bed. Pesci felt around for the small panic button, pushed hard; again, and then again.

Nicky grabbed Pesci by the leg and covered his right foot with another pillow. "Bite down." Pesci began to babble. Nicky fired a second time, POP, and the room stank of burning cotton and cordite. Pesci passed out for a time. Nicky sighed, got up, looked around for some liquor, poured himself a whiskey. Went back over to the bed and poured some ice water on Big Paul.

"No," Pesci whimpered, "please don't. It wasn't me."

"Don't bullshit me, Paul, I know it was you."

"Who said that? Who lied about me?"

"You embarrass yourself," Nicky said quietly. "This is how a man drowns, by panicking."

"I demand to know who fed you this crap!"

"It's simple, Paul. The girl told me."

"She lied."

Nicky shook his head. "First she told me because she thought I would call for help if she was honest. She said Big Paul. The second time I let her think I would end it for her with less pain. She swore she'd told me the truth. I believe her. It is a difficult thing to hold back on the way to the grave, Paul. Few do."

The door opened behind the two men. Pesci gasped with joy. He raised his good arm and pointed at Little Nicky. "Kill him! Kill him now!"

Cowboy Eric and Clyde entered the room, weapons raised. Nicky stiffened a bit and lowered the Firestar to the floor. He sat back in his chair, now calm. Pesci scrambled back into a squatting position on the bed, one hand and one foot dripping blood. "Get the doctor in here, Eric, but first, shoot this piece of shit."

Nicky sat quietly. "Should I explain?"

"Not interested," Eric said.

Pesci struggled to wrap his wounds in the bed sheet. "Take him in the bathroom and shoot his ass in the shower, Eric. Clyde, you cut him up. I don't want a trace of this bastard left behind. We'll say he ran off with the twins."

"I was just in their room," Eric said quietly. "One's gone, the other's dead."

"Okay, one of them. Whatever. Just kill him. Look what the fucker did to me! Michelle? Michelle?"

Little Nicky coughed. Everyone else in the room jumped. "Tell me how it all worked. Give me that much. You hired Faber and Toole from the start, yes? They were to get the money and the disc and set up Mr. Stone to take the fall. When this Callahan fellow came into the picture, you just took advantage of his presence to muddy the waters. You planned to keep all the money and the drugs, and then use Faber and Toole to sell the disc back to my superiors, when it was you who stole it in the first place. Have I put this together properly, Paul?"

Pesci was pale and sliding into shock.

"Clyde?" Eric said. "Maybe you'd better go get Doctor Edison."

Clyde left the suite.

"Well, Paul?" Nicky seemed genuinely curious and not at all afraid of his imminent death.

Paul Pesci shivered. His teeth were chattering. "I wasn't going to sell it back to *your* people, asshole. You're thinking too small. I was going to sell it back to the corrupt US government for a freaking fortune."

"I'm just wondering why you had Faber and Toole killed," Nicky said. "That part just doesn't make sense. Unless, of course, it was just that they were the only witnesses who knew you had anything to do with stealing the disc. By the way, where is it?"

Pesci fell back on the pillow. "Go to hell. Eric, shoot him."

Eric the Cowboy exchanged glances with Nicky. He lowered his weapon. "No can do, Paul. Sorry."

"What?"

"Me and Clyde, we sold out for a better price, too. I'm sure you can appreciate that. Just capitalism at work."

Pesci moaned. Nicky laughed, reached down to the carpet and retrieved the little pistol. He grabbed another pillow. "I want it all, Paul, especially the disc and the money. The drugs I've promised to Eric and Clyde, here. Tell me where everything is." Nicky placed the small pillow over Pesci's crotch. He raised the gun.

"ET hid the stuff," Pesci babbled. His eyes stayed on the gun as he shielded his shriveled penis with his one good hand. "He doesn't even know about the disc, just the drugs and the money."

Nicky sat back. He snapped his fingers. Eric opened the door and Clyde came back into the room. "Clyde," Eric said calmly, "haul your ass down to the party. Find ET and bring him here. Do it now."

"Please," Pesci said, hating himself for whining. "I'm sorry."

Nicky laughed again. "I'll bet you are. He is sorry, yes, Eric? We can all bet he is sorry now."

Eric stayed in place by the door. Pesci tried to crawl off the edge of the bed. Nicky grabbed his arm, pulled him back, shifted the pillow and covered his face. Pesci screamed. Nicky fired one last time, POP, and there was silence. Pesci twitched and died.

Eric stayed at attention.

"I want ET to see this," Nicky said, "before he gives us directions to where the goods are. I want him to know what awaits him should he ever think to betray me."

"Okay." Cowboy looked pale.

"Afterwards, get someone to clean this room top to bottom." He waved at Pesci's corpse. "Go make travel arrangements for our friend here. He is running with the money and the drugs, yes? Find some witnesses who will swear he took a plane to Mexico City at midnight tonight."

Eric said, "Consider it done."

Nicky stood up. He towered over Eric, who was not a small man. He poured himself another drink. "There is already a warrant out for Mr. Stone, yes? This Mick Callahan fellow could attract too much attention. I want him to stay out of Nevada, or at least be in the same predicament as his friend. How can we do that, and quickly?"

Eric shrugged. "We got two detectives downstairs. I'll get one of them to name Callahan a material witness in some murder case, doesn't matter which one. We'll make sure he finds out through his friend, the LA cop. That ought to either keep him from taking the risk or get him hauled in if he does."

"Do it."

Eric opened the door. Nicky motioned for him to wait. "I do not often share my thoughts, but you have assisted me greatly in this, and I shall make an exception. I think Paul actually had a good idea for once in his life."

Eric the Cowboy said, "Well, I don't know shit about any disc, but if it was worth a fortune then it seems that way to me."

Nicky waved a finger. "However, one should not try to bargain with the US government these days. It is quite corrupt. Besides, we would never survive embarrassing the organization that sent me to Nevada. However, quietly selling the disc back to my bosses through someone else? That may be the stroke of genius."

TWENTY-FOUR

Salt Lick, Nevada, was a pile of stones and decaying buildings that squatted several miles off the highway, less than an hour from the outskirts of Vegas. A survival freak named Jack Flanders had built a small ranch there in the early sixties, and put in a bomb shelter the size of an Olympic swimming pool. Several decades went by without a nuclear holocaust, but Flanders died insisting one was right freaking around the corner, sure as shit. His frustrated family sold the place before the ink dried on his death certificate.

The new owner tried to sell tickets to a genuine paranoid's bomb shelter, but nobody gave a damn. He sold it to a bunch of ex-hippies who had dreams of starting a commune, but the land was too dry to farm and the upkeep too high. So they sold the worthless place to someone who sold it to the mob.

Over the years, the concrete bomb shelter had been used to house drugs, sell dope, torture prisoners, and even film a few porn movies. Now the place was pretty much deserted unless the bent nose crowd had something going on that needed privacy and really thick walls.

A bit later that night, Bud Stone crawled quietly through the sage wearing NV goggles and black clothing, a hunting knife gripped firmly between his teeth. The ranch house was dark, but one of the guards lit a cigarette in cupped palms and the reddish glow gave his position away. Bone slid down into a gully, wincing at the light rain of pebbles and sand. He waited a full five minutes before continuing on. He took the glasses off, now that he was on top of them. The moon was full and bright, the desert like the surface of Mars after a meteor shower.

Bud had been watching two men go in and out during the day, trading shifts. They had no idea what they were guarding. He'd already taken stock of their weaponry and was unimpressed. They were wise guys, not soldiers. Neither man seemed terribly proficient or worrisome as an adversary. Bone waited patiently. The night was hot, and both of the men smoked. Sooner or later they would give in to temptation and stand in the same place to talk. They'd already done that twice. The second time he'd managed to get inside and poke around, then sneak out again.

Idiots.

Callahan's description of the murder of Faber and Toole had taken the gloves off, as far as Bud Stone was concerned. There was no longer any need to pussyfoot around. If these people were going to play hardball, he would, too.

Tires whined on the highway then thumped over pocked, dry earth. Headlights cut through the velvet darkness. A car left the highway and started towards the isolated ranch. The guard stiffened and called for his friend. The wind was still and his voice carried clearly.

"Lucky? We got company."

Bone swore under his breath. They'd both be in the same place again but who the hell was in that car? Bud couldn't move until he knew more. He'd surveyed the house well before sundown. In fact, this was his second trip out. The bomb shelter was below, and had one hell of a tough door on it. That's why Bone was packing some good, old-fashioned plastic explosives and two small mines. It had all been ridiculously easy so far. The two goons hadn't bothered to lock up the shelter. It was cooler than the cabin, and they'd wanted to take advantage of the large air-conditioning unit.

The two guards put out their cigarettes and stood together on the porch, watching the strange vehicle approach. Bud took advantage of the opportunity and closed the gap. He was behind them in seconds, right at the doorway and into the cabin. He flattened against the drapes and looked at the entrance to the bomb shelter. It yawned open like a dragon's maw, big concrete steps leading down into the cool darkness. Bud peered out the window, into the night.

The car bounced along and came to a stop a few yards from the cabin. The black guy called ET got out, the muscled card player. He'd come alone. Bone fondled his knife, knew he couldn't take all three without risking gunfire. The ranch was miles from any neighbor, but shots brought cops. If it went south, this was going to be sloppy.

ET stopped at the foot of the steps, looked up at the two men on the porch. "The deal is off."

The guard called Lucky said, "Huh?"

"It's off," ET barked. "Forget we ever fucking talked about it. You never heard of Frank Toole or Joey Faber or any of this shit, got it?"

"Okay." The other guard shrugged. "Joey who?"

ET rubbed his head. He seemed on the edge of panic. "Jesus fucking Christ, they're dead, man, and I mean the really, really wrong kind of dead. Joey and Frank both. It's all screwed up, bro."

"What happened?"

"You don't want to know, but we got a new boss."

"Huh?"

"And believe me, if Little Nicky ever finds out we were planning on double-crossing Big Paul for the drugs, we'll all get skinned alive, just like those two dumb shits did. How the hell

240

did I let Faber talk me into this?"

Guard number two said, "Seems to me it was your idea, my brother."

ET glared at him. The dim one called Lucky looked back and forth between the two like a stoner watching vigorous game of tennis. Lucky finally said, "So what do you want us to do?"

"We get the stuff together now," ET said. "I take it back to Nicky like nothing else went down. We keep our mouths shut. Word."

"Man that was a lot of money."

"It was a lot of dope."

"Ah, well. Shit happens."

ET said, "Let's do it."

Bone was trapped inside. They were coming. The situation was rapidly deteriorating. He looked down into the bomb shelter, considered trying to hide but feared getting trapped. Sure as hell, now they'd finally remember to lock the door. He backed into the room and placed an explosive charge behind the couch and then another near the fireplace. He put the knife in his belt and pulled his Glock as the door opened and Lucky walked in. Bone took him out with two to the chest and one to the head before the other two men had a chance to react.

The second guard was surprisingly fast. He dodged to the side and began firing one-handed through the doorway. Bone had to run like hell to stay ahead of a stream of semiautomatic fire. Meanwhile, ET made it back to the car, rolled over the hood and opened fire on the building from there.

When another man got out of the car, my friend knew he was in trouble. Bullets pounded the walls, filling the air with wood chips and plaster dust and covering the floor with broken glass. Damn it, the driver had an AK-47. Bud Stone ducked under a heavy wooden desk. The second guard peeked around the corner, fired some rounds. So Bud set off the first of the hidden

charges. Part of the ceiling came down around him.
And then the shit hit the fan.

TWENTY-FIVE

The calls began coming in at around four that morning, but my home phone was off the hook. Darlene and I both slept fitfully, waking up any time our bodies touched. We made love around five, hoping to relax and grab some sleep. Mary Kate was in the office again. Soft message tones from my cell phone kept her from getting any rest. I got up at dawn and made a pot of coffee black as a war profiteer's heart. Mary Kate passed me in the hall on her way to the bathroom. She told me the cell had been ringing. I found several messages with the same contact information. When Darlene and Mary Kate started making breakfast, I closed the office door, fired up the computer according to instructions and got in touch.

"It's about fucking time!" The panicked young man on the computer monitor seemed barely into his thirties but was already losing his hair. "Can I speak freely?"

I wasn't in the mood. "I don't know, can you?"

"Do you know who I am?"

"No, do you know me?"

"You're Mick Callahan, the radio guy. I was in the room when you first met Big Paul and Little Nicky. My name is Jacob Mandel. I have something for you."

My blood pressure dropped. "What's wrong, Jacob? What couldn't wait until morning? Did something happen to Bud?"

He dropped his voice, leaned into the screen. The effect distorted his face in a comical way, but what he said wasn't funny. "Our friend went into the lion's den, okay? And he won't be coming back."

"Are you sure about that?"

"He's dead," Mandel said. His voice cracked. "Jesus, they're all dead. It was on the news."

He droned on, explaining. Meanwhile, I shrank his face to a corner of the screen and did a search for Salt Lick, Nevada. The first reports described a gun battle at a remote ranch, with several explosions and no survivors. My eyes stung. Bud Stone had gone right at them and had run into some kind of trap. I covered by drinking some coffee. "You said you have something for me, Jacob. What is it?"

"Actually, I don't have it yet, but I will."

"Any idea what it is?" I knew, but did Mandel?

"Our friend obtained something, copied it, and was trying to put the original back when the events occurred. The copy he carried was almost certainly destroyed along with him. How long will it take you and your friends to arrive?"

"All of us?"

"Yes, all of you."

"Give us six or seven hours, I suppose. Later on today."

"I want to discuss the rest in person, Mr. Callahan, but for now, let's just say our friend also sent a package to me via UPS." He gave me the tracking number, I scribbled it down. "Now this package, it's arriving late this afternoon. I have to sign for it. My instructions are to get it to your team soon as possible and then disappear."

My blood sang opera. Bone had scored the disc. We had the upper hand at last, but at a heavy cost. "Where should we meet you?"

Mandel wiped sweat from his forehead. "I'm getting out of here, it's not safe. Let me call your cell later on. We'll meet and go to my post office box together."

"Jacob, I. . . ." Mandel signed off. I looked at the white screen and logo for a long moment, then called Jerry and Hal. Jerry was already pulling up in front of my house, and came inside during the subsequent conversation.

"Oh, my word. I am so sorry, Mick." Hal was in his hotel room, walking back and forth in front of the camera.

I drank some more coffee. "I feel sick. Bone was a good man."

"You are going, of course."

"Of course, even if it's just to keep these bastards from getting away with it. Maybe we can get the disc and ransom Brandi, if she's still alive. Hal, why can't I just go alone, grab the package and fly back? Leave everyone else out of it?"

"We both know why, Mick. You said this Mandel seemed terrified. Thus, it would be unwise to vary from the specific instructions left by Mr. Stone, because if Mandel panics for any reason and refuses to cooperate. . . ."

"Understood."

"How about my shipment, did it arrive on schedule?" Hal was now several feet from the monitor, packing his suitcase. Jerry walked in, heard the question, and grabbed the FedEx package. He held it up to our camera. Hal nodded, went back to work. "I have a flight out this afternoon. I want to be there, too."

"What? Why?"

"First, to supervise a legal team in case anything goes wrong, and I have also placed a call to good friends who live in the Las Vegas area. You may need their support."

I shook my head. "You've done enough."

"Don't argue with me, stallion."

"Listen to me, Hal. Stay away from Vegas, so that you are free to help. Besides, no offense, but you're in your sixties. You'd only get in the way."

His shoulders slumped. "I despise these rare, annoying moments when you are irrefutably correct."

Jerry examined the false IDs and plane tickets in the package and whistled. "Man, this is beautiful work, really first class."

Darlene was sitting on the couch cleaning her Glock. Her mouth was a thin, dark line. Mary Kate was in the easy chair, still a little green from seeing what had been done to Joey Faber and Frank Toole. Hell, I was pretty sure I'd have a bad dream or two about that myself, somewhere along the way.

Mary Kate sipped orange juice. "Mick, why did you tell Mandel it would take all day when we'd already made arrangements to fly out this morning?"

"I want to get there ahead of time, just to size things up."

"And we can't be absolutely sure it's okay to trust this Jacob Mandel dude." Jerry tossed his fake driver's license to one side. "All we really know about him is that he claims to speak for Mick's friend Bud. Am I right, or am I right?" He rubbed absently at his burn scar. My little buddy was nervous. I loved him for his courage and loyalty, always respected him for overcoming his fear.

I looked at my new ID. Some guy named Mark Kaplan had my size and general look, but was a resident of San Diego, California, and needed glasses to drive. The package contained fake glasses and some bogus credit cards to back up the license. "Jerry, according to Bud this Jacob Mandel guy has been working for Little Nicky and can't get loose. Bud knows his family. Mandel is in as much trouble as we are."

"Is Lopez still out of the game?" That was Darlene, speaking for the first time in several minutes. "We could use another gun."

"I don't want this to come to guns if we can avoid it," I said. My heart tightened with grief. Poor Bone. "There's been enough dying. Sure, I want revenge, but I'll settle for putting these assholes in prison for life. Maybe we don't have to kill them."

Darlene stared up at me. "You want to put them in jail, Mick? That means going through channels, and they're not going to allow us to. You know that. I say we take them on there, once and for all, or we're going down."

Hal asked, "Have we heard anything new, Darlene?"

"A little, Mr. Solomon. Vegas PD is still crawling all over that old ranch house, trying to figure out what happened last night. Like Mick said, there was a nasty firefight, and at least three large explosions. When the cops arrived they found body parts everywhere. At first glance, it appears to be several Caucasian males, and all of them are dead."

Hal found my eyes. "I'm sorry, Mick."

"So am I, Hal."

"Are you going to say anything to his wife?"

I shook my head. "California is already looking for him. Sooner or later they'll put it all together and tell her. I can't risk giving away our involvement."

"No," Hal agreed. "I guess you're right. What a terrible shame."

"He said he was going to take it to them, and it appears he died trying." I got up, leaned against the computer desk. "Now it's our turn."

Jerry coughed. "I hope you don't mean it's our turn to die trying." The joke fell flat.

Darlene snapped her weapon together. "Let's get moving."

We went to the airport, separated in the covered parking lot, and walked in like strangers for the flight to Vegas. Darlene and Mary Kate dressed up enough to pass for expensive working girls coming back from a gig in LA. Jerry carried a specially modified backpack with plastic weaponry hidden in it, and wore a cowboy hat. He went off by himself, toyed with his laptop. I came in last, wearing those phony glasses, some belly padding, and a loose Hawaiian shirt. Darlene had done a lot of undercover work in her day, and managed to scan the crowd and look casual at the same time. She quietly flashed her badge and some kind of Homeland Security ID to the woman at the counter and was allowed to keep her gun.

There was no assigned seating, so we simply staggered getting onto the plane. We carried our scant luggage by hand. The brief flight was uneventful, the attendants bored and the honey roasted peanuts stale.

When we touched down in Las Vegas and stepped off the aircraft, the savage heat knocked us backwards. I went down the metal stairs first, and into the busy terminal. The others followed, several yards behind.

As before, McCarran International sang with the jangle of slot machines, dazzled with loud carpeting and flashing lights. We walked briskly, rode the silver speedway and went directly to the upper level. We had no luggage, so we just bypassed baggage claim.

My cell phone rang. It was Mandel.

"Mr. Callahan?"

"We're on our way, Jacob. Should be boarding soon."

"There is a big bowling alley two blocks south of the Wagon Wheel. It's almost directly across from the post office. Meet me in the bar at four-thirty." He broke the connection.

Mary Kate was the only person in the group likely to still be anonymous to the Pesci crowd, so she rented the car while Darlene stood watch from a few feet away. Jerry and I went outside. Jerry stopped, leaned on a pole. I walked to the far end of the row and waited at the entrance marked for a different airline.

The women brought the car around and picked us up. We went straight to a cheap motel a few blocks from the Wagon Wheel, a black-and-white, polka-dot wooden dump called The

Rolling Dice. I went in with Darlene, Jerry with Mary Kate, and we rented adjoining rooms on the upper level. We kept the door open, turning the rooms into one small suite.

The rooms were awful but the air-conditioning felt arctic. It was wonderful. Darlene was certain we hadn't been followed. "So far, so good."

"Mandel's on top of it, anyway." Jerry had his laptop open. "ETA for the package has been pushed up a bit. Now you're looking at around four thirty-five." He checked his watch. "That's a little over an hour from now."

I looked at my friends, my sister. They all seemed tired. "Freshen up and stretch out then, guys. Get a little rest, we're probably going to need it." Mary Kate and Darlene found two cheap cardboard buckets with dice on them and left to get some ice. Jerry left his computer on, went to the sink and splashed water on his face. I took off the fake belly padding, went to the wall unit and held my shirt up to the air.

"So, we get this disc," Mary Kate said a few minutes later. She was lying on the couch with a cold rag on her forehead. "What then?"

I sipped a diet cola. "Hal is making some calls. With a little luck, he'll be able to cut some kind of a deal, find someone who can take it off our hands and get it back to the rightful owners of the information."

"I don't see how that helps you with the bad guys," Darlene said. "If anything, this Little Nicky dude is going to get even more pissed once he hears he's lost out."

"I hear you."

"So what are you planning on doing about *that* aspect of the situation?"

I shrugged, smiled. "Pray and then run like a stripe-assed ape, I suppose."

"Very funny."

Jerry called out, "One body from the shootout in Salt Lick has been identified. They say it's a guy name of Lucky Ligotti, and that he's a known associate of Big Paul Pesci."

"Big surprise, huh?" Mary Kate sat up and rubbed her feet. "Man, do I fucking hate high heels."

"Try working undercover as a hooker for a few months," Darlene said. "Gives you a new appreciation for drag queens."

"Oh, shit. Shit."

I sat up. "What, Jerry?"

"You're on the news, too, my man." He turned the computer. It was streaming a local TV station. The announcer said television and radio psychologist Mick Callahan was wanted for questioning. Something to do with the murder of a Pesci acquaintance named Sharkey Jackson. They cut to a commercial and Jerry hit MUTE. He rolled his eyes. "You ever even hear of this dude, man?"

"Nope. Okay, feedback. Why would they do this to me now?"

"Maybe they still just want you sweating bullets so you'll hustle," Darlene said, "but my guess is it's a bit more than that. They have to know Bud Stone is dead, along with their men. Could be they suspect he arranged to get something to you, and they want you in custody so you can't hook up with whoever it is Bud turned. If you're off the street, it's one less thing to worry about."

"I don't like that idea. That they're on to a traitor."

"Me, neither."

"One thing is for sure," I said, "if they had any idea it was Mandel, he wouldn't be above ground and setting up meetings."

Darlene shrugged. "Not unless this is a trap."

"Yeah," I said. "There's that."

It was pretty quiet from that point on. We left early and cruised around the block, checking out the bowling alley, the post office, and the general area. The bar had a long glass window that faced the street. We'd already discussed that Mandel would probably want to see a few people in my group, as per Bud's instructions, but there was no reason to stay clumped together in the same place. When the time came, Jerry and Mary Kate would stay in the bar, seated by the window. Darlene was armed, so she would stay in the doorway of the bowling alley. I would meet Mandel, cross the street with him, and pick up the package.

At four-twenty, I went through the bowling alley and into the cool, dark bar, again wearing the gut padding and the dumb shirt. The place was almost empty, except for a gum-chewing waitress with big hair, a young blond bartender with thick forearms who was busy drying beer mugs, and an elderly couple seated at a table counting winnings from the quarter slots. I passed them, walked to the window and sat down. Jerry and Mary Kate followed moments later and parked four tables away. As discussed, Darlene remained in the doorway, where she could see both the bar and the street. Our vehicle was parked a few yards away, and Darlene had the keys.

Jacob Mandel was prompt. He came in dressed in shorts and a green shirt, his balding head pink with sunburn. He was just a kid, shorter than I'd expected, and his eyes told me I was much larger than he'd pictured. Mandel sat down hurriedly, waved the waitress away. His arm pits were dark with sweat. "Where are the other people Bud wanted you to bring?"

"They're here, kind of blending in."

Mandel turned his head all the way around, but couldn't spot anyone out of place. "Okay, then. Ready?"

"Hang on a second, Jacob," I said calmly. "Take it easy. Do you know where you're going?"

"I know, but I'm not telling you."

"You're right, you shouldn't. I just wanted to be sure you'd made some plans. Do you need money? I have a friend helping me out, and he's got very deep pockets."

Mandel shook his head. "I've been saving up cash for months. Look, man, can we just get this over with before I crap my pants? I want to get out of town."

"One minute."

I surveyed the street. The post office seemed fairly quiet, just a customer or two coming and going. A couple of parked cars, no one sitting in them. A black rent-a-cop leaned against the wall, smoking and talking on a cell phone. A pretty red-haired woman in tight shorts and a halter waited at the bus stop, thumbing through a tourist magazine. A man was standing at the far end of the block, probably not close enough to constitute a threat. I caught Darlene's eye. She shrugged, as if to say, "I don't know, it's your call."

"Mr. Callahan? Please?"

"Okay, Jacob." I pushed away from the table, got to my feet. "Let's do this."

We went past the long, empty bar. The waitress was halfway to the ladies' room. The bartender with the immense forearms was mucking around in the cash register. He did not look up. We walked into the corridor, then the lobby. Mandel brushed past Darlene without realizing who she was, and I didn't bother to enlighten him. He went through the front door. I waited a moment and followed.

We went out into the afternoon heat. No one outside had moved more than a foot or two either direction. *Why not?* A tiny alarm went off in my gut, but Mandel was walking briskly, head down, arms pumping, and quickly entered the post office. I crossed the steaming black asphalt and went up the small staircase. I shaded my eyes, peered in through the glass door. Mandel was inside, at the counter. There was one man in front of him, an Asian in his thirties who turned almost immediately and came my way. I stepped to the side and allowed him to exit the building. He had some letters in his back pocket and did not look up or back once he'd passed.

Mandel paused in the lobby. I went inside to join him there, my body shielding us from the street. He was carefully opening the FedEx envelope.

"What's wrong?"

"Just take the damned thing, all right?" Mandel slid the disc out of the red, white, and blue envelope and handed it to me. I put it in the front pocket of my pants. Mandel pushed by me, still holding the empty envelope. He was wide-eyed, drenched with sweat. "I'm out of this, all right? Now just leave me the fuck alone."

He went through the glass doors, into the street and down two of the steps. He stopped for a moment, still toying with the envelope. I opened the glass door and started back across the street for the bowling alley. Behind me, Mandel looked around, spotted one of the mesh metal trash cans and went that way. What happened next happened faster than I would have believed possible.

First, everything went quiet. The pretty woman in shorts and a halter top trotted up the steps, large breasts bouncing joyfully. She smiled brightly at Jacob Mandel, produced a small automatic with a silencer on the end, pressed it to his forehead and blew his brains out all over the hot pavement. Mandel threw his arms up and dropped like a stone. The woman caught the flying FedEx envelope in her free hand, spun to face me. The gun inched up but I was already running. I could just see the black security guard out of the corner of my eye. He was raising another silenced weapon. I saw the large round cylinder on the end and small sparks appeared. I heard something that sounded like popcorn in a microwave.

I varied my pace and direction but always moved forward.

Now the noise exploded. I could see Darlene in the doorway, pressed against the wall as she returned fire. Bullets dug a neat row of divots in the sidewalk near her position. She shifted her attention up and over my left shoulder. Something nicked my cheek. I dove for the lobby and rolled over onto my back. A man in a construction hat was on the roof of the building next to the post office with a silenced rifle. The world was louder now, the popcorn sound and some booms; people screaming, glass shattering. I turned my head just in time to watch a row of bullets zero in on Jerry, who clutched his laptop computer. A bullet caught him in the shoulder. Blood splattered and pulsed. Jerry went over backwards. He hit the floor hard. I crawled his way, but another shot from the rifle drove me back.

I went flat on the floor, peered out and tried to check on Jerry's condition. That's when I noticed Mary Kate. The big bartender had her by the neck. She was kicking and screaming as he dragged her out the back door. I wanted to follow, but suddenly the two old people I'd taken for gamblers pulled weapons. They fired just as the shooters across the street began to retreat. I barely made it back behind the wall. Darlene was reloading by then. She saw my expression but was pinned down for a few precious seconds. Finally, she put just her hand and gun around the pillar and fired several rounds. The old people vanished out the back. The world quieted down. We heard them lock the big security door and then the squeal of tires.

The wail of police sirens in the distance. People shouting, wondering what was going on. Darlene and I locked eyes. "Did you get it?"

I nodded. We ducked low and went after Jerry. He'd taken a bullet high on the right shoulder. Darlene ripped his shirt apart, used scraps to stuff the wound.

"Ah, hell," Jerry said. "That hurts."

I looked at the locked back door, still thinking of Mary Kate.

Darlene shook her head. "No, Mick. Let's get him in the car."

Darlene was right and I knew it. We each took an arm and dragged Jerry out of the building, got him into the back of the car. "Give me the disc, Mick," Jerry said through clenched teeth. I slipped it from my pocket, checked the seeping wound. The improvised bandage was holding.

"Let's go!" I rolled over into shotgun position on the front seat. Darlene got into the driver's seat and we sped away. She cut down one alley, then another, and finally went straight onto the highway as if intending to head back to Los Angeles. I was already on the cell phone to Hal and told him we'd been ambushed.

"You can't go back to those rooms," Hal said quietly. "I just got a tip through Larry Donato via your friend Dave Lopez. Your identity was just compromised by someone who recognized you from your days on television."

"So much for the clever disguise."

"How's Jerry, son?"

I looked over my shoulder. My little buddy had the laptop open and was typing feverishly. His shoulder was bleeding a bit, but certainly not gushing. "He's going to be okay, but we'll need someone to clean and bandage the wound and score some pain meds."

"The friends I told you about. I'm calling now. They will help."

"Thanks, we'll need them." I turned back to Jerry. "What about the contents of the disc?"

"It's encoded, but your friend Mr. Stone did some of the work already," Jerry said. That puzzled me. Bud Stone wasn't an expert in computer science, at least as far as I knew. Jerry managed to chuckle. "Damn, there's even some operational stuff Mandel must have stolen from The Valley of Fire resort."

I remembered the back of Mandel's head vanishing into pink

mist and my stomach rolled over. "Damn it, Jacob was just a scared kid but they killed him. And now they've got Mary Kate."

"Yes," Hal said, "but you have the disc."

Darlene squealed around one turn in the highway that temporarily shielded our location. "Hold on."

We braced ourselves. Darlene skidded down an embankment and into a gully filled with brush. We bounced and heaved to and fro. I dropped the cell phone. We rolled to a stop in two feet of water at the bottom of a cement wash. By the time the slow traffic behind us had caught up again, we were completely hidden from view. It was as if we had vanished on our way back to LA.

Darlene sat back, exhausted. She had a small cut under one eye. I found a tissue, pressed it, put her fingers there. I recovered the phone. Jerry kept working, fingers clacking on keys.

"Hal? Can you find us a safe place to hide?"

"I'm working on that, too. Are you okay for now?"

"It appears that way."

"Then hang on. I'll get back to you in a couple of minutes."

I closed the phone. We watched shadows crawl across cement; cool darkness approached with the paws of a black cat.

"Damn," Jerry said. He stopped working for a moment. "You know what? This really hurts."

"I'll bet. Can you hang in there?"

"Yeah. Oh, I get it." Jerry was typing again, had already moved on. He paused to turn on a small light located above the screen and went back to work, the discomfort temporarily forgotten.

Soon it was dark. I was still trembling from adrenaline. Darlene held my hand. Hers was shaking, too. "Now what?"

"Now, bingo," Jerry said triumphantly. And then, as if in awe: "Holy shit."

"What?"

I looked back. Numbers and symbols were crawling slowly up the small laptop screen, their greenish reflections lighting up Jerry's blood-streaked features. I got Hal back on the line, held the phone up so he could hear.

"Guys," Jerry said, "what we have here is a list of sums paid to politicians in the United States and England by various Defense Department contractors in Iraq and Afghanistan. There must be two dozen different companies, and at least two billion dollars' worth of bribes."

I blew out some air. "Jesus."

"There's more," Jerry said. "This is the Oil for Food Scandal times two. It's got the private bank accounts of several world leaders, including a few key folks in Washington. Man, no wonder people would kill for this."

Darlene squeezed my hand. Our eyes met in the gloom. I brought the phone back to my ear. "This is far too explosive for us to broker," Hal said quietly. "My people won't touch it. Still, you can't give it back to Little Nicky and the mob, Mick. You know that, right?"

Not even for Mary Kate?

My cell phone throbbed. I had an incoming call. "Hal, hold on."

"Mr. Callahan?" My gut clenched. It was Nikolaou Argetoianu. "You will pardon the intrusion, yes? One of my people grabbed Jacob's phone before leaving the scene, so I took the liberty of using it to get in touch. You can imagine my irritation when the envelope returned to me was found to be empty."

I let Darlene listen in. Jerry went quiet in the backseat. The only light was the green cast by the computer screen. "Yeah," I said dryly, "and I'll bet that just about chapped your ass."

"Such colorful cowboy language." Little Nicky covered the phone, barked an order. I heard a muffled scream. "Someone wants to say hello."

Mary Kate. She was sobbing in pain. "Mick, oh God, Mick, give it to him, please just give it to him, Mick they hurt me. They really hurt me."

I wanted to vomit. Darlene began to reload her Glock. Little Nicky came back on the line. "Mary Kate has confessed to being your half sister. How charming that you finally met. You must tell me all about this."

"What do you and Pesci want, Nicky? A trade?"

"Just so." Another scream from Mary Kate. "What will be left of your sister for the disc? We both know the money and drugs burned up with your friend Mr. Stone."

"Easy. I'll meet you."

"Good. Naturally, we know you are still in the area because, as I am sure you already suspect, we are tracking your phone. Thus, you will soon use another. Let's just spare ourselves more drama. It will be so much better for everyone concerned to settle things quietly."

Jerry made hand motions indicating he'd find a way to block Nicky from locating our position. I closed my eyes. "Go on."

"Please listen carefully, Mr. Callahan. May I call you Mick?"

"Certainly, since we're getting to be really good friends now, and all."

"The disc is encrypted."

"We figured as much. So?"

"If you attempt to examine the contents of that disc, or to copy them, you will leave behind a record of having tampered with it. If my people discover such evidence, your sister will be executed immediately, and all of you will be hunted to the ends of the earth."

I looked back at Jerry. My eyes questioned him again. My pal smiled weakly, shook his head, mouthed something about "him and the horse he rode in on," and went back to work. Jerry wasn't concerned about leaving electronic fingerprints.

I sighed. "Understood."

Little Nicky said, "So, come and see me, all three of you, yes?"

"All two of us. My friend got shot back at the Post Office." I let my voice disintegrate. It wasn't hard. I was worried about MK. "Jerry is dead."

"Good. That will lessen your temptation to explore that which you should not. Please, come have a drink with me, Mr. Callahan, you and the lovely Sergeant Hernandez. The Valley of Fire should provide you the comfort of a crowd. I'll give you two hours."

TWENTY-SIX

Ten minutes later, with Hal directing us, we took several winding back roads and finally arrived at an isolated ranch-style house located out near the dam. A retired couple named Baxter lived there. They were expecting us. Dr. Baxter met us in the driveway, helped me get Jerry out of the car and took him right into their bedroom. The old man produced an old-style black bag. I tried to thank him, but he waved me away. "Hal Solomon took some heat for me thirty years ago," Baxter said. "I owe him. We'll look after your friend. You go do what you have to do." In a matter of minutes, Jerry was lightly sedated and heavily bandaged.

Darlene and I got ready to go. Jerry sat up straight, the laptop now plugged into the wall socket. "I have my cell right here, Mick. I made a copy of all the information on Valley of Fire. Hell, I can get into their computer system with this stuff. If you need my help, just call."

I paused in the doorway. "Jerry, are you sure they won't be able to tell they've been hacked?"

"Yeah. Piece of cake, my man." Jerry winced, touched his shoulder. He seemed so small, but so brave, like a little boy facing surgery. My heart cracked for him. I looked at Darlene, the determined set of her features. She had changed into another dress and borrowed a blonde wig from Mrs. Baxter. Years of undercover work were paying off. Darlene looked like a different woman. True friends. I was a very lucky man.

Jerry handed me the disc. "It's got timed worms on it now," he said. "They'll spot the first one. If you think you're going to escape safely, give them the password Lednam1, that is 1Mandel backwards. The screen will flash an okay, and Nicky will think he's in the clear." Jerry was tired and the pain had obviously begun to gnaw at him.

"However?"

"However, there's a second worm. I made it untraceable and nasty. Everything will seem to check out, but there are tiny errors that will take a while to show up, and within forty-eight hours the rest of that data will start breaking down, too. And if they screw around trying to stop my second virus, it will immediately spread out beyond the file and crash their entire system."

"Great job." I put the disc in my pocket again. "If we do make it out of there, and he passes the files along, Nicky's customers will probably think he tried to pull a fast one on them."

"That's the idea, anyway. Mick, you know he's going to kill you, right?"

I sat down on the bed. "Maybe not, Jerry. He's already got the cops after me, and a lot of underworld types thinking I deserve a bullet in the head. Why not let someone else take me out? He's the type that might enjoy watching me run."

"Ever the optimist." He picked up my cell phone, double-checked some clever modifications, and tossed it to me. I put it in my pants pocket. It made an odd bulge because he'd jammed it so that it was stuck partway open.

Jerry said, "Watch yourself."

"Always."

Darlene checked her watch. She had her Glock cleaned and reloaded and a backup .38 strapped to her ankle. She straightened the tight dress and checked herself in the mirror.

"Wow," I said. "A thousand a night, minimum."

Darlene flipped me off. "Okay, let's move."

Dr. Baxter saw us out and locked the door behind us. I drove this time. We went out the back roads again, caught Highway 15 and went north and east. The night sky was magnificent, packed with stars and lit by a moon that hovered like a bright, white balloon. The route took us along the edge of the wildlife preserve, and then into the low mountains. Darlene held my hand for a while before closing her eyes to grab some rest. I let her sleep.

It was a long drive. I was about to call Nicky via redial to double-check directions when we came around a long, wide turn. Suddenly I could see down into the Valley of Fire. I turned the lights off and coasted closer without giving our presence away.

Big Paul Pesci's creation simply dominated the mountain out of which it had been carved. It was more a creature than a building. Tall glass panels reflected and refracted light that seemed to dance like a towering flame. The part of the resort that had been completed flowed from the rock face like a huge horseshoe of color, with the glass-fronted lobby in the far center and twenty floors of rooms on either side. From the top of the hill I could see that the casinos were also on the left and right, set away from the parking lot; rows of empty gaming tables and sparkling slot machines. I squinted as I looked down. We coasted silently around a corner and back into the shadowy dark. I stopped the car.

"Nobody's there." My own voice startled me.

"What?" Darlene sat up and rubbed her eyes.

"It must not be officially open until tomorrow, Darlene. There's nobody here. It's another trap."

"Let me out, Mick, and don't go any closer until I've had some lead time."

262

I kissed her. "I love you."

Her eyes widened. "Why, Mick Callahan, did you really say that or am I imagining things?"

"You're hallucinating from stress."

Darlene kissed me back. "See you soon." She slid out of the passenger seat and into the warm night air. She was wearing tennis shoes and holding the high heels in one hand. She vanished into the gloom.

I waited by myself for a good five minutes, then flicked the headlights on, started down the driveway. A few minutes later I came into view. I drove to within twenty yards of the building and stopped, acutely aware that I was fully exposed. The absence of customers meant there would be no witnesses to my fate. My cell phone rang. I wiped my hands on my jeans and answered.

"Who told you it was satisfactory to come alone?"

"Take it or leave it, asshole."

"Ah, such colorful language. Welcome back to my casino, Mr. Callahan. Mick. Please get out of the car slowly, with your hands in plain sight."

"I think I'll just sit right here for a minute, thank you."

"You perhaps remember the sniper who gave you so much trouble this afternoon? Well, he has you in his sights this very moment. Exit the car, please."

"Looks like you have the upper hand." I slid out, but kept the car door between my body and the building. "Fortunately, I took a few precautions of my own."

Several seconds passed before Nicky answered. "And those would be?"

"Don't worry, Nicky, I have what you want."

"Please approach the lobby. We'll talk when you get here."

I closed the phone partway again, dropped it into the pocket of my jeans and walked across the asphalt. I kept my arms away from my body, palms forward. When I reached the bottom of the front steps, Cowboy stepped out of the shadows holding a silenced 9mm casually, barrel down. "Howdy, Callahan. You bored yet?"

"Eric." I stopped, lifted my shirt, turned around. "I'm not armed."

"I believe you, but I'll still have to pat you down." He set the gun down on the pavement, closed the distance and checked me out. He examined the disc and took a quick look at my cell phone, noticed it was slightly open, but put both back in my pocket without comment. He backed up, retrieved his weapon. "Let's go."

Cowboy followed me inside but stayed a few yards behind. The lobby was bright with light, green with tall ferns and moist from two fish ponds fed by waterfalls located on each side. Gold-plated elevators drew my eye to the far center. This time I noticed the see-through swimming pools located on the floor above, and one above that, probably going all the way to the top. The mix of water and light added to the always swirling colors. It was a stunning, if gaudy design.

Little Nicky exited from the elevators, dressed in slacks and a silk shirt open to his hairy chest. The thug called Clyde was with him, but remained behind to hold the door open. There was no one else in the lobby. I crossed the loud carpet in silence, my stomach tight with anticipation. I had forgotten how big Little Nicky was. We met in the middle of the room.

"We can go in there," Nicky said. He slapped me on the back. I almost fell down. He led me past the deserted reception desk, through wooden doors and into a spacious office complex hidden behind the plants. Cowboy waited outside.

"What's this, the hotel office?"

"Hotel *and* casino," Nicky replied. "The mainframe is here." He gestured. One of the computers had an oversized monitor showing a screen saver with rapidly shifting colored tubes. "You know, I really don't understand why you came alone, Mick. I'm not going to harm your friends, so long as you brought me the goods."

"I'd rather be safe than sorry." I took the disc out of my pocket. Nicky sat down and popped it in the machine. I remained standing. "You're going to see it's been tampered with. Call that my insurance policy."

Nicky lowered his head. "I am so disappointed to hear that." One big leg lashed out and the foot caught me in the stomach. I doubled over and dropped to my knees, out of air and hurting. The bastard kicked like a mule on loco weed. "Explain this to me immediately."

I couldn't talk yet, waved my palm for time. Caught my breath again and explained, "There's a worm in the file, and now it's in your computer system. When Mary Kate and I are out of here, I'll give you the password to dissolve it."

I made it to my feet, slowly rubbed my stomach. My vision had turned red. I wanted to stay calm, but my stepfather, Danny, was crouching in the back of my mind, gibbering, *you gonna let him get away with that? Shit, the bigger they are the harder they fall. . . .*

Nicky glowered, then began to chuckle. "You know, I don't even need to kill you, Callahan. You already have trouble coming at you from every direction at this point, the police and the mob. Soon my colleagues in Europe will also want to exact revenge."

I cocked my head. "You want to repeat that last part again?"

"Eric!"

Cowboy came into the room with his gun raised. Clyde was right behind, and he had MK with him. She was gagged and her hands were bound with plastic cop ties. She'd been beaten. Her lips were swollen and her left eye was closed and blue. Clyde pushed Mary Kate toward me. I caught my sister and

Harry Shannon

held her up. Now Cowboy and Clyde were all business. They spread out to either side of the office doorway to keep me covered. The rage was building, partly in response to the fear. My heart was thudding and my muscles felt engorged.

Nicky stepped away from the computer. "If I let you walk, you won't last a week. The cops want you for questioning, but our men on the inside will make sure you never make it out of the jail. You see, I just issued an executive order on behalf of Big Paul, who has, shall we say, taken an extended leave of absence. It's a hit on you and all your friends. The reward is two million, five hundred thousand a head."

Something worked behind Clyde's dim eyes. He wanted that money. I looked over at Cowboy, couldn't read him. Nicky stepped closer to me, but was too smart to give me an opening. "And as for my colleagues, once you have given me the password, I will tell them you ran off with the disc and intend to sell it on the open market. They would rather have the information destroyed than used against them, I can assure you. They will find and kill you all, Mr. Callahan, sooner or later. I would enjoy hearing about that."

"So let us go."

Nicky sighed. "Unfortunately, Ms. Hernandez is not here. Left to your own devices, and with her assistance, you are intelligent enough to approach the US government. And that I cannot allow. Now, give me the password."

"No."

Nicky produced a small handgun. He aimed it at Mary Kate's leg. "I will ask you one more time, and then I will shoot your sister in the foot, then ask you one more time before I wound the other foot. I will follow with her hands, elbows, and so on."

Mary Kate trembled against me. I gently undid her gag. "The password is Mandel's name backwards, plus the number one."

Nicky backed up, made sure Cowboy and Clyde were cover-

266

ing me and sat down at the computer. He typed for a moment. Satisfied, he rolled the chair back and got to his feet. "Kill them."

Cowboy motioned with his gun. "Sorry, bro, nothing personal. Let's take it outside, shall we? It's such a nice night."

"I want Hernandez hunted down, too," Nicky said. "She can't have gone far. Make sure you pick her up."

Cowboy nodded. "Will do. Clyde, watch the girl." He backed away from me, gripped his weapon in both hands and followed me, targeting dead center. All very professional. Clyde moved closer to Mary Kate. He wasn't as competent, but then she was too confused and hurt to pose much of a threat.

I stopped in the doorway to stare at Nicky. "By the way, don't sleep," I said, smiling. "And don't ever turn your back on anyone."

His eye twitched. "Excuse me?"

Clyde did as I'd hoped. He pushed Mary Kate past me and into the lobby. I knew Cowboy expected me to make a move soon. All I could do was hope he wasn't a great shot. Not much of a hope. I risked a look his way. Cowboy shook his head. "I wouldn't, if I were you."

I smiled again. "You're not me." I raised my voice. "Jerry? Do it."

A fire alarm blared directly overhead. Cowboy jumped back and looked up just as the overhead sprinklers came on, drenching us all. I could see Mary Kate through the open wooden door. She thrilled me by giving Clyde an elbow to the throat. His gun went flying into the ferns. Clyde went purple and sat down hard. I hit Cowboy low. The gun went off twice near my ear, but it was silenced, so the noise was not too bad. We sailed over the top of a desk covered with charts and blueprints and smashed into the carpet with me on top. We fought for the gun. My skin crawled because I knew Nicky was right behind us, looking for a shot. I rolled under Cowboy just in time. Nicky fired and Cowboy's eyes went wide. He said, "Ah, shit," and went limp.

I yanked his weapon away and fired back, driving Little Nicky further into the office. I had a gun and for once was glad of it. The air was thick with water and it was difficult to see. I slid out from under Cowboy, checked him quickly. He'd taken a round in the lower back, but it was to one side and mostly a flesh wound. He stared up at me dully, but oddly without rancor. I made sure he had no backup pistol and then went after Nicky. Two muzzle flashes drove me back to the wooden doors. I took the cell out of my pocket. The modified screen stayed dark, even though it was on and connected.

"Jerry, turn everything off."

The alarm stopped, the water dried up, and the room went black. I edged back out into the lobby, clothes soaked, shoes squeaking. "Not the lights. Leave them on."

After a moment, the room brightened up. They were over by the fish pond. Clyde was still clutching his neck, while Mary Kate covered him with his own gun. One eye was still closed, but the other radiated hostility.

"You okay?"

MK nodded. "I've got your new nickname," she said. "From now on, I'm going to call you Hero."

"If I live, I'll deserve it. Stay here, I'm going after Nicky. If he gets away, this will never be over."

I went back into the office. Stayed low by one of the desks. Cowboy was still flat, clutching a dark red stain low and to the side. I whispered, "Jerry, is there a back door out of the mainframe office?"

"Negative, not now. There are two fire doors, but I just locked them tight."

"Way to go. You have the cops on the way?"

"ETA twelve minutes, maybe sooner if the Highway Patrol can get loose from a big pileup on the 15."

"Okay. Here we go. Wish me luck."

I risked a peek over the desk. A huge sliver of wood nicked my cheek as Nicky fired again. *That little gun can't hold many more bullets,* Daddy Danny said from his little corner of my mind. *Make him use them . . . and then shove it up his ass.*

I fired back and ran along bent over, using the row of desks as cover. Nicky fired again and then again. I squatted near a long row of cubicles. "Jerry, the lights at the far east quadrant of the mainframe office? Shut them down." A moment later, all of the lights behind and around me went dark. Nicky, on the other hand, was illuminated. I could see his shadow on the wall near the fire door. I squinted, fired, trying to angle a ricochet off the metal door. Nicky yelped and fired back from reflex. That's when I heard the click I'd been waiting for. He was out of ammunition.

I left the gun and cell phone on the carpet and ran like hell down the row of desks. When Nicky raised his head I was sliding over the top of one and slammed into him at chest level. The force of that blow drove him back into the metal fire door and the locked bar struck him right in the kidneys. Nicky moaned in my ear. I grunted in satisfaction and began tearing at his face with my nails. I think he expected me to fight fair, try to punch him, but I wanted to rip his eyes out. I bit down on his nose and blood spurted. Nicky got his hands up enough to shove me away. This time it was my turn to take one in the lower back. The desk caught it and knocked the wind out of me.

Little Nicky towered above, nose bloody and eyes wild. He slammed a fist into my skull with enough force to make the world spin—and also maybe break a bone or two in his right hand. This man wasn't used to street brawling. I saw his look of anguished surprise, grabbed that fist in both my hands and slammed it down onto the wooden desk. Then I hit his nose again with the flat of my palm. His eyes filled with tears. Nicky may as well have been blind. I let him have it, kicked down into the side of his knee until he dropped to the carpet. Kicked him in the head and sent him over into a metal trash can. Kicked him in the bloody face once he was down. Again. Then I stopped because I knew I'd kill him if I didn't control myself.

"Mick?"

I looked up to see Darlene in the doorway. She had a bead on Clyde. Mary Kate was at the fountain, throwing cold water on her face.

"Hey," she said, "you about wrapped up in there?"

It was over. I walked back to the cell phone and just then someone burst into the lobby shouting. Darlene said something about being on the job. A cop drew down on me, and I finally made out the words.

"Freeze, motherfucker! Police!"

"Easy." I raised my arms. "I'm not armed. The main guy you want is over there on the carpet."

"Stand where you are or we will shoot you down."

Salt-and-pepper cops, one black and one white. They were the small-town variety; young and scared, therefore doubly dangerous. I kept my hands up and waited. I checked on the whereabouts of my cell phone. It was still a few yards away but that was close enough. I could see Mary Kate in the doorway, standing with Darlene. They waved. A second pair of cops had disarmed the two women and cuffed Clyde. There was no sign of Cowboy, and that bothered me.

"Careful," I called. "There's another one."

"Shut up and stand still." The black cop reached Little Nicky and bent over. He jumped back. "Christ, that's Big Paul's number-two guy."

"Damn."

"Oh, man."

"Okay. What the fuck should we do now?"

The white cop thought furiously. He called to the two in the lobby. "Rick, Eddie, listen up. Take the cuffs off that dude and get out of here."

"Say what?" A young cop with glasses stood in the doorway.

"Just do it."

"Okay, okay, but then what about the women?"

"Not your problem."

"Guys," I said, "don't do this."

The white cop jogged to my gun and the cell, thought the phone was off and left it on the carpet. He kept me covered and brought the 9mm back. Checked to see if there were any rounds left, tossed the gun to the black cop. "Give that to Nicky. We're going to retreat four miles and come back fresh, after they've worked things out. Believe me you don't want any part of this shit."

Nicky was on his feet, but bent over slightly. Blood was dripping from his shattered nose. He fixed me with a predator's glare and picked up the gun. I knew I was a dead man. Nicky raised the weapon. The black cop caught his arm. "No offense, but wait until we're out of here, okay? We're doing you a solid, so give us some slack."

"For God's sake," Darlene shouted, "you're cops. You can't just turn us over to these people and leave!"

Nicky nodded to the local lawmen, forced a smile. "Go. We'll make this worth your while."

The cops covered me as they backed out the door. Nicky smiled through flattened lips. Clyde had Darlene and Mary Kate covered again. *Oh, man.* We were seriously screwed. To top matters off, the cops made it out of the casino even faster than they had arrived. No time to think.

"Nice trick," Nicky said. He stumbled toward me, the gun centered on my chest. "Your cell phone, I assume?"

I didn't answer. "I don't suppose you'd want to put that gun down and settle this like men."

Nicky sneered. "That is a tempting thought, my friend, but I am more interested in winning than playing fair. Prepare. I am going to kill your woman and your sister in front of you, one at a time, and then shoot you in the head."

I heard a BANG from the lobby. Nicky and I turned at the same time. Clyde was sliding down the doorjamb with part of his face missing. Darlene was scrambling for his gun. Mary Kate was screaming. I ducked again and took off. Nicky knew he was low on ammunition. He followed me, but was reluctant to waste fire and end up having to get physical with me again.

A man's voice, unfamiliar: "Back up, back the fuck up."

What the hell is this, an Elk's Club convention? I came to the end of the row. Cowboy was not where I'd left him. There was a trail of blood smeared across the carpet. It led into some potted plants near the doorway. I risked a look over the top of the desk. Mary Kate's ex-boyfriend, Ed Talbot, stood four feet from the doorway. He was amped up, waving a .357 around like a kid in a rap video. Talbot had shot Clyde and was now ordering Darlene to stay back. I looked back over my shoulder. Nicky would be on me in no time. If I ran for cover, I'd be on top of Cowboy. If I stayed here, Nicky would blow me away. If I stood up, Talbot might do it for him.

"I'm coming out."

I got up slowly, arms high. Talbot spun around and for a second I thought I was toast. He was definitely on crystal meth, pasty faced, twitching and jerking and grinning like a sagging Halloween pumpkin. "We want the money and the dope, man. The money and the dope, okay? Just give us the money and the dope and we're square."

Mary Kate was pacing around, hugging herself, exhausted and also clearly embarrassed. I could read her body language from half a room away. "Ed, not these two. They're our friends. Just look out for the big guy."

Talbot blinked wildly. The gun swung to and fro. "Big guy?"

Oh, shit, he didn't even notice Nicky. It finally registered that MK must have said something to Talbot. I'd been double-crossed by my own sister. They'd made plans along the way, intending to score both the money and the drugs. Mary Kate would have rationalized it, justified things in her mind. After all, Mick only wants that disc. Why not call Ed and grab a hundred and fifty grand in cash and some premium dope to unload? Leave town and get a new start somewhere?

"Ed," my sister said urgently. "Give my brother the gun. Hand it to Mick. Trust me on this."

I shook my head sadly. "MK?"

She looked away. "I'm sorry, Hero. Guess I'm just a fuckup."

By now I could feel Nicky behind me. He was low on ammo, but this new guy was armed and just as capable of killing us, thus temporarily posing a bigger threat. I started to bring my hands down and move closer. Ed Talbot whirled and aimed at me. The floor seemed to drop away. A .357 has a damned big barrel when you're looking right down it.

"Ed," I said as calmly as possible, "you'd best let me walk over there."

Mary Kate stopped pacing. Her eyes narrowed. Something came over her. She charged Ed from behind, ignored the gun and attacked, kicking and screaming. Ed, enraged, fired once into the floor by accident. The noise seemed to startle him sober. He caught himself and brought the gun up. My sister froze and fell backwards onto the floor. Ed snarled, aimed. He was clearly going to shoot MK first, then me. . . .

Nicky arrived, and reacted without thinking. He fired. The

shot took Ed in the throat. Talbot dropped like a stone, grunting and wheezing. Blood went up and to the side in a fountain and the now slippery .357 skidded right towards me. I scrambled for the gun, ignoring the gore and the man now dying maybe five feet away. Meanwhile, Darlene was making a move for Clyde's weapon. Nicky fired again, just missing her, and she skidded away on her butt. MK went flat and covered her ears. She couldn't stop staring at what was left of Ed Talbot. She began to scream. Darlene rolled behind the fish pond for cover. Meanwhile, the pool of blood on the floor steadily widened.

I got the .357, rolled onto my back, and shot twice at where I expected Nicky to be. My ears rang. I blinked. Nobody was there. My hands were shaking. How many bullets had been fired from this gun, three? That left three in the chamber. No sign of Nicky. I swallowed and edged backwards through the muck, trying to get closer to Darlene and Mary Kate. The room felt like a combat zone. The air stank of gore and cordite. I made it to the doorway. Clyde's gun was in the middle of the lobby, several yards from Darlene.

"Get the gun," I called. "I'll cover you."

"Naw, I wouldn't move if I were you, lady," Cowboy said. His voice sounded hoarse. He shifted position so I could spot him. He was on his feet, in the potted plants, and now had an angle on Darlene. "Hey, Callahan, why don't you put that gun down so we can all have us a little talk?"

Little Nicky came out of the row of cubicles. "Yes, put it down now, Mr. Callahan, or Eric will shoot your woman. Come on, you're a proven survivor, why not buy some time?"

"No, Mick," Darlene said. "Don't give up your weapon."

I froze. My head pivoted back and forth between Cowboy, MK, Darlene, and finally, Nicky. With luck, Jerry was still listening. He had control of the computers that ran the entire complex. Jerry would be the U.S. Calvary, come to the rescue. He'd think of something. I dropped the weapon and stepped toward Cowboy. Nicky was a lot more pissed off at me than Eric. Or so I hoped.

Nicky smiled, held up my cell phone. He'd crushed and shattered it. There would be no calvary. "Now we finish it, Callahan. Yes?"

"Yes," Cowboy said, "now we finish it. It's your turn to disarm, Mr. Argetoianu. Just set it down on the carpet, if you please."

Nicky said, "What?"

Cowboy took aim at his head. Stunned, Nicky did as he was told.

I heard fresh movement in the lobby. A row of military types entered the building, true boots on the ground; brisk, efficient men issuing orders in low tones. Darlene sat up grinning. She flashed me an okay sign. Mary Kate had stopped screaming and was now crying instead. She stayed flat on the floor. I smiled at Eric, shook my head.

"Yeah, I kind of wondered about you from the start, Cowboy."

"He shot Ed," MK sobbed, "poor Ed." After a moment, "Are you okay, Mick?"

Several of the men in SWAT-style black entered the computer room, but now I could see that their uniforms had been stripped of all insignia. These guys were Black Ops for sure. Two of them flanked Nicky. They kept him covered, stood casually, as if awaiting orders.

Cowboy sighed. He lowered his weapon, slid down the wall. "Will somebody get me a fucking medic?" The crowd of men parted and their leader stepped into view. He was smiling.

"Hey, Bone." I sat down on the floor, too. Bud was amused that I wasn't surprised to see him alive.

"How goes it, Mick?"

Darlene looked puzzled. Mary Kate pulled herself together. Bud Stone, also in Ops black, knelt next to me. He dropped a big paw on my shoulder. "You done good, Callahan."

"I don't know whether to hug you or beat the shit out of you," I said. "Tell you one thing, you have a ton of explaining to do."

"Don't I know it," Bone said. "Look, we were trying to get here sooner, but the local cops were flat bought and paid for. They blocked the road and wouldn't move. We didn't want to start a firefight, and they wouldn't budge. Finally, my boss got some big, swinging dick in Washington to order them out of the way."

The medics appeared. They began to attend to MK, Darlene, Cowboy, and even Nicky. As for me, I waved them off. After all, most of the blood on my clothes had come from other people.

Mary Kate quieted down, stared at me, tears running down her face. "I'm so sorry, Hero. I'm so sorry."

I looked away. *We are what we are.* All the while, some guys in white canvas and plastic masks moved things around, cleaned up gore, and generally messed with the crime scene. Someone had given them specific instructions and they were out to make this look the way the brass wanted it to look. The covert soldiers were rushing everywhere; a few guys in street clothes, too, but they were all military nonetheless. It takes one to know one.

I wanted some answers. "You never left Special Ops, did you, Bone?"

A bad Pacino. "Just when I think I'm out, they pull me back in."

"Does the wife know?"

"Wendy? Oh, hell, no. I think she suspects, but they won't let me fess up all the way. And believe me, that part of it really sucks."

"Okay, I figure the information on this damned disc was too

hot for regular channels. If it fell into the hands of the real cops or the FBI or the press, all hell would break loose."

Bud Stone nodded. "You got that right. By the way, you don't look too shocked. How long have you known?"

"I finally got ahead of the curve this morning, when Mandel said you were trying to sneak back in to replace the disc with a phony. That tipped me off. Well, and the size of the explosions at the ranch. Sounded like professional grade. I didn't want to say too much to the others, in case one of them got captured and interrogated. Need to know, and all that."

"You always were a smart one."

"I told Darlene some of it, and had Jerry install a double worm on the most sensitive material. In case you're wondering, we're not putting anything right again until every single wrinkle that affects us has been straightened out. Screw us over, you've got nothing."

"I hear you," Bud said. "We'll take care of it all; the mob, the law, everything. You know, Callahan, you're still pretty damned good." He placed a hand on his heart. "Sincere offer. My boss says you can come and work for us any time you want."

"You can tell your boss to fuck off."

"Tell her yourself," Bone said. He smiled brightly. "She's mean as a fucking snake and flat scares the crap out of me. Anyway, you want something cold to drink? Let's get you patched up."

I tugged his sleeve. "Sit your ass down for a second and explain. So, you needed a beard, somebody who could do some of the legwork, somebody the bad guys would know didn't work for the DEA or CIA or whatever acronym currently covers what you do. Maybe everybody wanted into this for their own reasons, but me, I wouldn't care. I'd just want to help out a friend."

"Right you are."

"You told your boss about me. That I owed you big-time."

"Yeah, but not anymore, bro. We're even." Bone fixed me with a sincere look. "I never meant for you to get in this deep, Mick. I swear. It all just kind of got out of control."

I looked back toward the lobby. A young woman now sat with Mary Kate, consoling her. She wore a uniform, had blonde hair tied back in a ponytail. She looked kind of familiar. Then I remembered her face. It was Brandi DeLillo.

"Damn. So Brandi there was one of yours all along. That was just about having an excuse to get me into this situation."

"No, not exactly," Bone said. "Now you're overestimating your importance. Like I said, I never meant for you to get all that involved. It's like this. We planted Eric undercover more than a year ago. It was Nicky's people who first bought themselves a double agent and scored the disc. Next we heard they were trying to skull out a way to sell the material without exposing their own people. Well, what's left of the Vegas mob went for the deal. Now, we all knew from Eric that Pesci had toyed with making a personal move on the disc while it was in transit through Gordo. So it was Eric who went to Pesci and suggested the bullshit deal with Faber and Toole and using me as the fall guy."

I nodded. "In other words, he pointed all of them your way, so you'd be able to get the disc, change the contents any way you wanted, and put a phony back in the pipeline. A lot of crooked people on the other side would suffer, but your Washington friends would still have their asses covered."

"Yeah," Bone said. "I was to nab the disc when I went after Gordo for additional cash, take our people off and put it back. Intercepting it would look like an honest mistake. Eventually, Pesci would have everything he wanted; the drugs, the money, and the disc to sell, but only our edited version. We'd be playing them the whole way."

"But when the time came, Faber and Toole got there first,

killed Gordo, and tried to double-cross everyone else."

"Exactly, and all while working for the guy already screwing the mob. What a mess. Yeah, turns out damned near everyone was making a move of their own. It got to be one giant cluster fuck. Of course, Pesci went nuts. Hell, then even ET got into it, figuring he'd screw Pesci out of the drugs and the cash. Anyway, we just lost control of things."

"No kidding. Now, were you in on sending Eric and Clyde to the bar that first night we met up?"

"No, I didn't know they were going to be there, man. That was Pesci. And poor Eric didn't even realize I was actually playing for the good guys. Also need to know basis and all that. We both found out later."

"So why did you contact me in the first place? I still need answers. Why me?"

Bud Stone said, "Well, pretty much because you're a badass."

"Right. That's all?"

"Mick, you got quite a reputation, especially from that thing happened up in Dry Wells. My assignment was to look like a real sucker, a guy with an expensive mistress, someone who'd buy Faber and Toole and their bullshit idea for a big score. Now, that dumb guy would want the little mistress looked after. I picked you because we were old buddies, you are known publicly to be a wild card, you owed me, and they'd believe I'd ask you for help. But we never thought they'd grab you and threaten your friends."

"Like you said, it all got out of hand."

"And fast. Hell, the firm had to call Brandi back in because we were afraid we'd get your man Lopez killed. Sorry, I didn't know that had gone down, either, or I would have told you not to worry about her anymore."

"Major Stone?"

A young soldier stood in the doorway. Darlene and Mary

Kate were being herded away. MK seemed pretty much in shock but Darlene was resisting evacuation. She was waiting for me to join them.

"Mick? You okay, Mick?"

"Go ahead, Darlene. I'm fine."

"Take them out to the van," Bone said. "And close the door."

The wooden doors creaked slowly and clicked shut. I rubbed my temples. "You took your own sweet time getting here, Bone. Why didn't you just contact me when you knew I had the disc?"

"We *didn't* know. We saw that shootout from a distance, but our people said Mandel was holding it, and that Nicky's foot soldiers got away with the FedEx envelope. We didn't know Mandel had already passed the disc on to you until we overheard Nicky say so via satellite."

I looked away from my friend, stared back at Nicky. Speak of the devil. "What next, Bone? What about him?"

Bud Stone got to his feet. He grunted. "Shitfire, it looks to me like the fucking St. Valentine's Day Massacre happened in here, don't it? Big, big mob fight. Little Nicky and his boys shot a lot of people and then poor Nicky got killed his own self."

Nicky registered that statement and tried to break free from the two men guarding him. "No! Wait!"

The two agents just stepped back, kicked his legs out, and dropped him to the carpet. Nicky cried out. Suddenly a strange, haunted look came over his face. The crotch of his pants went wet. Nicky whimpered, wiped his eyes and whispered, "This is how a man drowns." The words made no sense, but the horror in his voice gave me a chill.

The two soldiers looked up for orders. Bud eyed me. "Now hear this, Callahan. The miserable prick had poor little Jacob Mandel shot down, and I know Jacob's daddy from the SEALs. So it's a done deal. Now, do you want to kiss him goodbye or anything?"

Nicky's eyes pleaded with me. I wanted to protest summary execution, do the honorable thing, but Bone wouldn't have listened, and Nicky certainly didn't deserve protection. I finally just shook my head. "I guess not."

Bone said, "Nicky, consider yourself kissed." One of the two soldiers fired. Nicky's chest exploded. He fell over.

I looked down and away. "Jesus, Bone."

"Oh, come on," Bud Stone said. He shrugged as if nothing of significance had occurred. "When did you go all girly on me? You're just like us, bro."

"I am?"

"Sure." Bud slapped my shoulder. "One of the wicked."

"St. Louis, as in *Missouri?*"

"Well, turns out it's television as well as radio, and they do have the Rams, so wouldn't be a total loss."

Darlene edged away. I grabbed her arm and held on. "I'm only kidding, honey. I don't know if I'm going to take the job. Honest. I'm just thinking out loud. And you could always come with me."

We were in my living room in our underwear, listening to some early Randy Travis. "Come with you? LAPD is the finest in the country, Callahan. Why would I want to work anywhere else?"

I kissed her neck. "I was thinking maybe so we could be together."

"Don't even think about starting up again," Darlene said. She rose and headed for the kitchen. "Are you thirsty? I want some juice or something."

"Sure. Grab me some ice water while you're up."

It was night and we had the lights dimmed low. The drapes were open to the backyard. I watched the twinkling lights of a jet liner that emerged silently from the clouds. Randy finished the song and the CD player stopped. Now I could hear the jet, the ice-cube maker, and glasses clinking in the sink. Darlene came back with our drinks. She set them on the coffee table and stretched out flat on my couch with her legs up and the juice balanced between her breasts. I watched from the floor.

"Service scantily clad. I like that."

"You would." She took a long pull of what looked like cranberry juice. "Did Mary Kate call again?"

"No." I shook my head, even though she wasn't looking. "Just that one time. I figure she's too embarrassed to pester me."

"Are you going to call her back?"

"Someday, but right now I'm not sure what to feel. She was setting me up, you know? MK and Talbot were going to rip us off for the money and the dope. On the other hand, that accidentally saved our lives."

"Can't argue with the result," Darlene said. "Maybe you should cut her some slack."

"I'm thinking on that."

She whistled. "Man, I'll tell you something, Bud Stone's people did a hell of a job on the LAPD. It's like the last couple of weeks never happened. You know what it takes to pull off something like that? Reams of paperwork have to up and vanish. From what I can gather, stuff got marked as clerical errors and deleted from the system."

I sat up, drank some water. "All in the name of Homeland Security, no doubt. One size fits all."

"So Jerry gave them what they needed?"

"Once we were all in the clear."

"You didn't pull a fast one on them or anything . . . like set it up to fail later?"

"I thought about that, but it didn't seem worth the risk. Jerry's smart, but these people run the world. They managed to twist everything around again within a couple of hours, so now the Russian mob is scouring the planet looking for Big Paul Pesci. Meanwhile, the crooks named on that disc go to bed every night believing it's still out there."

"Except for our homegrown Washington DC crooks. They can relax."

"Exactly."

"And Pesci is dead, at least according to your friend Cowboy."

"Eric? Actually, I never learned his real name. Now I probably never will. Hey, you want to maybe get something to eat?"

"I should get going."

I walked over to the couch, leaned down. "One of these days, you should be staying."

"Oh, really? You mentioned something about St. Louis a ways back."

I stole some of her drink. It was cranberry. "I'm going to turn it down, Darlene. I just decided."

"Why's that?"

"Well, you for one thing." I forced her to make room, snuggled close. "And LA is the show biz Mecca. Assuming I'm going to keep on working in radio or TV, I have to be here. Besides, I'd miss the desert. At least this way I can get out there by car in a couple of hours."

"Going to sell this house?"

"I'd rather not." I closed my eyes. "Hey, something will turn up."

A few moments slid by. I was almost asleep when Darlene whispered, "Are you doing okay?"

I twitched. "Huh? What do you mean?"

"You've seemed kind of down, Mick. You're doing a fair job of hiding it, but a girl can tell."

Quite a woman. "It's just something Bud Stone said."

"What?"

"He said that I was like him and 'just one of the wicked.' That really bothered me for some reason. It sounded familiar, so I looked it up. It's from Shakespeare, Henry the Fourth."

"Why let it get under your skin?"

I hugged her close. "Because I'd like to think I'm a good man. That people can change. That I can change. Bone made me wonder if I'm in denial about that, or just kidding myself."

"Look up neurotic in the dictionary, Callahan. It has your picture next to it."

I laughed. "I never should have told you that one. Looks like I'm going to get it thrown back in my face. So, you don't agree?"

"I don't know if we can ever really change or not," Darlene said. "All I know is that we have to try, and that there is something noble in the effort."

"That's all that matters?"

"Maybe. Anyhow, it's all we have."

Darlene tried to sit up. I hugged her close again and pulled her back down. "Wait a little while." My mind was replaying things she'd been lucky enough to miss. Like little Nicky saying *this is how a man drowns.*

"Sleeping here, Mick?"

"No, I want to stretch out on the bed."

We got up and helped one another down the hall, two of the walking wounded; just a couple of people trying to get by.

"Okay," Darlene said, just as I'd hoped. "I'll stay until you fall asleep."

Maybe that is all we have, I thought, as we lay down on the warm sheets. Trying to change for the better, and maybe steal a bit of precious time together.

You know what? Sometimes it's enough.

ABOUT THE AUTHOR

Harry Shannon has been an actor, a singer, an Emmy-nominated songwriter, a recording artist in Europe, a music publisher, a film studio executive, and worked as a freelance Music Supervisor on films such as *Basic Instinct* and *Universal Soldier.* He is currently a counselor in private practice. Shannon's "horror genre" books include *Night of the Beast, Night of the Werewolf,* and *Night of the Daemon.* He's also author of the Mick Callahan suspense novels *Memorial Day* and *Eye of the Burning Man,* and the thriller *The Pressure of Darkness,* all from Five Star Mysteries. Harry has been published in a number of genre magazines, including *Cemetery Dance, Horror Garage, City Slab, Crime Spree,* and *Gothic.net.* His first horror script, *Dead and Gone,* was filmed by director Yossi Sasson. Find out more at www.deadandgonethemovie.com.

As for Harry, he can be contacted via his Web site, www.harry shannon.com or via MySpace.com/HarryShannon.